SILENCE
INVITES THE DEAD

SILENCE
INVITES THE DEAD

SCOTT GREGORY MILLER

thistledown press

Library and Archives Canada Cataloguing in Publication

Miller, Scott Gregory, 1954-
Silence invites the dead / Scott Gregory Miller.

ISBN 1-894345-87-8
I. Title.

PS8626.I454S54 2005   C813'.6   C2005-900876-8

Cover photograph by Johner/Photonica
Author photograph by Laurel Reimche
Cover and book design by Jackie Forrie
Printed and bound in Canada on acid free paper

Thistledown Press Ltd.
633 Main Street
Saskatoon, Saskatchewan, S7H 0J8
www.thistledown.sk.ca

 Canadian   Patrimoine
Heritage   canadien

 Canada Council   Conseil des Arts
for the Arts   du Canada

Thistledown Press gratefully acknowledges the financial assistance
of the Canada Council for the Arts, the Saskatchewan Arts Board,
and the Government of Canada through the Book Publishing
Industry Development Program for its publishing program.

ACKNOWLEDGEMENTS

Books are a collaborative effort but any errors are mine only. I would like to thank the following for their significant contributions:

Laurel Reimche

Susan Musgrave, my editor

Allan Safarik

Dolores Reimer

R.P. MacIntyre

This is a work of fiction. Although the 1994 United Nations peace-keeping mission in Rwanda was commanded by a Canadian, the deployment did not include an armed forces contingent from this country.

The events and characters are products of the author's imagination and geographical and other liberties have been taken in the depiction of the village of Candle Lake and other locations mentioned.

For Laurel,
my love,
my wife.

These be
Three silent things
The falling snow . . . the hour
Before the dawn . . . the mouth of one
Just dead.

— Adelaide Crapsey, "Triad"

Prologue

Kigali, Rwanda — April 12, 1994

The Land Rover bounced along the blood-soaked road from Kigali Airport. Myles Sterling sat rigid. He took short open-mouthed breaths trying to ward off the stench. His chauffeur, Captain Ed Braun, looked almost obscene in his spit 'n' shine blues amidst the slaughter. Alongside in the River Akagera, bloated corpses, tens of thousands of them, stemmed the flow and lay in mounds along the banks. Cadavers had been reported downstream as far east as Lake Victoria in Tanzania. In the ditches, troops of the Interahamwe, the genocidaires, *stacked limbs and torsos in separate piles, as if taking inventory. The reporter watched some of the drunken soldiers laugh, elbow each other as they rolled sun-baked skulls over Rwanda's red, fertile earth. Nothing that Sterling had covered around the world compared to what he now saw.*

A blanket of black clouds choked the city. Angry gangs milled about roadblocks of flaming tires. Fueled by the frenzied voice of Hutu government radio, the enraged Interhamwe waited with Kalashnikovs, machetes and spiked clubs to check identification papers. The local militia hunted the inyenzi — *Tutsi cockroaches* — *and their Hutu friends.*

The acrid smoke cut deep into Sterling's lungs, stinging his eyes. Captain Braun steered through the carbon haze around block after block of burning buildings. As he slowed the Land Rover to navigate through a pile of bricks and rubble, a woman stepped into the street from behind a jagged wall where a home had once stood. At least six feet tall in her long cotton cream-coloured gown, her delicate features and doe eyes bore into Sterling. She raised her arm.

"S'il vous plait. Arretez."

Sterling didn't understand her at first. He thought she spoke Nyrwanda. She sobbed the words over and over. Her arms extended, a swaddled child's tiny head peeked from the blanket.

"Prenez mon bébé! Prenez lui s'il vous plait!"
Take my baby! Take him, please!

Braun shifted into first gear and Sterling's eyes locked on hers as they passed. The woman fell to her knees, prostrated herself on the ground, the red dust smearing her robe.

"Prenez mon bébé. Prenez lui s'il vous plait."

"You can't let it get to you," the captain shouted over the grind of the engine. "You'll go insane."

"We're sitting in pure evil." Colonel John McTaggart leaned his head against the screen window. "Just

watching." He gazed beyond the compound, sand-bagged and barb-wired, to a row of houses across the road. The commander of the Canadian unit of the United Nations Peacekeeping Force in Rwanda rapped his fingers against the sill covered in deep crimson dust. His foot tapped the floor to a tune only he heard. As usual at dusk, a stiff tropical wind moaned through the lush, rolling hills surrounding Kigali. The thermometer still read thirty degrees Celsius. "Watching evil with a Kalashnikov slung over his shoulder and a machete in his hand."

Sterling sat at the only chair and table in the small room, limited his movement to the occasional wiping of his brow. He tried not to see, to smell, to listen to anything beyond the sound of McTaggart's voice.

The camp sat, a fetid shambles. Beyond the office, human waste ran down the hall where a soldier sat, wild-eyed, gnawing a scrap of meat. The humidity and foulness suffocated like a heavy blanket. Outside, the snap and snarl of wild dogs never ceased.

McTaggart turned away from the window. He removed his hat, the famous blue beret worn proudly around the world where the United Nations saw fit to quell trouble. The burnt scarlet of dried blood and the Rwandan earth had stained the soft cloth. His large hands crushed it into a ball, rolling it smaller and smaller.

A gust of wind rattled the screen window and McTaggart stared unblinking. Sterling listened to the eerie sound of the breeze for a moment and cringed. His pen fell onto the wooden table.

"Your ears don't deceive you," the colonel said, "those are cries from Hell."

Placing the rumpled beret back on his head, he peered at the small neighbourhood across the road from the compound, his fingers on the window sill, drumming, drumming.

"Sometimes at night when the wind howls, it sounds almost human," he said. "See that house? Yesterday I took a patrol to check it. There were 132 bodies inside." As if trying to shut out the picture in his mind, he closed his eyes. "No one ever lives. After the machetes, they throw tear gas inside and track down the coughing."

McTaggart's foot on the floor rapped like a snare drum. He gestured to a dirty clapboard storage shed down the road from the compound. Two young Interhamwe, bare-chested and in over-sized camouflage trousers tied high above the waist with string, passed a can of banana beer between them, laughing. They guarded their post, rifles strapped over their thin shoulders.

"Evil also wears a pin-striped suit and sits in a fat leather chair at the U.N. in New York. That shed over there is a weapons cache. I'm not allowed to touch it. Strict orders. We can't take sides. Just monitor no matter what we see." McTaggart's sunken eyes narrowed, pin-holing Sterling. "This isn't war or peace. This is genocide." McTaggart's body vibrated. "But the big boys aren't listening," he whispered. "It's only Africa, after all."

The growling and yipping outside grew furious. Sterling rose to join the colonel at the window. Three dogs tore at a one-armed human torso from a heap of bodies across the road. The biggest and most corpulent of the canines, all fat and salivating after weeks of rich scavenging, ripped the limb from its socket. Trotting a safe distance away, the animal lay down and licked the raw flesh.

Sickened, the reporter stood there unable to look away. The colonel unlocked a cupboard from which he shouldered a bulging canvas knapsack. Sterling turned, watched McTaggart unholster his sidearm and walk out of the room.

The nausea that had gripped Sterling from the moment he stepped onto the airport tarmac now fused with dread. It dawned on him he should follow and he ran out the door to the compound gates twenty metres away. The pile of severed corpses across the road taunted the colonel's camp, its neutrality, its uselessness.

The pack had grown to seven or eight surrounding the human flesh, ripping from it. In the midst of them, stood McTaggart. He sighted his pistol at point-blank range and shot each dog, one by one. So tamed to the sound of gunfire, not one did more than raise its head as the others toppled. The colonel continued to fire at

13

the now motionless beasts until his weapon rendered only a muted click-click-click.

McTaggart's eyes shone, darted about. He walked down the road toward the weapons cache. Somehow, Sterling knew what the colonel intended. He could see that the two sentries, boy soldiers of fourteen or fifteen at the most, had stopped giggling at the sound of gunfire. The banana beer can glinted in the sunlight on the ground.

McTaggart raised his pistol, approached one guard and aimed at his head. The boys levelled rifles at the colonel who began to tower over them as each slow step took him closer. McTaggart's face, which in his small office had contorted through a circus of emotions, turned to stone. He didn't halt until the barrel of his gun entered the gaping mouth of one of the guards.

Time stopped as the three soldiers stood there. Beads of sweat rolled down the boys's foreheads. The sentries stood, frozen, eyes darting. McTaggart's hard glare never left his target.

He lifted his free arm, raised one finger and counted "un." He raised another finger and counted "deux." Another and "trois." The Kalashnikov in the hands of the other sentry began to shake. As a fourth finger raised, the weapon dropped to the ground and the boy backed away from the shed. He turned and fled.

McTaggart's eyes narrowed to slits. The man and the remaining boy held each other's gaze down the barrel of a gun.

Sterling watched this symbol of high authority, trained for decades and at his pinnacle, reduced to terrorizing a child torn from his own family, forced to slay his neighbours or be cut down by the same evil machete.

McTaggart pushed the pistol further into the boy's mouth forcing his head back, tears rolling down his chubby cheeks. The colonel squeezed the trigger.

Click.

The colonel lifted the young guard's rifle away and withdrew his pistol. A dark stain spread over the backside of the boy's trousers as he scrambled down the dusty road.

The door to the shed hung on a single hinge, the weapons cache left open, mocking. From his rucksack of grenades, McTaggart retrieved one, pulled the pin and tossed the explosive through the open door. The pouch followed. He turned his back and walked away.

Crouched behind the compound sandbags, Sterling watched a multitude of explosions blot out the purple horizon. Ignited bullets gave the staccato racket of a night firefight. For a moment, the brilliant show stopped the horror of daylight, kept him awestruck, until the building only smouldered in embers.

Sterling rose and strode across the yard to the colonel's office. He stood in the shadow of the doorway. The Canadian commander sat upright in the room's single metal chair. Beside him, Captain Braun stood at attention.

15

"I'm sorry, my colonel," Braun said, in a strong voice. "Kigali HQ saw the smoke and knows what happened. The general says we're under strict orders." The captain paused and cleared his throat. " You're under suspension, sir."

"It's all right, it's your job," McTaggart said, surrendering his holstered pistol. A silver ring of keys jingled as he handed it over.

The colonel turned to the door. Now his feet and hands remained still, his fingertips silent. "I can't abide by evil," he said.

The frigid air bit deep, the light not yet strong enough to throw shadows from the jack pines that skirted the endless lakeshore. The sun would soon burn off the dawn fog that shrouded the ice fishing shanty town on the mouth of Fisher Creek. Then sundogs —ice crystal rainbows — would hang from the sky.

Lights shone from the small frost-glazed windows of a few of the shacks, their tin chimneys already pouring steam. Inside, radios played low over hot cups of coffee. The anglers here awaited a fine catch of the rapacious jackfish, which, when hungry, didn't care a whit about a little commotion above. With its big ugly jaw and ripping teeth, the northern pike feared nothing but a bigger one of its own. This fish would eat any flesh.

Off to one side of the main bunch, a smaller cluster of occupied huts remained dark inside. These patient fishers huddled quiet over their holes above rifts in the lake bottom that hid the elusive pickerel. The least light or noise scared away these tasty morsels, their shy nibble at bait

17

all but undetectable — just a slight bob of the tip-up set at the ice hole. Only the flickering light of the propane heater burned, the single nod to comfort for these dedicated anglers.

About a kilometre further onto the frozen lake, a more upscale community thrived. Larger and more luxurious digs compensated for the longer haul. Cabins that held a comfortable party of five or six and travel trailers modified to skids sat over the deepest waters. Anglers idled away many hours in sedentary pursuit of the delicious but moody lake trout. One or two lights already flickered here, too.

At thirty below, all who had braved the darkness to get an early start huddled by fired heaters, waiting for the first bob of the tip-up. Along the path over the lake, a tall, erect figure with a walking stick trod through the grey mist. It was a walking stick of a different sort, tipped with a heavy steel chisel . The man stopped every so often to chip, poke and dig at the ice. He wore a snowmobile suit as most ice fishers did in this kind of weather. The thick binding outfit did not hide the precise nature of his steps, however. It was the walk of a military man. A blue beret peaked out from under his hood.

Despite the proud and determined visage he presented from afar, a closer look revealed haunted hollow eyes as if all inside had been drained away. He stopped a couple of metres from his shack, staring across the wide expanse of snowbound ice. Setting down his fishing gear and walking stick, he pulled off one glove and, from his pocket, retrieved a key. Stepping forward to insert it into the padlock on the door, he dropped from sight.

Vanishing for what seemed forever, the man bobbed up through a hole in the ice. He struggled to propel his chest and arms onto the frozen crust when another figure darted from behind the shack and shoved him back into the frigid water. The attacker grabbed the walking stick and swung down hard. The victim, arms flailing, grappled onto the edge of the opening, his legs kicking, boiling the water. The weapon arced through the air. Again. Again. Again. The body slipped back into the black liquid. Under the sole of a heavy winter boot, the head submerged. Only the blue beret still floated there.

Candle Lake — *Morning March 3, 2000*

The divers clambered out of the frigid water and pulled the corpse onto the ice. Sterling's stomach twisted. A string of onlookers blocked his view but their whispers confirmed his worst fears. It was John McTaggart , Mayor of Candle Lake.

The determined pulse of paramedic, police and fire department rescue activity almost stopped as word spread. Before they could cover the body, Sterling forced his way through the crowd. He had to see the colonel one last time.

Sterling glanced away from his friend's face. Once through the ice, no one dressed in winter clothing had much of a chance. The large insulated boots would sink like rocks on a man weakened by shock. The heavy snowmobile suit would also weigh a terrible burden once sodden. The material didn't seem disturbed in any way, no rips or gouges.

Sterling's eyes travelled the legs to the upper body. One missing glove revealed a bloated hand, the fingers swollen and black. He took a deep breath and looked again at McTaggart's head. No eyes, no cheeks, a bony skull stared back. Jackfish had eaten the soft flesh.

Sterling stumbled across the lake away from the crowd into the cover of jack pine, bent over and vomited. His guts heaved at will as if, at last, they'd had enough. The horror of war in Somalia, Rwanda and Yugoslavia had never become routine but somehow, no matter how bloody the sight, Sterling had never thrown up. Now, however, in the lap of peaceful Saskatchewan lake country, the Prince Albert *Sun*'s most recent scribe couldn't stop retching.

Exhausted, Sterling fell into the snow and closed his eyes. The new beginning had become a nightmare.

The noise from the woods sounded like a bear on a rampage. Whoever stomped in Sterling's direction didn't mean to be stealthy. He turned his head and opened his eyes as the cop lumbered toward him.

"Frank Milburn is the highest ranking RCMP officer around here," Joe, the editor of the *Sun* had instructed. "You'll want to develop a good working relationship with him. By the way, when can we expect you in the office, meet us in person?" Soon, soon, Sterling had assured his new boss.

The tall, heavyset Milburn made his point. It seemed he liked to crowd people. Prone in the snow, Sterling estimated the glistening black boots before his eyes at about size twelve.

"So this is our famous war correspondent come to tell us about the ways of the world," Milburn said. "Our tum-tum a bit queasy?"

Sterling had learned in his travels that all authorities loved respect. Police, especially, adored it. Wiping the string of saliva from his mouth, he rose to his feet, smiled. "Yes, sir? What can I do for you, sir?"

The officer stepped closer, his chest almost touching Sterling's.

As he spoke, his breath felt warm on Sterling's face: "Listen to me, pal. If I find you interfering, I'll tack your ass on the wall of the lock-up and leave it there."

Sterling didn't want to imagine the reputation that preceded him. Then again, the good staff sergeant could dislike reporters on principle. Wrenching away from his fiery blue eyes, Sterling called out to the crowd milling on the lake, waved hoping someone would see him. No need for violence.

He turned back and smiled. Their faces still so close, a hint of spearmint gum drifted into Sterling's nostrils.

"I won't tell you again," Milburn said. He turned and headed back onto the lake.

Sterling watched the staff sergeant's broad back as it diminished, melded into the slow commotion on the canvas of snow and ice. In the background, white smoke rose from the chimneys of the vacation cottages and year-round homes nestled in the evergreen forest that crowded along the lake's edge. In the foreground, two white-uniformed attendants zippered the corpse into the black body bag and slipped it inside the ambulance. The door closed. The colonel was gone.

The beginning of a dream come true met by more death. Sterling wondered if a curse would always hang over him. Was this a sign that the demons that sometimes rode the wind, which, without warning, appeared in store windows or rose from the roadside, would haunt him forever? Would Joanne's face, the circle of red at the temple, never fade from his mind? Or was he the one who wouldn't let the memories die?

After the horror of Rwanda, the unquenchable thirst for a story dried up. No matter where he looked, death gazed back. Nothing seemed to matter anymore.

Back in Canada, he lived life on a blurred edge, one crummy newspaper to the next, quit or got fired, each place a little smaller and a little dingier than the last. Then the call came. Somehow the colonel had tracked him down.

"Fishing all year round, my friend," McTaggart had said, only the month before. "You never told me this was some kind of paradise." It surprised Sterling that the colonel recalled the reporter hailed from Saskatchewan. "Remember Ed Braun, my captain in Kigali, the guy who grew up around Meath Park? He knows people at the Prince Albert *Sun*. We've convinced them to put a correspondent in Candle Lake." McTaggart laughed. "Probably all you'd ever have to do would be to take a few pictures of bake sales and prize catches. You could still spell everyone's name wrong."

Before the killing started, the peace held easy in Kigali when the U.N. first arrived. A day on Lake Kivu in the biblical Eden of Rwanda had spawned the dream of finding a quiet paradise. The sun high above, the waters calm, Sterling floated along in a dinghy with McTaggart and Braun. When he found out Sterling came from Saskatchewan, the colonel said he had someone the reporter should meet, reminisce about manure or whatever *stubble-jumpers* do. How else would a miserable journalist be invited to fish with the army? Over a few hours, the gentle ribbing of wishful thinking among strangers thrown together became a promise each one made to himself — somewhere, someday, he would regain this paradise. The dream slept six years for Sterling until the sound of the colonel's voice awakened him that day.

"Come on down," the colonel said. "Have you forgotten? The pickerel are here for the taking."

Sterling felt excitement jump from McTaggart's every word. Restless, always involved, the colonel had been courted to run for mayor and won. A more formal courting had also taken place. Sterling would meet "her" when he arrived. He'd never heard such joy in John's voice. McTaggart had conquered his demons. Hope lay ahead for Sterling.

He scooped a gloveful of snow to wash away the bitter taste. Now jackfish digested bits of the colonel's bloated corpse.

Keeping a wary eye for the hyper-sensitive staff-sergeant, Sterling walked back onto the ice. The onlookers began to meander away, many returning to their ice fishing shacks, about 100 metres from where a local resident had discovered the body.

Sterling spotted Ed Braun and a young constable sharing a joke, the mountie grinning at some punch line. McTaggart carted away in a black bag, his face devoured down to the skull and Braun already laughing.

Now close enough to see the strain in the army veteran's face, Sterling regretted his snap judgement. It would be petty to blame Braun for a brief moment of dark humour. Stress hit people in different ways. The test lay in how you survived it.

Captain Braun had seen the worst of Rwanda and had come out of it better than any of them. Now the owner of a thriving trucking firm, he had managed to give McTaggart the choice between certain promotion to general in Ottawa or a new career as owner of the Wheelhouse Bar and Restaurant in Candle Lake, Saskatchewan. The army had decided to withdraw McTaggart from the field, kick him upstairs. Riding a desk as a general, however, would have ground his very core into dust. He jumped at Braun's offer.

Sterling knew, however, that more than paper mountains had sent the colonel fleeing. Demons, too, chased him. To remain still risked encounter with voices in the wind, haunted visits from the slaughtered of Rwanda. Sterling understood this. He had come to Candle Lake for the same reason. Of the three of them, only Captain Braun had the strength to survive the wounds that genocide bestows upon its spectators.

Braun clapped the constable on the shoulder. Sterling didn't know what the big staff sergeant's problem had been a few moments before, nor if the same poison had been spread among the rest of the local constabulary. Milburn's underling, however, didn't seem to notice Sterling.

Braun waved and walked over.

"I thought I saw you a few minutes ago," he said. "Then you disappeared."

The man stood solid as a tree trunk. A little taller than Sterling and twice as wide, Braun still carried himself like a drill instructor. His heavy parka bulked him even more although Sterling wondered if a shaved head proved the best defense against the glacial wind. The elements wouldn't matter at the moment, though. Braun looked shaken, his face grey.

"I had a short interview with Frank Milburn," Sterling said. "He bit my head off."

"He's a good cop, usually on an even keel. You must have done something."

"I was hoping you could tell me."

Distracted, Braun shook his head. His eyes followed the ambulance as it crossed the lake, wound its way up a pine-curtained road. He seemed to shrink within his heavy winter clothes as the vehicle grew small, disappeared.

"John was my best friend," he said. "For a long time after the search for him was called off, I was certain he'd pop into the office one day and say he'd been visiting his sick mother in Smuts, or something." He gestured to the ice fishing shanty town. "But when I looked out of my shack this morning and saw the cops and divers, my guts told me it was him."

As Sterling spoke, he hoped Braun would understand the intent, wouldn't take the comment personally: "I spent fifteen years covering dirty little wars and I never believed in heroes until I met John."

"A lot of us were good soldiers but he was that special one in a million." Braun looked away for a moment, as if reflecting. "He proved that over and over."

The colonel's captain understood perfectly. He gazed after the departed ambulance once more. When he turned back, his composure hardened. Sterling had seen the look before. Work beckoned. Braun had changed little since Kigali.

"John was an expert out here," he said, "it couldn't have been an accident."

Braun's roots in the community ran deep. He knew everyone in town, his ear close to murmurs and rumours.

"Did that young cop tell you anything?" Sterling asked.

"You mean Emil Cuthand. He said every winter people fall through the ice. Some of them drown. It sounded as if they'd already made up their minds."

"I'll see what I can find out," Sterling said.

"Start there." Braun pointed to a couple being questioned by the supposedly even keel staff sergeant. "That's Bonnie Matheson, John's fiancée, and her brother. It was Brendan who spotted the body."

Even from a distance, the blonde woman's face captivated. It had the classical beauty found in glossy magazines, the kind of looks to which merely pretty women aspired. Still, dark crescents shaded her eyes. She glanced about, her gaze landing nowhere long, as if hesitant to linger.

Sterling had trouble taking his eyes off her.

"Close your mouth, ace," Braun said, walking away. "The colonel isn't in the ground yet."

The brusque remark took Sterling aback. That's what he got for being so obvious. He watched Braun amble across the ice, a solitary figure on a blanket of white. The man was right. Something about Bonnie stirred the reporter. The colonel's taste was excellent.

Sterling watched Staff Sergeant Milburn shut his notebook and peer about. The reporter slipped behind an onlooker's truck bed, one of a number of pick-ups, suv's, snowmobiles and all-terrain quads that sat scattered about the hole in the ice. The big cop looked different than he had in their initial encounter. Now he moved with slow and measured gestures, his countenance gentle. He put his hands on the shoulders of the brother and sister, consoling them.

The colonel's flesh-eaten face flashed across Sterling's mind. The sudden loss of her fiancé would be tragic for Bonnie and finding the body no less frightening for Brendan. In peace, too, death cut a jagged swath.

Devastated or not, the young man stood out. It took only a moment for Sterling to recognize the face: Brendan Matheson, the famous painter of whom the art world made such a fuss. Tall and slim with a flamboyant air, he looked like he should have been strolling the downtown streets of Montreal, New York or Paris. On the frozen surface of Candle Lake, Saskatchewan amid tuques, parkas and florescent-striped snow suits, he wore a knee-length navy blue cape and matching beret at a rakish slant. A heavy wool scarf wrapped around his face and neck, and worn Kodiak work boots constituted his only concessions to the cold.

Winter clouds kept the noon sun grey and solemn yet Brendan sported wraparound mirrored sunglasses. Snow blindness wouldn't trouble the star this day. He stood a head taller than Bonnie who wore a more sensible baby blue ski suit. It may have kept her warm but it also accentuated rather than hid the supple lines of her body. Brother and sister made a striking couple.

Milburn marched away allowing Sterling to take a stroll, observing the Mathesons while pausing to overhear conversations among the small crowd.

Even those who had found themselves on opposing sides from John McTaggart voiced begrudging respect. The community had taken him into its bosom, made him its mayor. The tragedy had hit the village hard. Still, although some questioned the apparent drowning, stranger things had happened.

"You have to keep an eye out," an old fisherman warned a couple men standing beside him. "Only last year two guys on their snowmobiles went through ice a foot thick. It was old, crystallized and weak. Darn shame, too. American tourists spend good."

As Sterling approached, Bonnie leaned her head on Brendan. While her hair gleamed full and blonde, her brother's hung white, thin and flimsy against his head as it fell to his shoulders.

Now the shades made sense. Still some artistic caprice, perhaps, but he needed them even on a dull day. An albino, the tall, spare young man's eyes would hate much of any kind of light.

Sterling introduced himself. The brother and sister stepped apart, their postures straightening. Bonnie ran her hand through silken tresses.

Experience taught that some people valued privacy more than others. Sterling had seen Brendan's face in enough magazines to know the prodigy often found himself in the spotlight. Yet a shyness tinged his demeanor as if he still hadn't come to terms with the attention. And, despite Sterling's many years as a nosy scribe, he still believed grief deserved some seclusion.

He would be brief.

"I'm sorry to bother you."

"That's all right," Brendan said. "John spoke of you from his time in Africa."

"He spoke fondly of you," Bonnie added. "This must be difficult for you, too."

Sterling nodded. "Perhaps we could meet later under better circumstances?"

"There isn't much to tell, anyway," Brendan volunteered. "I was out for a walk. I have trouble with sunshine so my time outdoors is confined to cloudy days. I still need fresh air, though, especially when I'm working." His arm gestured across the purview of Candle Lake. "And the landscape for inspiration."

Confused, Sterling asked, "You were strolling across the lake and came to a hole in the ice?"

"No. The police used a chainsaw."

"I don't understand. What about the body?"

"The wind gusts up the mouth of the creek and leaves this area quite clean of snow," Brendan explained. As if trying to clear the picture from his mind, he shook his head. "I looked down and his face, what was left of it, was staring up at me through the ice."

Bonnie's throat emitted a small cry. She turned away.

Her brother flushed. "I'm sorry, I wasn't thinking."

Her hand reached out, touched his forearm. Her gesture of forgiveness said this was going to be tough for everyone.

"I'd like to do a memorial piece on John," Sterling said. "What he did in the army, his contributions here. I was hoping you could help me." Looking at both of them, he hoped Bonnie would answer.

"That would be very kind of you," she said. "John told us although he hadn't known you long, he considered you a true friend."

"Not kind at all, it's what he deserves."

The feeling of an ominous presence crept up on Sterling. Even so, it took some effort to tear away from Bonnie's soft blue eyes. When he did, he met the hard glare of Staff Sergeant Milburn from about twenty metres away. The big mountie talked to an even larger man who, going by the size of his gut and unlike the cop, owed his bulk to fat rather than muscle.

"Acting mayor Dan Farrow," Bonnie said, an edge to her voice. "He and John didn't get along. Something about progress."

The cop eyed Sterling as Bonnie explained that Farrow had mayoralty aspirations of his own but had decided to run for alderman instead when he saw McTaggart's strong popularity. With the mayor missing for almost a month, the council had voted Farrow as a replacement. It seemed the temporary position was now permanent.

Milburn began to stride toward them, a bear on hind legs.

"Where do we meet?" Sterling asked, back-pedaling toward his parked car.

"The Wheelhouse about seven tonight," Bonnie called, glancing about, searching for the reason behind Sterling's abrupt departure. Her eyes twinkled and she stepped in the policeman's path. They began to talk.

Brilliant, Sterling thought. And beautiful. A potent combination. The Wheelhouse, of course, that's where Bonnie waited tables, at John's bar.

Sterling watched as the policeman's eyes bore into him. Sterling remembered why he so often got in trouble. Whenever someone like Milburn ordered him around, he had the greatest urge to do the opposite. With a big grin, he waved to the cop.

Late Morning March 3, 2000

CHAMBER
OF COMMERCE
WELCOMES
YOU TO
CANDLE LAKE
SNOWMOBILE
CAPITAL OF
SASKATCHEWAN
500 KM OF
GROOMED
TRAILS
MINOWUKAW
SAND DUNES

The thirteen billboards greeted tourists just before the turn-off into town. Sterling pointed his baby down Highway 120.

Was this stubborn love or just bone-headed stupidity? Bent over the steering wheel and arm through the sliding window-vent, Sterling scraped frost off the outside of the windshield as he drove. The cold engine did not purr so much as rattle and whine.

"Saskatchewan! You're taking a darling like that to Saskatchewan! It'll be certain death! She's almost thirty years old. Here, let me write you a nice cheque. I'll keep her warm here where she belongs."

Sterling had heard offers like that a few times once it got around that he'd no longer claim southern Ontario his home. However, he refused to abandon his mustard-yellow Triumph TR6 to some sports car collector. Perhaps stubborn love did describe it best.

Was he being cruel? The ice wind skittered up his sleeve. Chills vacuumed his spine. It had been over twenty years since he left Prince Albert. He'd bragged about weather this bad; he didn't expect to live in it again. The interior warmer took half the day to clear the windows of the two seat cockpit. The new block heater entirely misunderstood its task. The stupid thing directed most of its energy toward short-circuiting the electrical system. Sterling had to dress warmer to drive than to walk. He'd been forced to empty his wallet so his car could cozy up in a heated garage while outside the frozen wind howled. Cruel, no; he took care of her.

Now, though, any thoughts of leisure days winding the TR6 through the boreal forest hills of home seemed far away. The colonel's death had left a pall over everything.

Sterling had watched John McTaggart and a handful of U.N. soldiers in Rwanda negotiate for the lives of thousands of unarmed civilians. Sometimes the colonel lost, watched prisoners led away, listened to their death cries. In the slaughter of almost a million people, however, the few hundred troops had only their wits on which to rely. Small victories, hiding away ten people here, twenty there, kept the peacekeepers going each day. In the red dust of Kigali, only the begrudging respect of both the Tutsi and Hutu for McTaggart kept the Canadians alive.

To survive that genocide a world away only to die at the hands of some miscreant on a pretty lake in northern Saskatchewan spoke of gallows humour. Or did the colonel die by some simple misadventure? Braun, for one, insisted it couldn't have been an accident. Even if the mounties pursued the case as just another annual winter drowning, they'd still have to wait until the autopsy to close the file. And who knew what the coroner might find?

Sterling would never forgive himself if he didn't uncover the fate of the only hero he'd ever met. A good place to start would be with Dan Farrow. He had replaced McTaggart in the mayor's chair and Bonnie said the two men grated on each other.

Sterling ground his teeth for thinking like a rookie, stumbling over his own feet. What young Constable Cuthand had told Braun rang true. So far, evidence of nothing but the usual winter unpremeditated drowning had surfaced. Still, Braun's insistent words echoed in the reporter's mind. The harm in nosing around was getting one's nose cut off. However, after such a rude reception, anything that stuck it to Staff Sergeant Milburn made the effort worthwhile.

The cockpit of the little TR6 warmed at last, the windshield clearing. Sterling's fingers numb and tingling, he drew his hand inside and slid closed the vent. He continued along Lakeview Drive and onto the three kilometre stretch of Highway 265 until it came to Highway 125 where he turned west. The twenty-one kilometre stretch to the junction of 55 at Meath Park would give him time to settle his nerves. His stomach still rode a stormy sea.

Sterling stepped hard on the accelerator. In spite of himself, the rumble of the in-line six cylinders and triplet of two-barrel carburetors pulsed adrenalin in his veins. He travelled through the gears into over-drive testing the racing clutch's friction point. Its sweet spot hit like a hammer. When the clutch grabbed, Sterling's head reefed back. The ancient speedometer paid no heed to metric, talked only in miles per hour. It said 95.

Wide snow-covered ditches guided the grey two-lane asphalt through the forest of pine splashed with swatches of larch and aspen. At this speed, it all blurred.

Ahead, the curve looked gentle enough but why take a chance? The engine growled with his downshift. Sterling noticed the road lay flat through the turn, no banking to the pavement. Too late, he feathered the brake. The rear tires squealed, lost adhesion. Jerking the steering wheel in the direction of the slide, for an instant, momentum held under his touch. Then the rear end broke loose again and his world began to twirl. And twirl and twirl and twirl.

At last still again, Sterling shook his head, erased the huge vision of a steel guard rail spearing the windshield. The TR6 now straddled the double solid line in the wrong direction. After several deep breaths, he eased the sports car over to the shoulder and got out.

Sterling walked back over the curve. Did road engineers produce Friday and Monday lemons — too excited about the upcoming weekend or too hungover from it to come up with their best stuff? How tough was it to handle a transit, get the angles right? The curve's flat camber would throw off many vehicles even at lawful speed. Perhaps that explained a guard rail where seemingly no danger existed, no sharp drop off from the road shoulder.

Once back in the car, Sterling decided to return to town. He'd had enough excitement for one day. Out on the highway, he accelerated to the speed limit. He glanced up as a huge silver grill filled his rearview mirror.

Downshifting, Sterling revved the engine until the speedometer needle bobbed at 75 mph. Now enough distance split the two vehicles for him to see what followed: a Volvo tractor pulling a B-train. These new turbo-charged semi's could move with just about anything on the road. In no time, it again hovered over the little Triumph's rear bumper.

Through the glint of windshield, Sterling could only make out that the cowboy behind the wheel preferred the goofy look wearing his baseball cap backwards. He seemed to know how to handle his rig, though. Perhaps he didn't realize driving in Canada was supposed to be an easy Sunday stroll and not a demolition derby. Sterling clinched the wheel.

The double-trailered tractor edged closer, the mammoth chrome-plated bumper about to swallow the boot of the British sportster. Then the truck veered into the on-coming lane, easing past. A shadow fell over the cockpit and Sterling held his breath. The speedometer read 80 mph and he eased off the gas. The giant rig flew by as if the TR6 stood still. Sterling exhaled as the words "Sons Trucking" on the truck's door panel interrupted a case of deja vu.

The rearview mirror darkened once again. He slammed down the accelerator, the TR6 lurching, gaining a little room. Behind him another elephant bone-white Volvo attacked driven by an identical grinning maniac, except that this jockey wore his cap with the peak to the front.

Sterling shut his eyes then opened them. His knuckles ached white on the wheel as the truck in front slowed while the one behind charged. The Triumph's brake lights flashed frantically.

The fun over, the trucks played serious now. Sitting in the jaws of a rolling crusher, Sterling downshifted, jerked the wheel hard left. The TR6 squirted into the oncoming lane. An air-horn screamed, headlights flashed as he reefed the wheel right again cramming the little car back between the B-trains. An on-coming semi wailed past.

The Volvos squeezed again, oozing the breath out of him. With no space between the three vehicles, the acrid taste of diesel choked the cockpit. The semi behind nudged the TR6 into a kiss with the big truck-twin in front. Sterling wanted no part of this ménage à trois. His heart pounded. Once the two rigs had their way with the little thing, the TR6 would be like a bug squished on a windshield.

The blinking signal light confused him. Sure enough, the trailer in front of him began easing to the shoulder. In the rearview mirror, the other trucker followed suit.

The Triumph's inline six screamed, raced beyond its two suitors before they could change their minds. Sterling didn't breathe until the mirror reflected two small dots. The thick stink of oily fuel hung in the air and he opened the windows.

His fingers tingled and his face flushed hot, a reminder of what had drawn him into the war zone. He hadn't expected such a pure rush of adrenalin in Saskatchewan's sweet pine-scented lake country.

In the clear, he backed off the gas. The TR6 eased along. The crisp air soothed Sterling's lungs. He leaned back, loosened his shoulder muscles, took in the rolling vista of green forest pine.

The explosion of a thousand nuts and bolts in a tin can thrashed under the bonnet. This time the mirror darkened in blue-black smoke. The Triumph's innards rattled into silence. The car rolled to a stop at the side of the highway.

Sterling laid his head on the walnut steering wheel. The unmistakable grind of heavy gears gnashing, the squeak of huge wheels rolling to a stop and the stink of diesel all engulfed him. He looked up to see the passenger door of the first of the two elephant-bone Volvos open and the young driver lean over. He appeared to be in his early twenties, broad-shouldered like an athlete. The face grizzled from a few days growth, he grinned like a hunter coming upon a fallen buck, barrel smoking. This close, he looked familiar although Sterling couldn't place him.

"Bad luck, buddy," the trucker said. "Unless you're running a diesel in that little tinker toy, that smoke means a blown engine." He tipped his cap. "I've radioed a tow truck for you."

The two B-train grain haulers pulled away. In black letters on the doors of both tractors glossed the words "Braun & Sons Trucking."

Afternoon March 3, 2000

Ed Braun kept his small, spare office neat and clean. A wooden desk and two grey metal folding chairs sat near one wall. A couple of filing cabinets stood against another. A black card table sporting an electric coffee urn rounded out the furnishings.

Beside the computer on the desktop lay the day's edition of the Prince Albert *Sun*. It had gone to bed before news of McTaggart's body surfaced. A headline circled by a felt pen drew Sterling's eyes to a small story in the bottom corner.

POLICE WARN OF TOXIC STREET DRUG

RCMP have issued a news release warning that a toxic batch of methamphetamine, the street drug commonly known as crystal meth is circulating in the area and has sent two people to Prince Albert Hospital with psychotic convulsions. The drug's active ingredient is ephedrine but laboratory tests of a sample obtained by police detected a significant amount of a lye-based drain cleaner. RCMP caution that ingestion of the tainted crystal meth could cause permanent brain damage. Other street names for the drug include crank, go-fast or, in its smokeable form, glass or ice.

The two victims, thirty-seven-year-old Larry Fredericks and twenty-year-old Megan Milburn, are now reported in fair condition. CRBI-TV will only say that the station has released Fredericks from his employment as anchor of the evening news. Milburn is a community college student.

Sterling walked to the window, gazing at the view as he waited in the empty office. The gravelled yard covered half a city block. The similarity to the Kigali compound the Colonel's unit had erected, at least before the encampment became a fetid ramshackle, struck hard. A twelve-foot-high chain link fence topped by three strands of barbed wire strung at an outward angle kept intruders at bay. Access over the top appeared impossible without a catapult. Signs warned of nightly electrification.

Sterling became lost in the forest of spruce and pine beyond the barrier, the evergreen hue softening the sharp white of sun-glistened snow. The hills of Rwanda rose in tiers of lush green with their banana, pyrethrum and corn crops. His mind drifted to the road from Kigali airport.

Prenez mon bébé! Prenez lui s'il vous plait!

Sterling shivered. Spiders crawled over his skin. A bead of sweat walked down his brow. The trees staggered like drunken soldiers, thickets of dark branches became cadavers, hacked limbs piled in rows of mounds. The air keened with the howl of blood-slaked hounds.

He closed his eyes. At last, his breath returned in sharp stabs. The swaying forest became still and silent once more.

Escape wouldn't come easy. Yet the colonel had found it. A sudden thought struck. Could it be that in some way McTaggart's death was connected to Rwanda? Could it ever be left behind?

"So you've met my boys."

Keeping his back to Ed Braun as he walked into the room, Sterling said, "Let's say they introduced themselves."

He opened his eyes. The Kigali compound vanished, the corpses gone. Only semi-trailers and their tractors, coupled and uncoupled, single trailer 'A-trains' and the double trailer 'B' trains stood guard along the rear fence. A brown and black rottweiler paced back and forth, sniffing the air along the chain link interior of its pen adjacent to the office.

Inside the overhead doors of the hangar-sized garage, sparks flew from the intense blue of a welder's torch under the open hood of a truck. The two turbo-charged Volvos Sterling had encountered on Highway 125 glistened by the front gates like a couple of white stallions.

"How's that little car?"

Sterling turned as Braun closed a drawer in his desk, the newspaper gone. No doubt, the dutiful father would use the story to warn his boys, should they be inclined to indulge.

"At home sick," the reporter replied, taking a chair, "the *Sun* set me up with a rental."

The small office was attached to the garage. Ed Braun sat behind the old wooden desk, his eyes never leaving the stir of activity in the adjacent shop for long. "Zeke and Zak are naturals with anything mechanical," he said. "They can drive it or tear it down and rebuild it. By the time they were twelve, they'd run everything with an engine on their granddad's farm."

The B-trains had squeezed the Triumph into a dangerous vise of bare inches, a feat of daring and talent, no doubt. But what would the proud father think if he knew how the twin "naturals" handled the "anything mechanical" he'd left in their care?

"They looked like they knew what they were doing," Sterling replied. "I was stunned."

47

It must have been the tone because these words brought Braun's eyes away from the bustle of the garage to where Sterling sat. They stared at each other.

Braun shook his head, frustrated. "You mean they were showing off. They've been ticketed a couple of times for monkeying around. Between them, they played around with half a million dollars of rolling stock and cargo."

He cursed under his breath and glared at the floor.

"Are they about?" Sterling asked. "I'd like to thank them for calling a tow truck."

"At home sleeping off a round trip to Winnipeg. Probably won't wake up until noon tomorrow." Braun rose, closed the office door before walking over to the window. "Their grandparents raised them on a farm near here." Braun watched another B-train pull out of the yard. "My wife died in childbirth. I was a mess and took a posting to Germany. When the Berlin wall came down and they closed the base at Lahr, I just kept signing on for U.N. tours."

From habit, the former captain stood at ease — feet shoulder-width apart, hands clasped behind his back. "I think I got back here three times. I told myself it was okay; I was saving the world and my parents could do a much better job with the boys than I ever could." His hands separated and balled into tight, white fists. "The last month of her pregnancy she got sicker and sicker. She knew. She knew it was twins and she knew she was going to die." His voice softened to a whisper. "The truth is, for the longest time when I looked at the boys's faces, all I could see was her. That's why I stayed away."

Braun walked over to the table, filled a Styrofoam cup from the urn. Sipping, he said, "A few years ago, my mother died and right after my old man got sick. It was time to come home. When my father kicked off, I sold the farm and put the money into this." His arm swept the breadth of his commercial enterprise. "I know trucks and you can just keep your head above water hauling grain these days. You can't make money growing it."

"It looks like you're swimming along quite nicely," Sterling said.

He nodded to acknowledge the compliment. Braun eased back down into his chair. His fingers tapped the pitted varnish of the wooden desk. "We have to find out what happened to the colonel, no matter what the mounties think."

"Accidents can happen to a careful man."

"No!" The big man's fist came down hard, the cup jumping. Hot coffee bubbled over his hand but he didn't wince. Rising, he ripped a paper towel from a dispenser on the wall. In the time it took to wipe the spill, the fire in his eyes dulled.

Sitting down again, he uttered a small laugh. "Remember the day we borrowed some rods and tackle and high-tailed out of Kigali? Lake Kivu must be the most beautiful fishing hole in the world." He grinned. "The only water around without crocs and hippos and with the right lure you could actually hook an old fashioned trout." The soldier's training would never leave him. He didn't stop scrubbing until the table shone. "John used to joke that if we ever found angling heaven, it better not freeze over." He tossed the sodden towels into the waste basket.

"The first time we went ice fishing here, he was as jittery as a cat. He only stayed out for half an hour before he made an excuse to go back to shore. It was a few more episodes like that before I got the truth out of him. He'd fallen through a frozen dugout as a kid and almost drowned."

"He wasn't a man to display his weaknesses," Sterling said.

"Exactly. It was almost as hard for him to tell me as it was to walk on the ice."

"But he became an avid ice fisher. What cured him?"

"A spud," Braun smiled.

"A potato?"

The army vet grinned. "No, it's a walking stick with a heavy metal wedge at the tip. They use them in Michigan to poke the ice as they go. I picked one up special for him. Even had his name engraved on it."

"And he used this spud whenever he went on the lake. Perhaps that one morning he forgot his stick," Sterling ventured, "there was the excitement of the party the night before."

"Never." Braun's unblinking eyes pinned the reporter. "Being able to test the ice himself was the only thing that made him comfortable. If the surface even smelled soft he wouldn't go near it. You'd never catch him ice fishing without his spud. So where is it?"

The beginning of March didn't leave many weeks of safe ice. When Sterling had made his retreat from Staff Sergeant Milburn on the lake, he'd noticed a couple of mounties nosing around McTaggart's shack. If the colonel had made it that far, the elements would have erased any tracks long ago. Still, it wouldn't hurt to go over the same ground the police had covered.

"I wouldn't mind getting some fishing in myself." Sterling paused. "From John's shack first thing in the morning." The metal folding chair scraped the concrete floor as Sterling rose. "I wonder if something happened at the engagement party."

"I wouldn't know." Braun became sheepish. "That was the night me and the twins spent in P.A. hospital. We were loading round bales on a flatbed and one of them got away." Shaking his head, he covered his eyes with his hand in mock embarrassment. "Mowed all three of us down."

Braun stood, unzipped his green quilted vest. He unbuttoned his plaid shirt to reveal a cloth bandage around his chest. "I still have to wear this or it feels like my ribs will fall out. It's my own damn fault, though. I should have kept a closer eye on the boys." He winced as he did up his shirt. "I was invited to the party but I didn't make it."

"There was something else," Sterling said, as he turned to go. "Bonnie doesn't seem to like the brand new mayor. Dan Farrow certainly had something to gain by John's disappearance."

"Think Farrow, think progress. Slickest damn campaign you ever saw for a simple Candle Lake councillor."

"Big money means somebody wants something and is willing to pay for it."

"In this case," Braun replied, "it's a casino. The Minowukaw First Nation filed a huge land claim that includes Candle Lake. It's making us property owners pretty jittery. Word is Farrow's been talking to the band about allowing a huge hotel and casino development with tax breaks in exchange for dropping the town from the claim." Braun began to button his shirt. "John accused him of going behind council's back and vowed to fight it all the way." He zipped his vest, let his hands fall by his sides. His eyes bore into Sterling. "This is what I've been trying to tell you. McTaggart was a very careful man on the ice, but he'd made a few enemies on land."

"He won the election easily," Sterling pointed out. "It must mean the voters didn't want a casino."

A bitter edge ground Braun's laugh. "I shouldn't have to tell you about money and politics. What the people want and what they get are often pretty different."

Sterling walked to the door and opened it. In one work bay of the garage, the entire front body of a Western Star flipped forward to reveal the mechanical cornucopia of the engine compartment. Two welders stood amidst flying sparks, like statues drowning in fireworks. The odour of diesel and steel reeked an artificial sweetness.

He looked back at Braun. "I noticed John's shack was set off from the rest."

Braun nodded. "He bragged he'd landed on a pickerel hole."

Evening PM *March 3, 2000*

Inside the Wheelhouse Bar, a diaphanous blanket hung along the ceiling, slow whirling fan blades cutting through the blue haze. Sterling stood inside the door allowing his pupils to expand to the darkness. The rented tin trap the *Sun* had arranged had needed a boost to start, making him half an hour late.

An Old World ambience touched the room. Just as in the pubs of England, Ireland and Wales where he'd tipped a few, church pews lined the walls. The shiny varnish of the seating contrasted with the grimy pine slat floor covered in a gravel of peanut shells and cigarette butts. Along the middle of the room, tall stools surrounded narrow tables.

A young woman, auburn hair cascading down her back, in a short black skirt and shiny white silk blouse, served customers. She splashed glasses of one-for-the-road draft toward some grim old patrons about to allow the young night crowd its noisy shenanigans. A flick of her wrist cleaned ashtrays, spilling butts and ashes across the raw floor. The men resumed peanut shelling after their eyes returned from silent praise of her hips. While the sullen guys stared, a party of men and women sporting jackets from the Minowukaw First Nation laughed loud, boomed jokes and quips at each other. The waitress kidded with them and asked that the volume be turned down a notch.

A giant of a guy in his twenties, head shaven, wearing dark glasses, emerged from behind the bar and ambled past Sterling. After stringing across the rope barricade, the bald behemoth stood before the entrance foyer, arms folded, biceps's tattoos winking. No one got past this bouncer without his okay.

Sterling then spotted the sign. Someone named Big Jim McLeod and his band played tonight in a one night stand. The cover charge raised the reporter's eyebrows. It seemed pretty steep for some unknown bluesman playing an out of the way small town bar. Outside, the March wind howled to the chords of a thirty below lament, not much of a formula for drawing a crowd.

Laughter and chatter filling the foyer turned Sterling's head. He saw that the local folks took no stock in his judgement. A long line-up had already formed out the door.

He couldn't see Bonnie and Brendan among them, however. Walking past the bandstand, he followed the long mahogany bar and came upon the doorway to a games room. One guy in a cowboy hat and denim jeans and jacket racked for a game of eight ball on the pool table. His buddy chalked a cue. The bodiless electronic bark of video arcade games, flashing and blinking lights, cheered the players.

Sterling glanced at his watch. Perhaps the Mathesons had left in a huff, stomping through banks of snow to their car. Then he noticed the passageway to an alcove at the end of the room.

As the reporter approached, his heart went out to the lonely figure he saw. Muted blue light bathed Bonnie's face, painting it pale as she slouched on a stool in front of a garrison of video lottery terminals. Otherwise, the chamber loomed in darkness, Brendan nowhere to be seen.

Sterling halted and stared. John McTaggart's body had surfaced only hours before and the woman he loved now sat grieving the final truth. Sterling knew he would have to keep his little used heart in check.

Still, gazing at this young woman, a strange old feeling stirred inside. He thought his heart had gone cold years ago, as cold as his fiancée's brain after a sniper's bullet had pierced it when they'd been on assignment together in Serbia. As much as he tried not to think about Joanne, some-times her face crept into his mind like dapples of light. At least the constant dreadful pining no longer hung over him, the weight that had pushed him to chase into the most dangerous theatres the world offered. Bonnie and Joanne didn't even look alike. Why did he feel an old excitement?

Bonnie strained toward the machine, the three icons on the screen resting only a split second before sent rolling again by a press of her thumb. Even though the activity was as passive as changing television channels with a remote control, her eyes sparked hot at the fruit symbols scrambling for a jackpot.

Stopping a metre away, Sterling waited to be acknowledged. Bonnie, however, showed no sign any world existed outside the electronic rays of her VLT. Her thumb never stopped moving, like tapping Morse Code. Sterling coughed but that drew no attention so he spoke her name. Only upon repeating it louder a second time did Bonnie glance around. A blank stare and a nod greeted him. She turned back to her game.

In a moment, the machine cried, hungry again, needing more food, more coins. Bonnie pointed to a nearby chair in which he should sit. From her purse, she pulled a roll of two dollar coins and tore it open, the crumpled paper wrapper falling to the floor.

Sterling liked to play the occasional hand of blackjack but the VLT's had yet to seduce him. The stack of silver and bronze toonies told him he would be waiting some time as Bonnie played.

The reporter leaned back, took the opportunity to study this beautiful woman. Most of her long blonde hair curled and waved on top of her head in a style more fitting to ball gowns and diamond tiaras. Her tan leather coat remained buttoned but pink satin slacks flared over red pumps with the tallest heels he'd ever seen.

Sterling frowned. She was dressed to kill in the Wheelhouse Bar with its carpet of peanut shells and cigarette butts. Then the answer came. Tonight, Bonnie served tables. A silent whistle blew from his lips. The other waitresses had better go back to their closets for more ammunition.

"Sorry for making you wait."

At the sound of her voice, Sterling looked up. Only her coffee cup sat on the ledge of the VLT table, the stack of coins gone. He checked his watch again — fifty dollars swallowed in fewer than five minutes.

The shock must have showed. "This is my only vice," Bonnie looked away from him and down at her hands, spreading her fingers, studying them.."I don't drink much or anything like that so when the tension seems too much, I'll sit in front of one of these machines for a few minutes." Her sad, subdued laugh wavered. "It's almost as good as shopping."

She seemed nervous and kicked a pile of wrappers further under the table with the pointed toe of her pump. The quiver in her voice begged for reassurance. Sterling's fingers squeezed her shoulder. "I'm sorry. He was a good man."

Her hand covered his as she stood. "Thank you. Let's get a table. I'd like some coffee."

It had been so long. The warmth on his skin frightened him, burned. He withdrew from her touch. "Is Brendan here?"

Bonnie shook her head. "One of his migraines hit when we got back to the house and he headed for his bedroom. He won't be up again until tomorrow at the earliest."

Sterling eyed her satin slacks and spike heels as they made their way to the front of the barroom and sat in a quiet corner.

"It looks like you're ready for work," he said.

Bonnie's slim white hand played with the top button of her coat before dropping to her side. Her nails glowed scarlet.

"I feel so awful." Tears formed in the corners of her eyes. "It's my only chance. Big Jim won't be back."

The urge to touch her again overwhelmed him. "Big Jim?"

Bonnie nodded at a framed photograph above them, one of many lining the walls featuring musicians who had played in the club over the years. A tall husky man wearing a Montreal Expos baseball cap and a grin as wide as the stage on which he strutted played a big Stratocaster guitar. Beside him, a beautiful blonde woman poured her heart into the microphone she gripped in both fists, her body bent backward almost in a swoon. Her halter top, as if studded with diamonds, glittered in the harsh spotlight revealing a tiny milk waist. She tilted on very tall heels, her shiny slacks flaring in the light. Sterling could almost hear the soul flowing from Bonnie's lips.

"That was last summer," she explained, "when John brought the band up here. He knew Big Jim from some dates he played for the army in Ottawa. I got up on stage for a couple of tunes and now he's going to audition me for his next tour."

Why was a woman who was about to marry a man almost thirty years her senior thinking about going on the road with the boys in the band? "What did John think of that?"

The tears disappeared and Bonnie's eyes cleared. "It was only going to be for a few weeks at a time. John knew my dream was to become a singer." She glanced down at the floor. "That's why I loved him. He was so understanding." She looked back up at Sterling. "I feel terrible. The very day John's body is found."

"What did Big Jim say when you told him the news?"

That same sad smile tugged at her mouth. "I know the words sound corny but they weren't, coming from a professional like him. He said, 'the show must go on.' That's why I want to sing tonight. For John."

The colonel had seen more than beauty, he had seen the strength of her will. "Then you should," said Sterling. "And don't worry about what anyone thinks."

"Thanks." Again the warmth shocked him as she put her hand on his. "I'm sorry, I'd just like to freshen up." she said, and rose, "You wanted to know about John's life in Candle Lake. I'll be right back."

Sterling's eyes followed her to the washroom door, her tall heels giving her saunter an unsteady rhythm. Why had she looked away when she talked of John's love and understanding?

As Bonnie disappeared, sharp voices erupted from the entrance foyer. Although obscured by the crowd, Sterling could just see two men glaring up at the hulk blocking the doorway. The next moment, from out of the throng, the young titan flew through the air. He landed on his back over an empty table and, before he could move, one of the two intruders walked over, hitched the bouncer up on the wall by the scruff of his denim shirt.

"We don't pay no cover charge." The snarl rumbled through the room in the sudden silence.

The doorman nodded, slid to the floor.

The two new customers found themselves a table, called to the waitress for a couple of beers. She looked to another woman behind the bar. By the lines around her eyes, the one in charge appeared about ten years older. She glanced at the door, saw that, although worse for wear, her man once again guarded his post. She nodded and uncapped two bottles.

The Braun brothers laughed and removed their hats out of an apparent sense of decorum. It seemed they preferred a few drinks over sleep to get out the road rust.

Ed's boys had grown up liking a little fun. It would pay to keep an eye on them. The manager knew enough not antagonize a couple of punks. What else did she know about them?

Sterling waited for a lull before walking past a couple of the other waitresses on a hurried smoke break. The cigarettes would be the servers's last respite of the night. The line-up now extended into the parking lot.

"You're Myles Sterling," the bartender said, her smile easy. She handed him his change and a mug of something dark on tap. The reporter offered his hand.

"I'm Monique Leblanc, the manager," she added. Her grip held firm and her eyes flirted. "John told me you'd be coming out here from down east." As she spoke the dead man's name, the grin vanished, a sadness lining her face. "We'd been hoping he'd walk through the door and say it was all a mistake. He'd just gone on a little holiday, that's all."

"Did you know him well?" Sterling edged onto a bar stool so he could keep an eye on his table and Bonnie's return.

Just as he'd spoken, a bellow from the waitress station broke through the quiet chaos of the growing crowd. "Chi-chi, pina colada, brown cow, two silver clouds, three rootbeer floats and four paralyzers!"

"Boys drink beer." Monique raised her eyebrows. "The girls have arrived."

Sure enough, women dressed for a night on the town crowded a couple of tables. Glossy lipstick shone and tight jeans pinched all around.

Monique didn't miss a beat. As if from the deft hands of a magician, a row of glasses of differing shapes and sizes materialized on the bar and filled with colourful liquids. She juggled bottles like rubber balls while at the same time giving Sterling's question some thought.

"I knew him well. I knew him very well once."

Her scarlet nails wrapped like claws around the kaleidoscope of drinks as she set them at the waitress station.

"I'm doing a memorial piece on the colonel and I'd appreciate your thoughts," Sterling said.

At first, this had the desired effect. A smile lit Monique's face but left as quickly as if she'd decided her reaction inappropriate. "What's going to happen to the Wheelhouse now?" he continued.

This question hit home. Monique became grim as the bellow of another drink order floated across the bar.

"The lawyer phoned this afternoon and told us to keep working until the will is read." A mug of lager slipped from her hand foaming over the ice-filled sink below. No harm done yet she seemed agitated. "I have a job for awhile anyway."

"A good crowd for Big Jim." Sterling gestured at the Braun boys downing more beers. Several empties now littered their table. "Not everyone thinks they should have to pay to see him."

Monique's eyes flashed, her hand now steady on the draft lever. "I'll speak to their father one more time." Her focus narrowed, ice blue. "Then I go to the police."

"So this wasn't the first time?" Sterling prompted.

Monique sloshed another round of frothy mugs on the servers's counter. When she turned back, she paused as if deciding how much to say.

"My family moved here from Quebec when I was a kid. Ed was about the only one in school who took the time to listen to the broken English of the Frog girl. Let's just say we grew up together."

The crowd buzzed in anticipation of the first set. Sterling found himself shouting.

"Do you know anything about your mayor, Dan Farrow?"

The bar manager's shoulders stiffened. "Look. I can't answer any more of your questions right now."

Even in the din, the anger in her brittle voice emerged. Something had snapped when he mentioned Farrow's name.

"Mind if I call you to arrange that interview?"

Monique said nothing, uncapped another beer.

"Thanks," Sterling said, sliding from the stool before she could refuse.

He halted. Bonnie had returned to the table and one of the Braun boys had slipped over. His thick shoulders hung over her chair, his lips moved inches from her face. Her back straight, she glared as he jawed something at her.

Sterling strained, still couldn't hear the words between them. Then Bonnie cried out, "No! Stay away from me!"

Her hands shoved at the young trucker's chest. Braun just stared, let her push him back a step. He turned as Sterling reached the table. The young man hadn't yet shaved, his eyes glassy, like a bear just arisen from his cave.

"How's it going, tinker toy man?" he said, stabbing a forefinger into Sterling's shoulder as he walked away.

"What words to describe the power of song? Of the Singer? Many can make music. Only a few can make it absolute magic. It is rare that the song fuses with the heart and soul through the singer's voice to become a storm of emotion on stage. Such power is bestowed sparingly. It may take years for the gift to surface or it might shine early on. When at last its heat sears the public, people go on bended knee to be blessed. Last night, the crowd genuflected before Bonnie Matheson."

Sterling browsed the screen of his laptop. Another couple of paragraphs should round it out. After he'd phoned the editorial desk to file his stories on the colonel's death, he'd gotten on the line with the entertainment editor. Yes, a review of Big Jim Mcleod and special guest at the Wheelhouse would be just lovely, my boy.

Sterling's fingers left the keyboard for a moment to turn up the stereo. A Mozart violin

concerto serenaded his thoughts. Bonnie's beautiful, anguished voice still haunted him. It soared
and cried as if in her young life she'd stored a
thousand years of sorrow. For John, she told the
crowd.

Sterling thought of her sad eyes as they sat at
the table and talked for an hour before she went
on stage, mostly about her fiancé, how his death
had followed those of her parents not long before,
but also her reaction to her confrontation with the
Braun twin: "I wish I wouldn't lose my temper
but I'm just a bundle of nerves these days. He
sure wouldn't be the first drunk to hit on a waitress." She'd laughed. "I'd like to apologize to him
but was that Zeke or Zak?"

Apologize! Was she nuts? Sterling shook his
head. Perhaps she stood closer to the cliff edge
than anyone knew.

How thick some guys could be picked at
Sterling's craw. The young trucker couldn't have
missed the news that the body of her fiancé had
been found. Yet only hours later, he circled,
making his move.

Sterling hoped the boys wouldn't come
between him and their father. At least if the police
labelled the colonel's death murder, they had an
alibi. Ed said the three of them stayed in hospital
until the Monday after McTaggart went missing.
It would be very touchy to have to investigate the

Braun boys in the death of their father's best friend.

Even at 2 AM Sterling didn't feel any cobwebs, sleep for him always a slipshod affair. He felt numb with cold, however, and rose to squeeze another log into the already roaring fireplace. He fanned his hands to the flames, which didn't generate near enough energy to warm the whole cottage.

The uninitiated would think it ridiculous to run the electric wall heaters only in the garage so he could work on the Triumph while leaving the little cabin frigid. For that very reason, he'd keep the situation to himself. Finances forced him to choose and choose he did. Any visitors would just have to bundle up, no questions asked. Sparks flew as he jammed more wood into the little inferno.

The bungalow-style home nestled midway in a one block dead-end street, the preferred arrangement for residents in the pine-forested village. Sterling had browsed through the general store's bulletin board and the cottage fell in his lap like a gift — fully furnished with a handyman's garage. Only Sterling and a few deer wintered in the neighbourhood, the solitary existence heartening in its own way. There would be no complaints about his music. Rachmaninoff, Shostakovich fought off the enemy. Silence invited the dead.

Sterling sat back down at his makeshift desk, watched the second hand move around the face of his clock. The colonel had discovered sleep. Bonnie said that when the voices, the visions disappeared, learning to relax gladdened John most about becoming human again. So much so, he could take in stride the sight of a butcher shop.

Not Sterling, though. The very thought of raw meat still inched his last meal back up his throat. A glimpse sent him reeling to the toilet.

Bonnie told him that on the first date with her future fiancé they drove to Prince Albert for lunch at the Vietnamese. Strolling downtown afterward, the sun shone on a picture window featuring mounds of ground beef. McTaggart's eyes had grown large like those of a frightened animal and he tore away from her. She chased after him into an alley where he slumped against a dumpster, retching.

Almost a year later, the week before the engagement, they met for another plate of dim sum. He'd seen a nice bit of tenderloin on sale, he'd told her. He smiled, proud, the sight of meat no longer sickening to him.

Sterling downed a finger of scotch on ice, placing the porcelain cup back on the coffee table. Would he ever find such peace?

The only belongings the TR6 had room to tote rested on the carpeted floor of the living room —

a suitcase that fit in the boot and the cardboard box of files that had ridden the passenger seat. He rose, carried the piece of luggage into the bedroom where he wrapped the quilt around his shoulders and returned to the front room and the box. Dragging it across the rug, he sat cross-legged in front of the fire, released the bungee cords holding the cardboard together. He stopped, got up again. He needed the fortification of another drink before browsing through the newspaper clippings of the stories he'd penned in Africa. Full cup in hand, he turned the pages.

Rwanda made for a sordid tale. The pleas and demands from the head peace keeper on the ground for more troops rang desperate and hollow. For months, the commanding general warned his bosses in New York that the country teetered on the edge of a monumental bloodbath. Kill the *inyenzi*, slaughter the cockroaches official radio broadcast day after day. An orchestrated massacre cooked in the government's kitchen. New York didn't listen. Instead, U.N. headquarters withdrew most troops leaving McTaggart and his men among the few that remained. The world sat on its hands and watched.

The U.S. decided it no longer had the stomach for African adventure. Without help from its biggest player, the U.N. decided it hadn't the means to stop the "conflict" in Rwanda. The two bit players were no help, either. Belgium, the old colonial master, couldn't pull out its chips fast enough when ten of its own peacekeepers died at the hands of Hutu death squads. France stood pat, complacent, handing out arms behind its back to the *genocidaires*. The Hutu spoke French. The Tutsi attacking from Uganda spoke English. Fait accompli.

The bloodbath that followed still haunted Sterling's waking hours, terrorized his dreams. Almost a million people cut down by the ancient machete or the even cruder spiked stick in a mere three months.

Sterling pondered the impossible —describing the enormity of genocide. The words he wrote seemed useless. The numbers spoke for themselves but who listened? For most Westerners, Rwanda existed on the dark continent, best known for the life and death of American Dian Fossey among its mountain gorillas. The deluge of human blood over the land staggered the mind. For that reason, he wrote about the Tutsi woman and her child. *Prenez mon bébé. Prenez lui s'il vous plait.*

Sterling refilled his glass with four fingers, no ice this time. Braun proved to be the strongest of the three of them. He'd been through even more than the colonel and no demons seemed to haunt him. He ran a thriving business. He wasn't the first to have sons who would weather hormonal tirades before settling down.

The scotch, all of it, burned going down. It was Sterling who'd cracked. But where, when — in Somalia, in Rwanda? Or in Serbia, his fiancée's head lolling lifeless on his shoulder as he drove the cratered highway?

Early Morning March 4, 2000

Sterling jumped and wrenched around. The horn blasted the air as if the mammoth diesel locomotive roared mere metres from his back. Embarrassed, he turned forward again. The railroad tracks ran across the forest ridge at least a kilometre away. In the tranquility of twenty below zero, sound magnified, twisted.

Sterling's footsteps crunched in the hard crust of Candle Lake, his breath billowing through the thick wool scarf draping his face. His insulated Kodiak snow boots, quilted nylon ski pants, mitts and hooded parka left only his eyes bared to the chill wind. He toted a fishing rod and tackle box borrowed from Ed Braun.

Sterling felt silly, glad of the darkness. He'd grown up on the prairies, played outdoor hockey wearing not much more than a sweater and a jacket. Now at forty-two, after travelling the world, he waddled along like he just fell off the turnip truck from the tropics. His chosen attire, he figured, protected him to about seventy below in a blizzard.

He halted his brisk walk before the Matheson estate to avoid breaking into a sweat. Perspiration freezing to the skin would only mean trouble and defeat the purpose of all the warm layers. He'd need them, however, if the colonel's fish shack turned out to be one of those bare bones affairs for the tough and hardy — a wooden stall over a stool and a hole in the ice, not much different from a frozen privy.

Sterling's eyes travelled the sprawling three storeys of Bonnie and Brendan's home. Even in the moonlight, the lakeside view of their cottage presented something more akin to a mansion. The pine log beauty preened, all picture windows, balconies, turrets and alcoves. Their parents, Bonnie had said during their talk, had left them this inheritance. She'd given Sterling the address on the pretense he should drop by to see if Brendan had emerged from his migraine.

He would do that later. For now, he continued along Lakeview Drive until he reached a walkway that darted between two houses. This connected with a path skirting the frozen edge before curving onto the lake proper. Looking back, he saw the well-packed trail veered by the rear of the Matheson yard. On his final walk to his fish shack, McTaggart would have taken this route.

Stamping his feet to keep warm, the reporter trudged along the trodden snow a couple of hundred metres further onto the ice where the trail forked. One path headed to the middle of the lake and the shadowy outline of a cluster of huts. The other meandered toward the nearer shacks at the mouth of Fisher Creek.

"Is there a storm coming, buddy?" The deep voice resonated, somehow familiar. "I don't want to freeze to death."

Sterling turned. The moon off the snow lit the silhouette. The elder man in a wool lumber jacket and Montreal Canadiens tuque stood about equal height but barrel-chested, his body the V-shape of an iron anvil and, the reporter remembered, just about as tough.

"Noel Parenteau! Is that you?"

The fellow said nothing, his grin fading. Sterling studied the man he'd known since child-hood. Noel didn't seem to have changed in twenty-five years. He sported the same salt and pepper crew-cut, matching goatee. His brown skin showed none of the wrinkles of age and his almond eyes still sparkled.

Those eyes, however, darted in fear as Sterling clomped forward, arms open wide in a bear hug. As if under attack by a mummified monster, terror flooded the man's face.

Sterling stopped, unwrapped the scarf from his face and pulled down his hood.

"Myles Sterling!" the elder Parenteau laughed. The two men shook hands, clapped each other on the shoulder. "I was just reading about you. The *Sun* said it's hired a world famous war correspondent." Noel claimed ancestry with the Metis buffalo hunters and would tell his son Kevin and friends stories passed on from his grandfather. Young Myles had never known whether to believe the wonderful tales. Noel Parenteau had liked to pull your leg, make the kids laugh.

"What are you doing around here?" Sterling smiled.

"We moved into our summer cabin for good when I retired from the pulp mill last year." Parenteau tapped the folded newspaper under his arm. "When I read who it was, I said that's no war correspondent, that's little Myles from the high school paper. Probably here to do another story on Kevin."

Noel's son Kevin, Myles's best buddy through high school, could skate like the wind, throw a football with the force of a bazooka shell. As editor of the school newspaper, Sterling often featured the hero's picture on the front page scoring the winning goal or passing for the last second touchdown. Making passes and scoring wasn't a one-sided affair either. Myles managed more than one date from his friend's cast-offs. To top it off, Kevin also hit the honour roll every year.

But Myles had punched and scratched to enough grunting draws, slipped in and out of enough scrapes with Kevin to know he was as human as the next teenager on a cyclone's tail of hormones. Sometimes the hero blew a game and Myles wrote about that, too.

"Does your son still make his living by keeping rapists and cokeheads out of jail?" Sterling teased.

"He works both sides of the fence now. When crown counsel is short-staffed, Kevin gets a few cases thrown his way." Noel Parenteau grinned. "Good conviction rate, too." Lacking a high school education himself, Noel tracked his son's career through the courts like a hound. From the occasional word Sterling had received from back home over the years, it seemed Noel had become as knowledgeable about jurisprudence as any lawyer. "Otherwise, the boy's got a nice little practice going. As a matter of fact, the Lac Minowukaw Indian Band has laid a claim to this very land. Kevin's their man up front. You should give him a call."

Noel's and Kevin's brown eyes held the same unmistakable twinkle. Both men flashed a smile with the same ease and cut the same broad-shouldered swath.

Sterling's gaze fell. "I'm pretty caught up with the new job, the death of John McTaggart and all." The reporter didn't tell a lie, not really. Then again, perhaps Kevin rolled in enough dough now that he'd have forgotten all about an ancient debt of a few bucks. "I will when things have settled down."

Parenteau nodded. The spark in his eye deadened. "Terrible thing that, the colonel's death. I helped him build his shack. He hardly needed me, though. John was quite the perfectionist."

"Did you see him the weekend he went missing?"

The older man scratched his beard. "From what I hear, I was probably one of the last people to have seen him." He pointed to the scattered community in the middle of the lake. "I've been after trout this year. Mine's one of those travel trailers on skids. It's rigged for winter, nice and cozy so I can take the occasional nap or sleep overnight. That weekend, my wife was visiting her sister in Saskatoon so I just stayed in the trailer to get an early start." He frowned. "The damn chainsaw sounded like it was right outside the door. You know how sound travels at thirty below. I got up and peeked out the window just as the racket quit."

Parenteau glanced up at the starry sky. "It snowed that night but then it cleared with a bright moon. I could see John working around his shack." He shook his head. "It seemed early to be making such a racket but I thought I should ask if he needed a hand. He must have finished what he was doing though because right then he went inside and didn't come out again."

Parenteau laughed. "I was glad to get back under the covers. Now that I'm retired, I like sleeping as much as I used to like working. I went over after sun-up hoping he'd filled his freezer again. He'd been giving pickerel away. No-one around, but everything looked okay."

"You found it strange that McTaggart would make a commotion at that time of the morning?" Sterling asked.

"I was a little surprised." Parenteau shrugged. "John was a smart cookie. He would have known there might be a couple of overnighters on the lake. It's just common politeness to wait until daylight before making much noise."

"Perhaps he didn't realize how the sound carried?"

Parenteau's face twisted, doubtful, then grinned. "Well, you're the famous war correspondent."

Sterling knew when an old sage put the young guys on. "I'll keep what you told me in mind."

"Call Kevin," the father said, "he'd be thrilled."

"Tell him when I'm settled I'll give him a shout," Sterling said, shaking Noel's hand, "but it won't be for a while."

Parenteau gave the reporter's cumbersome clothing another once over. "Are you sure a storm isn't on its way?" The old man opened his stocky arms to the winter moonlight. "A geezer could catch his death."

Sterling shook his head as Parenteau headed down the path to his trailer. Knowing Noel, he would be fitter than most men half his age.

Sterling stepped along the icy path thinking of the one lucky summer he spent at Candle Lake with the Parenteau family. That year, Nurse Mom Sterling almost lived at the hospital covering extra shifts and Judge Dad Sterling took the opportunity to bone up on his international law at a conference in Stockholm. At fourteen, a boy's nerve endings danced with the devil and Myles couldn't have been happier when he'd been invited to test his forest mettle with Kevin.

The lake had steamed with July heat, and after supper, the boys promising not to wander far, had dressed in their uniforms of jeans, T-shirts and sneakers. They tramped near a bog at the north end of the lake. Kevin took the lead following a path of solid ground, careful not to veer where they could sink to their waist in seconds.

"Wolves don't attack humans," Kevin pronounced, "they're afraid of us." Listening to his friend, Myles patted the rectangular outline in his pants pocket, a box of wooden matches given to him by Mr. Parenteau. Never go into the forest without them, he'd warned.

"You know why they call it Candle?" Kevin continued his lecture. He stopped, pointed across the water. Slow ripples lapped at their feet. "Some nights you can see the light of a ghost out there. It's like a giant candle flickering in the wind."

His eyes narrowed, shifted from side to side, his version of a man haunted. "The Cree say evil spirits invaded their graves here. The light is a warning never to set camp, never to sleep at this end of the lake where the spirits can creep into your body."

Myles laughed but didn't hesitate to step from the shadows into the light and hard earth of an opening in the copse of trees where he could breath more easily.

Sterling surveyed the rolling ground of high grass and wild daisies shouldered on each side by aspen and pine. His eyes halted. Five wolves, four black and one grey, stood there, each the size of a very large dog.

"Kevin!"

"It's okay," Young Parenteau breathed, "they won't attack humans."

The pack moved in a direct path towards them from about fifty metres away. The closer the animals came, the harder Myles's heart pounded.

"Are you sure?"

Kevin nodded, cleared his throat. Myles glanced at his friend. Beads of sweat trickled down Parenteau's forehead. The wolves broke into a trot. Despite his claim, Kevin joined Myles in a slow-stepping retreat.

The beating in Myles's chest thundered in his ears. The pack was not more than fifteen metres away. Long canine jaws hung open, their tongues cradled between fangs. The eyes of the leader, the grey alpha, hypnotized him with the palest, purest yellow he'd ever seen. The animal split to the left and a black went right. The wolves slid through the grass in attack formation.

The boys turned heel and ran back to the forest edge. The closest branches of a jack pine waved above their heads but fear and adrenalin gave them the legs of hunted rabbits. A deep growl tingled Sterling's spine and a sharp yank ripped at the heel of his runner as rough bark and pine needles dug into his palms. He scrambled up limb over limb until a heavy thicket stopped his progress. Underneath, the grey sat on his haunches as two blacks circled and leaped,

leaped and circled. Their jaws snapped only air, splattering the boys shoes with saliva.

Myles did a slow dance, lifting the nearest foot as each attacker reached the apex of its futile effort. Kevin stood alongside in the tree, shaking his head, eyes wide as he stared down.

Young Sterling's voice had matured to a lower timbre but at that moment sounded as if it had lost some years. "What now?"

Kevin's voice cracked in reply: "I'm thinking," he said. "I'm thinking."

The futile lunging ceased. Now the four blacks circled the pine, snarling, their tongues dripping saliva. A few metres away, the haunting eyes of the grey stared, silent, motionless.

"What if they never leave?" asked Myles. He lifted his foot, inspected the sole of his runner. Sure enough, a tooth-shaped hollow had been carved in the rubber.

Kevin's face wrinkled, the question disconcerting. "They can go for days without eating."

The sun settled just above the treetops. Cooling darkness would soon overtake the forest. How would they keep warm? Myles shivered, then remembered.

"What about fire?" he said, pulling the box of matches from his pocket.

A small smile crept over Kevin's face. He closed his fist, gave Myles a soft punch. Looking upward, he broke some twigs from the thicket at their heads.

"Light these," he said.

After several attempts at igniting the moist bog wood, Myles muttered, "We're wasting matches." Gazing at his friend's shirt, he said, "Cloth burns." He pinched the cotton material. "Rip off a piece."

Kevin stared at Myles, glanced at the darkening sky. "Rip a piece of your own."

The boys glared but after a moment each began tearing his own sleeve. Myles held out a swatch of his t-shirt which began to smoulder under Kevin's match. The blacks jumped, yelped when the flaming material landed in their circle. Their noses cringed at the smell and they turned away. The grey, however, remained still and soon the pack of betas resumed its vigil under the boys.

"Not them," Kevin directed, nodding at the leader, "him. Light mine." Flames consumed the piece of cloth. The fire wafted through the air seeming to hypnotize the grey. The perfect toss floated, floated, dropped on his snout. The big wolf barked, scampered away, the pack quick to follow. At the edge of the opening, the alpha halted. Those pale yellow eyes stared at the boys, etching them in memory, then he disappeared into the forest.

Sterling frowned. Other moments made him feel less proud. Would those have dimmed in Kevin's mind? Or was that too much to ask?

He took the snow trail leading to the head of Fisher Creek. A few rays of morning light sneaking between the clouds licked the burnished metal of a structure about twenty metres apart from the others. Glinting like a distant star, this signalled the colonel's pickerel hole.

Here the path lay bare. Just as Brendan had said, the wind funneling down the creek left a swath of nothing but black ice. Any tracks made in a snowfall would soon be covered and last only as long as the calm. Sterling glanced down the lake to the spot McTaggart's body turned up, 300 metres away.

"Shack" might have been the appropriate term for some of the four-sided lean-tos on the lake but not this one. From the outside, every fit and corner looked perfect. Rivets secured the walls of aluminum alloy sheeting and two sides of the building had windows, with thermal panes, no less. Rubber insulation framed the door. Every detail spelled McTaggart's work, all right. Some frozen privy. Sterling should have known better.

He faced the entrance, the heavy padlock. Over the years, the reporter had become handy with both a credit card and a screwdriver. Setting down the fishing rod, he opened the tackle box and pulled out a multi-headed driver. He afixed the appropriate bit. Within minutes, the plate that secured the latch to the wall dangled loose, its four screws in his mitt, the padlock still snapped tight.

The door swung open. Darkness shrouded the room but the flashlight illuminated a propane lantern hanging from a ceiling rafter. Once fired, the warm light shone on an impressive sight, at least for an ice fishing shack. If there were Rolls Royce models, this met the standard. A military precision set everything neat and in its place.

A bench, padded for warmth, ran along all four walls broken only by the doorway. About three metres square, wooden planks underfoot on one side and bare ice on the other divided the little building. An axe, nets and wooden clubs hung from the walls. Sterling opened a cupboard drawer to find filleting knives in a range of sizes.

McTaggart knew how to live. In the corner, a propane heater sat atop a twenty pound tank. Within minutes, warm air washed the small area and Sterling's parka lay on the seat as he browsed.

One section of the shelves that covered most of the walls contained an array of hand tools but nothing specific to angling — no lures, line or even needle-nosed pliers for removing hooks. However, the mandatory wooden club to seal the fate of any catch deemed a keeper did dangle from a hook.

The heavy duty and high-tech equipment on the end wall provoked more interest. The colonel liked his toys. A motorized auger and chainsaw made preparation of the fishing hole fast and easy. An oily-smelling gasoline can labelled "two-stroke" sloshed half full. Behind one cupboard door rested a leather satchel. Sterling picked it up and peeked inside. Setting the bag down, his gaze caught on four broad-headed steel spikes scattered on the floor. Only these items appeared not to be in their special place, as if just tossed there.

Sterling kneeled and wiped away the glaze of frost. The ice shone smooth and clear with an aquamarine tinge, the silk texture of a newly flooded skating rink. The colonel had last been here the month before yet left no sign of a fishing hole. As a matter of fact, the whole open area of the shack had the same sheen.

With a little fuel and some coaxing, the tin roar of the auger rattled the small building. By the time Sterling trimmed the new opening to about six inches across, he'd peeled off a couple more sweaters that sat on the naugahyde seat. Shutting down the chainsaw, he replaced it on the shelf and wiped his brow.

He went back to the cupboard, eyed the toy he'd found. Playtime! Unzipping the satchel, Sterling pulled out an underwater viewing system. McTaggart had spared no expense. A spool of cable attached a fist-sized camera to a semi-rectangular control pod. Infra-red made the darkest waters no problem. Not only that, the video could be recorded on tape for posterity.

Sterling glanced at another reminder of how little the colonel had left to chance. Batteries powered the viewing system. For occasions when juice ran low, a gasoline generator for re-charging sat ready on the shelf.

The camera sunk into the black ice water as Sterling watched the viewing monitor. No surprise, the equipment worked fine. Even through dark and murky water, clear images appeared. Stopping the descent just above bottom, the depth chart in the corner of the monitor read three metres.

Sterling studied the screen. The picture didn't make sense. Turning the cable, he rotated the camera a full 360 degrees. It still didn't make sense. The lake bottom spread flat and featureless as far as the electronic eye could see. No ten metre rift, no crater broke the open expanse of underwater prairie flatland. No rocks, no weeds provided shadowed cover for the notoriously shy and absent walleye. No fish of any kind, even the garrulous and voracious northern pike plied these barren depths. Only a solitary log, like a broken fence post, jutted from the rippled sand.

Where was the colonel's bountiful pickerel hole? Where was the heaven-sent marine treasure chest that forced McTaggart to give away his catch so not to exceed his daily limit? Any venture into this stark waterscape would be a bold invitation to the bony and vicious jackfish, the walleye's mortal enemy, to come to dinner. The reporter stared at the monitor. This didn't make sense at all.

Sterling looked closer. Something he hadn't spotted before protruded from the sand beside the log. Spooling out cable and maneuvering the camera, he moved the red eye in for a closer look. Jigging over the log, the picture of the object cleared.

Rectangular and over a foot long, two metal latches on the face, it didn't appear natural. Reeling in a few feet of cable for a top view, what had to be a handle appeared. Could it be?

After hauling the camera out of the water, Sterling browsed through the supply of lures he'd brought and chose the six spoons with the largest treble hooks. Each of these he attached to a leader and tied to his line an inch apart from the one before.

Only one small detail remained. The augered hole was too small. Once again the thin metal ring of a tiny two-stroke engine consumed the shack with its lingering odour of smoke and oil. When he'd carved the hole in the ice to satisfactory size, Sterling exchanged the chainsaw for his fishing rod. First he lowered the camera back into the dark liquid then his flotilla of hooks.

The task demanded the patience of Job, or perhaps just the calm of a fisherman. Even guided by the camera, time after time, Sterling's grappling rig grazed over its prey or fell into the sand, empty. Finally, the hooks grabbed snug. With utmost care, the taut line dragged close to the water's surface. Sterling's arm dipped into the frigid lake and his bare hand snaked around the handle pulling the object onto the ice.

Who would have guessed? Water spilled from the brown plastic tackle box as he flipped the latch, opened the lid. The usual array of tackle now tangled in a bundle from its tumble into the deep. Exposed to the atmosphere, ice formed on the metal spoons despite the hut's shirtsleeve warmth.

Sterling pulled and prodded at the mess when something peaked out from the bottom. He retrieved the leather billfold and, with gentle fingers, unfolded its flaps careful not to tear any sodden papers inside. The only item he found hid behind the protection of a clear plastic window. It read:

Province of Saskatchewan

Angling License — 2000

John Robert McTaggart

A sudden crash bolted Sterling, his head yanking up. The door flew open, slammed against the outside wall of the shack. A gust of frigid wind stung the reporter's face. He squinted into the twilight. In the muted glow of the propane lamp, a huge silhouette loomed.

"You're under arrest."

The empty lock-up stank of stale piss and puke, the calling card of drunks embracing their home for the night. Sterling sat down on the grey steel bench anchored to the grey cinder-block wall and stared at the grey cement floor. He pulled his sweater over his nose, tried to mouth-breathe through the wool knit. It didn't help.

The ride to the small detachment at Meath Park had been silent, Staff Milburn a dark silhouette behind the wheel. The reporter had heard the iron clang from this side of the gate before but the odour never seemed this rank. As if the bars had become a solid barrier to all the senses, the flow of human waste stopped at the door.

Other encounters with incarceration had all occurred oceans away at border crossings where the thunder of artillery and machine gun fire rattled against the prodding of nervous soldiers. All Westerners were spies, especially journalists with their endless questions. American dollars and gold watches, though, proved good currency for passage. The hours locked in a stinking room drove up the price those sweating out a looming deadline would pay.

Sterling's hands slipped into his empty pockets. That was then and this was now. The few crumpled bills and loonies, the reporter's dime store timepiece, all among his possessions taken by the constable, would do little good here.

He studied the scrawl of graffiti that gave the bare, unpainted walls their only ambience. The jailors confiscated belts and anything pointed but where there was a will there was a way. Sharp pebbles dragged in on the sole of a muddy boot or even fingernails served prisoners struck by the muse. She raged sick and angry from what Sterling could read of the often illegible chicken scratch.

He leaned back, rested his head against the cold concrete wall. He'd been fortunate to get through on the phone. Even so, it would be a couple of hours before his rescue from this cesspool.

Milburn had confiscated the tackle box and billfold as evidence. Evidence of what, though? The mountie's face remained a stone mask when Sterling explained his own genius in spotting the box and grappling it out of the water. The cop didn't believe a word he'd said. Of course, he'd probably seen enough by now that his faith in other human beings hung pretty low. The reporter knew about that.

Still, Sterling had recovered new evidence. Milburn, though, wasn't tipping his hand either way. Brendan discovered McTaggart's body about 300 metres from his fishing shack. Yet his gear had fallen to the lake bottom directly under the shack. Where had McTaggart gone through the ice? Where was this famous pickerel hole?

Sterling turned his ear to raised voices. They came out of the front office just down the hallway from the cell. "That's an order!" He caught no other words from the flare-up. The conversation returned to normal, too low to decipher.

He rose from the unforgiving bench, began to pace the small room, his fat Kodiaks padding on the concrete floor. Was it possible the colonel had drowned with his tackle box and in time floated downstream? Sterling remembered lifting the kit out of the drink. Once the plastic container with all its metal lures and hooks filled with water, it's heft would sink it to the bottom where it would stay. Strong currents, however, could move a bloated body and McTaggart's hut sat at the mouth of Fisher Creek where it flowed into the lake.

The corpse might have drifted but Noel said nothing looked amiss around the hut, certainly no break in the ice through which a man could fall. Although there was no sign of it now, the only hole would be the one McTaggart fished in his shack and that one need not be any larger than the auger head.

Sterling halted his circle-march, slid onto the steel bench. If McTaggart had gone under where his body was found, the break in the ice wouldn't have been noticed. Away from the trodden paths, the wind-whipped snowdrifts in the middle of the lake made good camouflage, any rifts quick-frozen

Still, the scenario didn't answer why the colonel's tackle rested at the bottom so far from the body. Did it fall through by accident before the colonel drowned?

Sterling rose and again paced back and forth. There seemed to be something missing, something he hadn't thought through. Noel Parenteau said he saw nothing amiss around McTaggart's shack when he went by later that morning, no one about, the door padlocked. What was missing here?

Of course! Sterling himself had to enlarge the fishing hole to retrieve the tackle box. Whether it went into the water intentionally or accidentally, it had to pass through an opening in the ice. But big enough also for a man to go through? He stopped pacing. Perhaps, the problem didn't spell a dead-end, after all. Wouldn't there be a difference between new and old ice, the new ice that filled the hole and the old which surrounded it? A veteran fisherman would know and Sterling just happened to know a man who had winter-fished going on seventy years. Noel Parenteau might just be the one to determine if the colonel's own ice fishing hole had been the one to swallow him.

The door to the outer office slammed and Sterling heard boots stomping down the hall, echoing off the walls. Milburn and Constable Cuthand stopped in front of the cell. The staff sergeant rubbed his hands as he looked Sterling up and down. The young policeman, however, appeared sick and nervous.

"I see a troubling trend around here," the staff sergeant announced, furrowing his brow to show his consternation. "It seems some reporters think they're above the law." Sterling twitched. He could see Milburn enjoyed this too much. Wherever he headed, the destination looked ugly. "Some members of the so-called fourth estate, for instance, think they can imbibe illegal drugs with impunity." Now the cop glared. "They think it makes them look suave and sophisticated in front of college girls even though the guttersnipes were stupid enough to buy poison."

Sterling held Milburn's eyes without blinking. The circled story in the P.A. *Sun* on Braun's desk

Scott Gregory Miller

said tainted crystal meth had sent two people to hospital. One of them had been a talking head for the local television station. The cop's imagination worked overtime. Now he saw guttersnipes everywhere.

Cuthand appeared unhappier as each second passed. He pulled at his collar. Too tight? Or did his shoes pinch? He wouldn't stand still. At a signal, he opened the cell gate and guided Sterling out by the elbow. Milburn grabbed the other arm and they marched along the hall to a small windowless room furnished with only a table and three chairs. As an interrogation room, it appeared no better or worse than most he'd seen around the world.

Over the years, a few of Sterling's comrades had been tortured but he had never been. Even in Canada, cops behind closed doors sometimes rolled up their sleeves, got down to the business of softening up the hard cases or, as the phrase went, "instilling in them the fear of God." Sterling kept his face hard, blank. How bad could it get?

"I detected a funny smell in the ice shack you broke into," Milburn said.

It would do little good to protest. Still, Sterling countered, "I was running the power auger and chainsaw."

"Forget your incense?"

The big staff sergeant nodded at Cuthand whose shifting from foot to foot and fidgeting grew worse. Sterling hoped not, but the thought struck him the constable might burst into tears. The young man opened a cupboard, hesitated, then retrieved a pair of rubber gloves.

"Before the calvary arrives, I want you checked over." Milburn said. "We call this T.T. and B. Take off your clothes, turn around and," the cop paused and his malicious grin grew huge, "bend over."

He stepped out of the room and closed the door behind him.

An hour later, Sterling dug his fingernails into his palms, hoped to draw blood, as if the pain would make him feel better. Did he want to jump over the desk, grab a lip in each fist and rip the smirk off Milburn's face or would it be better just to crawl in a corner never to be seen again. He burned with pure fury and shame.

He stood in Milburn's office. A million words fluttered about his mind. He turned to his lawyer beside him, slick with his black razor-cut hair, his navy pinstriped suit cuffed like a knife blade. The man put a gentle finger to his mouth indicating that Sterling should shut up.

"Was a full body search of my client absolutely necessary, Staff Sergeant Milburn?" the lawyer asked.

The policeman, preoccupied with his computer, glanced up for only a moment before returning to his keyboard, two-finger style. Sterling steamed. Cyberspace technology and the cop still typed like an oaf. "There was a suspicious odour in the shack," Milburn said.

"I'm advised that was the exhaust smell of a chainsaw and power auger, and nothing more."

Milburn grimaced as he studied his monitor. "Some toxic crystal meth has surfaced in the area and people have been hurt. Any hint of illegal substances and I can't be too careful." He glanced at the accused and his legal counsel. "Especially where reporters are concerned."

"Now that the colonel's tackle box has been found, are you going to send some divers down?" Sterling interjected.

The sharply dressed legal representative grabbed his client's arm, glowered at him to be silent. With rage fueled by the memory of probing digits, Sterling glared back.

"We mounted a full scale search for McTaggart and found nothing," Milburn said. "Whatever else we do, it will be without your direction and without informing you." The policeman studied the reporter, seemed to find him lacking. "I warned you, no interference." Glancing at the lawyer, the staff sergeant corrected himself: "Mr. Sterling."

"For the public record then, what do you claim happened?" the reporter snapped.

The cop stared at the two men, shrugged. "Perhaps this will put an end to it. The coroner's report indicates John McTaggart's lungs were full of water. He drowned. The slight contusion on the back of his skull is consistent with him hitting his head as he fell through the ice. The shock of the frigid water in freezing temperatures took over. Death occurred approximately six weeks ago. It happens around here." Milburn raised his two fingers in preparation for more keyboarding. "The colonel's gear went down with him where it stayed. The current from Fisher Creek pushed the corpse farther into the lake where it was discovered by a local resident."

Sterling watched Milburn poke at the keys. From the evidence so far, the scenario made sense.

"Where did he fall through? Why didn't anyone see the break in the ice?" the reporter asked. "There's a whole village of fishing shacks there."

"A snowfall could have covered the hole as it froze."

Plausible, perhaps, but Sterling didn't want to give Milburn even that much satisfaction. A quiet knock broke the angry current between the two men. Milburn's poised typing fingers fell to his desk.

Young Cuthand stood in the doorway avoiding eye contact and pulling at that damn collar. Poor guy he'd never be the same.

The constable cleared his throat. "Excuse me, sir. I just got off the phone with Bonnie Matheson. She said Sterling was a friend of McTaggart's and she gave the reporter permission to use the shack."

Milburn didn't look surprised, just suspicious. "Why didn't he use a key?"

"She said she couldn't find one."

"I'll bet."

Sterling nodded. A darling. Bonnie was just a little darling.

"If that will be all?" the lawyer asked.

Milburn resumed his pecking. He didn't look up. "I don't want to see your client again. Understand?"

"Tell me, Staff Sergeant," Sterling said, "why didn't you do the body search? It seems like the kind of work that would be right down your line. Not as tough as typing, for instance."

Before the cop could respond, Kevin Parenteau whirled Sterling around and hustled him past a grinning Cuthand and out of the office.

"I was just going to call you," Sterling said, shivering despite the short walk to the detachment's gravel parking lot.

"You just did call me. Why else would I be here?" Parenteau slung his passenger a quizzical glance.

Sterling leaned back into the sumptuous leather of the Jaguar X-type. Sinuous curves graced the sleek little sedan. He removed his mitts, fanned his fingers over the air vents bathing his hands in the luxurious heat. Things had changed from the sixties when the British couldn't make anything that ran well in below zero weather. The rich odour of tanned cowhide laced the air: that sweet smell of success. Would a couple of hundred dollars mean much to a man of such stature? Of course not. Such an ancient debt would have slipped from his mind years ago.

"I meant that I meant to call you as soon as I had a chance, old buddy," Sterling said, slapping Parenteau on the back.

Despite the icy road, Kevin manipulated the little missile as if it rode on rails. With one hand on the wheel, his other arm dove up to the elbow in the briefcase beside him, rummaging. Pulling out a piece of paper at which he first glanced, the lawyer laid the single sheet on Sterling's lap.

"You owe me two thousand one hundred forty-seven dollars and," Parenteau said, "forget the cents." He smiled. "Old buddy."

"TWO THOUSAND ONE HUNDRED AND FORTY-SEVEN DOLLARS!" Sterling gulped. "For a forty-five minute drive from Prince Albert?" His eyes widened as large in wonder as he could make them.

"I haven't billed you for that yet." One old buddy looked over at the other. "This is for the parking tickets."

Sterling slunk down in the seat, so soft. Not cows but baby lambs, squealing to the heavens above, had given their lives for this leather. The reporter stared at Parenteau behind the wheel. How could anyone be so cruel?

He studied the paper: $328 in parking tickets; $375.89 fees for legal representation arising from unpaid parking tickets; $500 fine; $943.27 interest. "NINE HUNDRED FORTY-THREE DOLLARS AND 27 CENTS INTEREST!"

"It was over twenty-five years ago," the lawyer replied. "I paid your fine for you. At least now you're not a hunted man."

"I did you a favour," Sterling pouted. "Your first court case, I gave you my business."

"You sure did give me the business. You skipped town."

The frost on the passenger door window melted into condensation. In it, Sterling drew an unhappy face. "There was a war in Argentina I had to cover."

"Angola."

"What?"

"You went to Angola."

Sterling gazed through the windshield. "After awhile they all look the same." Two and three storey pine homes lined Lakeview Drive, their south faces mostly plate glass. In the summer, the morning sun heated the sands of their private beaches. "I'm somewhat financially embarrassed at the moment."

Sterling laid the bill on the seat. Parenteau grabbed the piece of paper and stuffed it in his client's pocket. A heavy silence settled on the Jag's interior.

At last Parenteau, eyeing his rearview mirror, said, "Do you know anyone in a big blue pickup?"

Sterling twisted around, looked through the back window and turned back. "No."

"He's been behind us since we left the police station."

Sterling turned around again and watched the truck turn off into a side street. "It's a small place, not that many roads," he said, "a guy like you could get paranoid here." He straightened in his seat. "Do you know anything about the new Candle Lake mayor, Dan Farrow?"

"Why?"

"Why what?"

"Why do you ask?"

Sterling took a long look at his old friend. Over the last twenty-five years, they hadn't talked much, the occasional visit home and a letter or two. What did they know about each other now? Was there much trust left?

Not all lawyers parried with sharp minds but many of them did. Their training and their jobs honed them so. Kevin would be one of those and there would be no putting anything over on him. Sterling decided to tell everything he'd discovered so far about the colonel's death.

The Jaguar turned down the one block dead-end of Second Street.

"Pull in there," Sterling said, pointing to his house and driveway nestled in a clump of snowy pine. He waited until Parenteau had exited the car before stuffing the bill back into the lawyer's briefcase.

Inside the cottage, their breaths clouded the frigid air. Parenteau's expensive London Fog overcoat may have weathered the conditions fine from office to car to courtroom and back but offered little warmth in this igloo. He stomped his feet, clamped his arms over his chest.

"You live like this?"

"I'll make some coffee and bring it into the garage," Sterling said. "We'll be warmer there."

"You're still not convinced it was an accident?" Kevin sat on a wooden chair in the corner, his coat unbuttoned, his tie loosened, his legs stretched in front of him. He set his empty coffee cup on the floor. "What are we waiting for? Let's hang somebody."

In greasy cover-alls, Sterling afixed a block and tackle to the Triumph's engine. He wiped his brow with his sleeve leaving a black smear across his forehead.

"I told you. The colonel's best friend can't believe the man would let himself get into a dangerous situation on the lake. McTaggart had a healthy fear of ice. I knew John and I believe what Ed Braun says."

Sterling drained his coffee and set the cup on the TR6's fender. Thinking better of the perch, he removed the vessel to the workbench and returned with a cloth to wipe the ring from the mustard-gold metal.

"If Milburn is right," Sterling continued, "and the colonel went down with his tackle box near his shack, why didn't anyone see the hole in the ice? It was the weekend and the path was well-travelled. An opening large enough for a man to fall through would have been visible for a day or so, especially to fishermen wary of that very thing. Your father said everything around the hut seemed normal. He also said it stopped snowing that morning."

Parenteau gazed at the little sports car. "So now the way is paved for Mayor Farrow and his casino."

"Exactly. What do you know about him? Your dad mentioned you were doing some work for the Minowukaw land claim."

"Which means I have client privilege to protect," the lawyer said. "I can't talk about any dealings we have with Farrow."

"I understand he put an awful lot of money into his campaign. He wanted to push through the development McTaggart opposed."

Parenteau's eyes narrowed. He almost looked like a fox. "If you're hinting that I should suggest this was a motive for Dan Farrow to commit murder, your knowledge of our slander laws are sadly lacking, even for an ink-stained wretch."

This was like trying to get blood from a stone. So much for buddyhood. Sterling snorted, rummaged through his tool chest. When he found a hammer, he leaned into the engine compartment and whaled on a stuck motor mount.

Without looking up, he said, "Did Farrow propose a deal to the tribal council in return for exempting the town from the land claim?"

"Well," Parenteau sighed, as if fed up, and rose to his feet. "Thanks for the coffee." He buttoned his overcoat. "There's nothing I can tell you. The proposal is public knowledge ,if not a little premature. It hasn't even gone before your village council. What the band thinks of it, for the moment, is another story." The lawyer retrieved his cup and placed it beside Sterling's on the workbench. "You're still quite the clown." The hammer became silent. "When I phoned Bonnie Matheson before going to the detachment as you instructed, she said she hadn't given anyone permission to use the shack. When I told her you were in jail for breaking in, she suddenly remembered she had said it was okay."

Sterling put the tool on the valve cover and straightened. He kept a straight face. "She looked everywhere for the key," he said, his voice trailing off.

"I'm sure she did," Parenteau said, returning the grave tone. He strolled along the low-slung car trailing his hand down the fender, over the windshield, across the soft convertible top. "Joanne picked this baby up in England?"

Sterling ducked back under the hood, still afraid of his emotions when he heard her name. A glimpse of her face passed before his eyes. "Mustard yellow TR6, just like her daddy's old one."

The reporter had written only two letters to Kevin over a few decades, both when Sterling had nowhere left to turn. Joanne carried their child when a rifle shell pierced her brain as they raced through the streets of Sarajevo in a rusty old truck. She might not have known about the foetus. She never mentioned that she suspected anything and they'd been engaged for a month. The doctor at the hospital said he thought the reporter should know about his fiancée's condition. Now Sterling would better realize the tragedy of the war that ravaged the once beautiful city. No more pompous lecturing from lofty heights with pen or microphone.

The doctor was right. The up close and personal almost brought Sterling to his end. For weeks there seemed no reason to go on. In the first letter he intended to say so long, but in

Scott Gregory Miller

writing it he began a debate about the value of life and the release of death. Page after page the argument raged. In the end, he concluded nothing. Exhausted by the question, he choose to try another day.

Sterling tore up that letter. A month later he sent a short missive explaining what happened so Kevin could reassure the folks at home who'd heard the news. But he felt compelled to explain that if he let go of the car, he would be letting go of Joanne. And still he didn't seem able to do that. How many years did he need? How many were too many?

"How are your kids?" Sterling asked.

"They want to be hockey players."

"Two girls, isn't it?"

"Smart as the dickens." Parenteau turned to go but stopped at the open door. "It's good to see you again, Myles. I'm glad you called." He smiled. "By the way, if you're looking for property, take a gander at the three lots on the north side of Highway 265 and Lakeview Drive."

Looking for property? Before Sterling could say anything, Kevin Parenteau disappeared. Sterling pondered for a moment. Was that a drop of blood from a granite face?

Sterling felt something in the back pocket of his coveralls, retrieved the piece of paper there and unfolded it. How did Kevin do it? Somehow, once again Sterling held in his hands the outrageous bill for legal services rendered, the words "payment overdue" now scrawled across the page.

Morning March 5, 2000

Sterling knew this to be a fact:

Editors the world over were all the same —
bullheaded. Commensurate with their bullhead-
edness was another universal quality —
shorthandedness. These combined always led to
"Ineedyoutoness."

"Josephine's got the flu and Joe's been
working double shifts since two weeks ago
Tuesday. I need you to . . . "

In this case, the Annual Candle Lake Junior
Girls Volleyball Tournament needed the
discerning eye of a veteran reporter. The key to
journalistic excellence, Sterling had long ago
observed, lay in the art of bargaining with
management. He had granted the keen interest in
the prestigious event, the importance of sports as
character builder and the possibility of the
budding of a future Olympian or two and countered with an interview with Brendan Matheson
about his new exhibition due to open in Toronto.
It would give "Arts and Entertainment" a scoop
before the two big boys featured the young
painter in their weekend sections.

The big boys, the two self-declared national newspapers, ruled the country from Toronto. Having returned to Canada, Sterling found their claim of dominion confusing. Whenever he browsed their pages, he always found himself reading about Central Ontario.

He pondered this as the tin trap rattled to a halt in front of the Matheson home. The shotgun report of the engine backfire signalled that the three cylinders of the four that had a mind to function had come to rest. He shook his head. The worst thing about the pathetic heap was that it *would* start again. Even so, Sterling swore he'd make the rental agency his first stop on his next trip to P.A. The orange-mopped kid at the desk had to have something better idling in his stalls. Sterling reminded himself to pacify the editorial desk with volleyball scores and a few snapshots.

He exited the junk pile and approached the Matheson estate. Someone had shovelled the walk clean. Under its soft, white blanket, the yard looked well-kept although some of its bushes and shrubs stood out in the oddest shapes. The lovely scene struck the reporter as an older couple's dream home, not one of two siblings in their twenties. Of course, he remembered, Bonnie and Brendan's parents had been taken from them.

The front of the house didn't boast the expansive windows and balconies that adorned the rear lake view. From the road, however, he could make out the three sweeping log storeys. A massive stone chimney centered the east side wall and swirls of white plume beckoned from the warmth of a fireplace inside.

An intricate forest scene carved into the pine door greeted him. Sterling reached up for the old fashioned brass knocker just as the door flew open. Bonnie's dazzling smile lit her presence like a spotlight.

"Myles, you criminal," she laughed. "Brendan said you'd phoned." The collar of a thick, luxurious fur coat caressed her cheeks. "I'm just on my way shopping." Her voice bounced with a musical lilt and good humour as she folded what appeared to be a cheque and placed it in her purse.

"Thank you for what you told Staff Sergeant Milburn," Sterling said. "It saved me from a lot of trouble."

"John said you were a friend. I'm glad I could help." Her tone sobered. "Were you just fishing or were you actually looking for something?"

"Both. I found John's tackle box but the police don't think it means much. They're still calling it an accident." Sterling looked into her blue eyes. "I haven't had a chance to ask you. What do you think happened?"

Tears formed but Bonnie shook them away. "I just don't know. The nights since he went missing, I've spent awake. Now that his body has been found, all I know is that he's gone forever."

Bonnie's face greyed, a reminder to Sterling that she would always carry the burden of the loss of her fiancé.

"I'm sorry," Sterling said. In his head, he kicked himself for being so abrupt. He could be such a klutz. "Do you have a key for John's shack? There's some expensive equipment in there that I should bring back to you and I'd like to look around a bit more."

"Sure, I went looking for it when the police called," Bonnie replied, scrounging through her purse. "Here." She handed him the little metal billet attached to a plastic fob advertising The Wheelhouse Bar. "I'm heading into P.A," she said as she buttoned her coat. She motioned with her head. "Brendan's round back cutting wood. He's working off the smog and grit of Montreal."

"Did his show go well?"

"Very, " she grinned.

Sterling's eyes travelled the fur in which she snuggled head to ankle. "Nice."

"Mink. The colour of elm bark, don't you think?" A thin white-gloved hand combed the coat's thick hair. "I love it."

Was that a little light returning to her face? Like a model down a runway, a little sashay courted Bonnie's stroll to the rusty red Mazda sedan in the driveway. She waved as she got in.

The mystique of the fashionable woman went up in smoke when she turned the ignition. The engine backfired, rattled and missed, and almost made Sterling's rental look like a hot rod. Blue clouds trailed the car down the road.

Sterling stared. Did Candle Lake hold a curse over automobiles?

The distinctive crack of sharp metal having its way with soft wood led to Brendan behind the house. The lakefront lot looked to be a good half acre, as large as any in the upscale lake country neighbourhood. A wooden fence, painted and in good repair, separated the Mathesons from each of their neighbours. Alongside the east barrier stood a large wooden shed, also well maintained. Attached to this, an open-sided port sheltered the young painter piling firewood. Sterling estimated the stacks at least a couple of cords, more than enough for the remainder of spring. Brendan, it seemed, had them well prepared for the cold.

As he strolled towards the young man, Sterling realized what the odd snow-blanketed shapes were that dotted the yard. One, bared by the sun, he discerned as a fish, a pike perhaps by its size and prominent snout. But who could tell?

SILENCE INVITES THE DEAD

Through the jack's belly a spear rose from the ground, acting as a stand for the metal sculpture.

Brendan hefted a maul, probably an eight pounder, a heavy implement many could not swing around with near the same ease. Two days ago on the lake, Sterling had seen a tall, skinny lad in a cape and hat, not unlike the stereotype of the emaciated yet flamboyant artist. Now in a red plaid lumberjack coat, denim jeans and work boots, a strong physicality revealed itself. Not even the dark shades seemed as mysterious now that Sterling knew they protected light-sensitive eyes. Wisps of filmy white hair sprouted from under his tuque.

Sterling watched Brendan swing the axe in a long overhead arc slicing through its victim. The reporter's mind began to swirl, confused. In the young man's hands the tool danced, light as a machete. The stack of logs rose well over the tall man's head. Each piece of wood, bucked and split to a fireplace fit, varied in length from the fingertips to where the elbow sliced away or of a leg from the foot hacked off at the knee. Lighter and darker browns and blacks shaded the skin of the wood. Where was the blood? It must have run off in a stream under the snow. Have to remember to be careful, the road home will be red slick. And where are the heads? They always pile the skulls near the limbs.

The yard and the frozen lake began spinning, called to Sterling in the voice of the wind. He closed his eyes and willed himself to stay on his feet, not to faint, not to vomit out the sickness within him.

"Are you all right, Mr. Sterling?" Brendan's voice pierced the fog in Sterling's brain.

He opened his eyes, saw the artist, maul in his grip, hanging over him. Sterling nodded, reached down for a fistful of snow and washed it over his face. The ice cold felt good, calmed the panic. His breathing evened, his heart quieted.

"Something I ate, I guess," Sterling said.

The alarm on Brendan's face remained for a moment but then dissolved. He smiled. "Come inside. A coffee should make you feel better, sir."

Sir? Was that a sign of respect or acknowledgment to a doddering invalid?

Once inside the lobby entrance, a cathedral ambience reigned, the sun glazing windows that extended up the full south wall. The second and third floors stopped short and became balconies overlooking the high open space into the lobby and main floor living room. The high gloss finish on the bare log interior gave the pale wood a comfortable solidity. Underfoot, plush carpeting cushioned their steps as Brendan conducted his tour.

"You have a very nice home," Sterling said.

"Thank you, sir," Brendan beamed. "My parents finished it when I was in high school." His eyes caressed the room as he gazed about. He pointed to the fireplace, its massive stone chimney the foundation of the east wall. "There's one on every floor connected to forced air venting. As big as the place is, we rarely need electric heat."

"You have every reason to be proud. Call me Myles. Please."

Brendan and Bonnie basked in the lap of luxury compared to Sterling's igloo. The novelty of the shirt-sleeve warmth beguiled. The reporter considered saying to hell with it and snuggling his bed along side the TR6 in his toasty garage.

As they went up the spiral staircase to the second storey, Brendan stopped for a moment. "This is where we entertain." Again, a fireplace centred the east wall with a couple of leather couches and chairs arranged before it. A proper-sized snooker table, six feet by twelve feet, with fat carved oak legs and braided leather pockets sat in the middle of the floor. Three dart boards hung on the cork-lined west wall. A floor-to-ceiling entertainment monster on the northern face dominated the room. Stacks of audio and video components surrounded a huge screen, their burnished chrome faces like worshipers to a god. "Actually, we don't have people over much." Brendan corrected himself. "The engage-ment party was the first time in a while."

Sterling found the air did have a musty tinge to it.

"My studio is this way," Brendan said.

They climbed to the third floor. At first glance, a tornado appeared to have ravaged the artist's work. Several easels with unfinished canvases stood haphazardly about the room while bundles of paper, huge sketch pads, lay strewn underfoot. To one side, stand-up lamps flanked an adjustable-angle drawing desk. Like ammunition for a snow-ball fight, wadded paper balls littered the floor — rejected ideas not worth aiming at a garbage can.

Sterling followed Brendan on a winding obstacle path toward the window and a faded green chesterfield, its cushions rumpled with time and rest. Soon Sterling realized that the mess mislead, that under it a sense of order held sway. Each easel represented a work station, the scat-tered sketch pads containing pencil drawings of different elements to be conveyed in paint on canvas. And, no matter where he laboured, the artist looked over the lake. Today under cloud, the expanse of frozen white and its community of ice fishing shacks, hazy streams rising from their chimneys, presented a serene picture.

The works celebrated the vibrant style of the young artist. Only the eyes of someone who found the world fluid and surreal, awash in a rainbow kaleidoscope could envision those landscapes. It seemed the Montreal exposition had not drained much of the painter's artistic energy. At least seven works in various stages of progress awaited the next dab of colour. The reporter had made the acquaintance of a few professional artists and, by the standards he'd seen, the young man would be considered prolific.

Brendan gazed out the studio window, flanked by both shutters and heavy cloth for days when the sun burned.

"All the inspiration I need is here," he said. "I can't see ever leaving."

Brendan sat on a stool at the drawing table and motioned Sterling to the couch.

"Does Bonnie feel the same?" Sterling still felt a little shaky. Where was the proffered coffee?

"Yes," the young man nodded, his pony tail bobbing like a stalk of bleached straw. "John had to agree to live here before she would get married. He'd already moved most of his stuff when they announced their engagement." Brendan paused for some time, once again studied the outside icescape. "Two years ago our parents were killed in an accident," he said at last. "A truck driver from Ontario who hadn't slept for three days took a nap on the highway to P.A. and wandered into the oncoming lane." The young man stopped again and he turned away. His voice hushed to a whisper. "He didn't even lose his license."

Sterling felt his face flush. No one had mentioned the tragic circumstances. "I'm sorry. I didn't realize."

A sudden loss like that would be devastating for both of them. Not long after, fate had ripped Bonnie's fiancé from her arms which must have made an already gaping wound huge.

"Bonnie was going to university in Saskatoon at the time, pre-law. She didn't go back after the funeral."

Brendan dug his thumb into the palm of his hand, scraping and scraping as if excavating memories. He looked up at Sterling and, for the first time, removed his dark glasses. "You have to understand." The weak, translucent eyes welled with intensity. "It was the darkest time of my life, too, but being a hermit is almost normal for me. Bonnie loved to be in the middle of life. It was amazing all the things she did on campus. She always seemed to be joining another club, or playing a new sport, and she still kept up her average." He appeared wistful for a moment. "She was even captain of the debating team." He shook his head as if recalling another world.

SILENCE INVITES THE DEAD

"When she came back here after Mom and Dad died, she didn't leave her room. She probably said five words the whole month. I feared she was dying, too. But one day she just walked out the door and stayed away for the afternoon. When she returned, she had a part-time gig as a waitress at the club. She also got back the dream of hers that she lost on the way to university. She would have a chance to sing." Brendan's dark glasses again shaded his eyes. Against his pale features, they gave him a bug-eyed look. "It was this house that gave her the strength to get back out there."

"But she didn't return to school," Sterling noted.

The young painter's countenance didn't waver. "Before the accident she was doing what she thought she should, what my parents wanted. Now she's doing what she wants. To sing has always been her dream. The blues seemed to come naturally." He rose from the stool. "I'll get that coffee."

Once Brendan had descended to the main floor kitchen, Sterling decided he could make good use of a toilet. The studio laid claim to the whole third floor forcing the search onto the second. The first room he tried turned out to be the bathroom. When he flicked on the light switch nothing happened. Opting for aim over modesty, Sterling urinated by the light of the open door.

Returning upstairs, he stopped to study a cork bulletin board festooned with newspaper clippings of the painter's exhibitions. One interviewer asked him to "articulate his artistic vision." The response made Sterling's eyes water: "The inclusion of both the banal and the exalted in my work seeks to discover the function of context in the orchestration of importance, and reflects my own attempts to reconcile both the yearning desire to create and the need to escape the anonymity of mass politicalization."

Right on, brother, whatever you say.

"I found some food to go with the coffee," Brendan said, as he topped the stairs. He beamed as if the offering ranked as an accomplishment.

The two men sat at opposite ends of the couch with the serving tray of two cups of coffee and the plate of "food" — one broken cookie — between them. Sterling decided not to complicate matters further by asking for cream and sugar.

"You go ahead," he said, gesturing at the plate. The coffee refreshed like a sip of tepid water. He put his cup on a side table and picked up his pen and notepad.

The host's face fell. "Sorry, I guess it's not much. Bonnie usually deals with guests. Actually, she deals with just about everything. The money, the house. I paint, weld my sculptures and play woodsman." A small grin lifted the corner of his mouth. "She says I should stick to what I'm good at." Brendan toyed with the cookie reducing it to crumbs. "It wouldn't be such a bad life," he ventured, pausing, "if these awful things didn't keep happening."

"Life seems to have been even tougher on Bonnie," Sterling suggested.

Her brother glanced up with a start. "I suppose that sounded as if I was thinking of only myself. I meant for both of us, all of us, really."

Although Sterling no longer found the dark glasses disconcerting, they still hid Brendan's eyes, their demeanor.

"When she started singing and John came into her life, Bonnie seemed on her way to becoming genuinely happy. Before that, she worked to please others, mostly my parents. It never seemed as real."

Brendan dumped the crumbs into his hand and tossed them in his mouth. Sterling felt relieved he wasn't asked to share.

"They seemed to make each other happy," Brendan said, chewing, wiping his mouth with his sleeve. "The colonel was pretty much a drag when I first met him but Bonnie seemed to lighten him up."

Sterling sipped his coffee, now downright cold. "You didn't mind John moving into your house?"

The painter gazed at his questioner. "You mean, was I jealous of him?" He paused, considering. "I suppose, but I tried not to show it. Bonnie's life was turning around. The last thing I wanted to do was spoil it for her." His tone lightened as his arms made a sweeping gesture. "Besides, it's such a bloody big house. There was room for everyone."

Sterling put his cup down on the side table.

"Would you like some more?" Brendan asked.

"No!" The reply came with more force than Sterling intended. "Please no." The young man took no offense, waited for the next question. "The last time you saw John, how did he seem?" Sterling continued.

"That would be the Saturday night of the engagement party. He looked very happy." Brendan leaned back on the couch and stretched his long legs. "Most of the time he seemed uptight but that night he let his hair down a little." The artist's long fingers played with his pony-tail. "What hair he had." His face reddened. "I'm sorry, I shouldn't speak that way of the dead."

"That's all right, I'm sure John wouldn't mind."

Brendan seemed reassured and nodded.

"How was Bonnie that night?" Sterling asked.

"She had a good time. Not quite like him but she doesn't drink much and said the wine had given her a headache."

"And you didn't see McTaggart leave to go fishing the next morning?"

"No, I left early for Montreal to set up my show. I had a 7AM flight out of P.A." Lines wrinkled his brow as if reminded he wasn't yet the veteran of success he pretended to be. "I slipped away from the party before midnight. It was my biggest exhibition so far and I had a case of the nerves. I wanted to be ready."

"The noise didn't keep you awake?"

The young painter shook his head, pointed to a closed door at the rear of the studio. "My room is there. Everyone was on the second." He shrugged. "I didn't sleep much anyway but I wanted to get away. Lights and noise and smoke can trigger a migraine."

The curious mind of the artist is prone to want expanding, by whatever means at hand sometimes. Did Brendan indulge? "It seems some drugs around Candle Lake carry quite a wallop, deadly almost."

Pretending or not, the painter appeared puzzled long enough that Sterling prepared to rephrase the question. However, the painter's eyes brightened. "You mean the crystal meth that put those people in hospital? I read about it in your paper." Brendan grinned, as if his information source should please the reporter. "There wasn't any at the party, if that's what you mean. Not that I saw. The colonel would have blown a gasket, thrown out anyone who even lit up a joint."

"The reason I ask," said Sterling, " is that I was wondering if something changed John's normally careful behaviour on the ice. Perhaps he drank too much and went out the next morning with a hangover."

The young painter's eyes narrowed as the reporter continued.

"He was such a careful man. I have trouble believing the misadventure story if there were no extenuating circumstances."

Brendan jumped from the couch, stood facing the window. A hard, tense line squared his shoulders, his voice tightened, just under control. "Why don't you leave her alone!"

It wasn't a question. Sterling waited, reached for his coffee cup, found it empty. He had no answer except he owed John.

The artist turned. His voice didn't so much spark with anger as implore. "The coroner and the cops are calling it an accident yet you still come around saying it wasn't. You have no proof." The young man's face reddened. "It was bad enough when my parents died." He paused for a deep breath. "Now Bonnie walks around on eggshells. She cries at most anything and hardly says a word. I'm afraid for her, afraid that she'll go over the edge." He levelled his gaze at Sterling. "All you're doing is pushing her."

Sterling felt his own face flush hot, anger rising. He wanted sharp cutting words, weapons with which to strike back. He stared at the young man. No proof. It still rang true. The only evidence pointed to McTaggart as just another of the routine winter drownings every year on northern lakes. The reporter's eyes fell to the floor then rose to gaze out the window. It hurt to think he made Bonnie's life more miserable. The anger dissipated, the knives he had at the ready back in their mental sheaths.

"Look," he said, "the colonel was my friend and I have to be able to convince myself everything is as it seems. I'll tell you what, though. I won't bother you and Bonnie with anything I'm not certain about, no more questions."

After a few moments, Brendan nodded. "I just don't want her hurt."

"Neither do I," Sterling replied. The painter appeared mollified, the tight lines of his body easing as he slid back onto the couch. An awkward pause passed. Sterling, reading from his notes, asked, "How the hell does the 'exalted and banal' in your work 'seek to discover the function of context in the orchestration of importance?'"

Brendan's eyes glazed, his mouth parted. "What?"

Sterling pointed to the bulletin board. He read out the remainder of the artist's self-analysis. "Those are your words. I just wondered what they mean."

The painter blushed, stammered. "I don't know. They're from a textbook. *The Globe and Mail* interviewed me once when I was in Toronto. I figured a good quote wouldn't hurt." A sheepish grin crept over his face. "I dropped out of university because I couldn't hack the art theory classes, flunked them all. After the article appeared, I got a call from one of my old professors." He giggled, looked very much the boy, shaking his head in wonder. "She invited me to be a guest lecturer in her class."

Once he got going, the painter spoke of his art with dedicated exuberance. Brendan had various routes on and around the lake he'd trek for inspiration. The landscape was limitless! He even confided the source of his trademark, the signature fluid kaleidoscopes that made his work so unique: not quite landscape, not quite abstract. Ironically, a hazy peaceful calm, waves that bathed his vision in various scrawling hues preceded his worst migraines an hour or two before the juggernaut of pain crashed. The brightest visions presaged the worst episodes. Some of the drugs prescribed by doctors for the condition contained hallucinogens which enhanced the pre-pain trip. Suffering for your art took on new connotations.

After the interview concluded, Sterling shot a few photographs. He glanced at his watch. Three hours had passed.

"Now that your secret of migraine visions is out, aren't you afraid of a legion of imitators?" Sterling asked, as they descended the stairs to the front lobby.

"There have already been copycats and there'll be more." Brendan's earnest tone now sounded confident beyond his years. "There have always been migraine sufferers yet my work remains apart. You still have to be able to put the banal and exalted on canvas."

"I know someone at *Art World Magazine*. I'll do a story for him after I file with the *Sun*," the reporter said, studying a mountain of shoes and boots by the door, certain his must be among them. "You'll be even more famous,"

"*Art World!*" Brendan grinned. "All my profs read that. I'll be turning down jobs." Sterling's footwear remained out of sight and he flipped the wall switch for more light. Nothing happened.

Brendan's smile disappeared. After a moment, he said, "Sorry, it must be burnt out." Squatting, he rummaged through the pile of boots and shoes, came up with an offering. "These are yours, I think."

"You'll need a couple of bulbs," Sterling said, tying his laces. "The second floor bathroom is out, too."

Brendan's face reddened. "Thanks."

They shook hands and then once again Sterling stood on the front step, the fresh chill filling his lungs. Did burnt out light bulbs somehow injure Brendan's sense of propriety? The painter hadn't said anything but something bothered him.

The cold air bit Sterling's face and he shivered. Moving into the garage didn't seem like such a bad idea, at least for a paycheque or two, or until warmer weather arrived.

He glanced along Lakeshore Drive. Once more, there it sat. Candle Lake was a small community but that blue GMC seemed to be everywhere. The body shone an unmistakable buffed turquoise, the pickup's suspension jacked high over some mean looking tires. The truck had lingered outside the Valu-Mart when Sterling shopped for the macaroni and cheese for his last evening's cuisine. The rig had also filled his rear-view mirror a few times while on the main drag through town.

The four-by-four idled half-way down the block, an exhaust cloud wafting at the tailgate. Black-tinted glass prevented sight into the cab but a muted light flashed on the passenger side — a cigarette being lit? Had the driver shifted over or were there two of them?

No sense in being shy. It seemed as good a time as any for introductions. Just as Sterling crossed the Matheson driveway on his stroll toward the GMC, an explosion cracked the air from the opposite direction. A little Mazda back-fired, bounced down the road at a reckless clip. Sterling dove into a snowbank as the car veered at him in a wild swerve into the front yard. The import spun to a halt in the reverse direction at the front steps. The driver's door flew open and Bonnie dashed up the steps of her home.

Sterling remembered the happy woman who had charmed him in her fur coat. He rose brushing snow from his parka and pants.

"Hey, Bonnie! What's the hurry? You almost sent me into the lake!"

His voice froze the young woman in mid-stride. She appeared angry anyone dare be about. She wheeled around, looked at Sterling then away.

135

"I'm sorry," she said, her voice cold, "I lost control on the ice."

Sterling laughed, shrugged and opened his arms wide. "Hey, no problem."

Her eyes remained hard. She stood there dressed in only jeans and a light sweater, rapid frosty clouds blowing from her mouth.

"What happened to your beautiful coat?" he asked, "the colour of elm bark, don't you think?"

Her eyes widened with fury. "None of your damn business!"

The front door slammed behind her.

Dumbfounded, Sterling's face reddened. What happened to the woman he'd watched drive away three hours earlier? How did he provoke such anger?

A big bore growl turned his head as the over-sized pickup rumbled down the road. The blackened windows didn't even give away a silhouette. The metal monstrosity vanished around a forested curve.

Sterling made his way to his rental where he sat as the engine warmed, frost retreating from the windshield in a wave rising from the dash. What could have triggered Bonnie's Jekyll and Hyde transformation? Considering everything, she had flirted and was in good spirits when she left. Something must have happened.

And what about that truck, was it some sort of tail? Ten to one it wasn't the executor of some late, great aunt's estate wanting to leave the *Sun*'s newest reporter a small but significant fortune, not driving that mean four-by-four.

The icy glaze on the windshield melted into a wet film. The wipers flipped back and forth in their rhythmic dance as hot air from the vent blasted his face. Something about the big blue GMC, however, chilled him inside.

Afternoon March 5, 2000

A laughing Staff Sergeant Milburn burst through the door from the Mayor's office. Sterling looked up into the red face that sharpened to a nasty edge as the mountie brushed past. So, the community's top dogs liked to share a good joke, spend some time together.

Sterling took a seat, ten minutes early for the 2 PM appointment. The nameplate on the desk read "Mrs. Irene Dankewics — Secretary."

She said, "Mayor Farrow will be with you shortly."

Forty minutes later, he shifted in his chair one more time. The Mayor of Candle Lake, population 1053, it seemed, found time a tight commodity. Or, perhaps, he practiced the power management techniques celebrated in airport paperbacks, the ones aimed at hungry executives scratching to the top. The technique in this case would be described in the chapter titled "Showing just whose time is more important anyway."

Sterling didn't mind too much since once the interview ended he was in for an inauspicious introduction to his employer. He'd been summoned to Prince Albert to be called on the carpet by no less a personage than Mrs. Candace Lord, the publisher of the *Sun*. Somehow she'd gotten wind of the reporter's brush with Staff Sergeant Milburn and his version of the law. "We are not pleased" her voice had crackled on the reporter's message machine. He had yet to set foot in the edifice in which the newspaper operated. Opting to pass through P.A. on to Candle Lake, he settled in before reporting for work. Then McTaggart's body had turned up.

Sterling squirmed in the old wooden chair, one of those designed to be comfortable for a maximum of ten minutes. The ripped vinyl-padded seat needled and gouged in all the wrong places, a reminder, as if he needed one, of his horrible jail episode.

The mayor's office was tucked into the back of an old building that also housed T & A Confectionary in front and Giovanni Real Estate at the side. The structure smelled of crumbled plaster and tar-scarred linoleum. A cold draft found an easy right-of-way through the waiting area.

Mrs. Dankewics and her desk looked to be about the same age, survivors of an era when Elvis dieted on something healthier than barbiturates. She sat tall and thin with bony hands and wrists. Her eyes darted as if she always lagged a task or two behind her self-appointed schedule. Her blue flowered dress bulged at one sleeve with a supply of tissues that she put to good use. Sniffling often, her red nose seemed to be forever in need of wiping, a result, no doubt, of the relentless cool breeze.

In the middle of the desk huddled the focus of Mrs. Dankewics's occasional hushed cursing and ferocious glare — a vintage computer, an Apple circa the 1980s in need of a good overhaul or, perhaps, just a trip to the dump. Whacking the screen with her fist didn't do much other than provide some very momentary stress release. The secretary didn't look happy.

The telephone rang and she let out a long sigh. After glancing at Sterling, she put the receiver to her ear and said, "Yes, Mr. Farrow." She grimaced. "Sorry. Mr. Mayor."

The secretary pursed her lips as she replaced the phone in its cradle. Sterling rose with a hopeful smile which vanished as she glanced at him, shook her head. He flopped back into his seat.

He buttoned his coat and stared at the desk's yellow table cloth, shivering. Parenteau was a sharp lawyer. His quip about the land had to be some sort of riddle. Kevin knew damn well if Sterling couldn't afford to repay his parking debt — isn't there a statute of limitations on those things? — then he had no money to buy property. The *Sun*'s young errand boy, some journalism student on his practicum, had dug up a grid map of Candle Lake from the land titles office in P.A., emailed it overnight along with the name of the owner of the properties, Edith Dolmage, and some other research Sterling requested. Then the kid had quit. He said he could make more money as a plumber and work half the hours, just as his old man had told him.

This set the editor, Joe, off, whining on the phone. Do you know anyone who would be interested in the job? Sterling used soothing words to mollify the poor man, begging off. He'd keep an eye out.

The map showed that Dolmage Holdings purchased the three lots, totaling over eight acres, in the last year. Vacant crown land sat adjacent to the south while to the north nestled a small residential property owned by one Veronica Milburn. Could she call a certain nasty cop her relative? The Dolmage parcel ran along the main drag, Highway 265, at the edge of the village. But who was Dolmage Holdings? The answer to that would, no doubt, count for a few points in Parenteau's little game.

Mrs. Dankewics opened her desk drawer and, with the care due precious crystal, withdrew a flat square object draped in a white towel. Holding with both hands an obvious gem in her eyes, she rose and stepped over to a wall dotted with framed photographs. Removing the towel and, with it, polishing the glass, she revealed a portrait of His Worship John McTaggart that she hung in the line of pictures of Candle Lake's other former mayors. She stepped back, studied the picture before adjusting it several times, and dusted the colonel once again.

The current mayor's portrait sat apart and distinct from the others. The secretary's elbow knocked Dan Farrow's picture crooked. An accident? Mrs. Dankewics and Sterling's eyes played hide and seek as she glanced back while he pretended to study his notebook. Twirling around, she clipped Farrow again and returned to her desk, the photograph hanging wounded and listing.

This time when her telephone rang her eyes sparkled. "Yes, Mr. Mayor!" Her voice boomed loud and brusque.

She eyed the reporter. "His worship will see you now."

Sterling checked his watch. He'd been kept waiting for almost an hour.

The pungent odour of new carpeting greeted Sterling as he entered the inner office. Everything, from the paint on the walls to the furniture and curtains, looked new. About twice the size of the reception area, deep, dark browns and purples dominated the space as if to emphasize the gravity of political office.

Dan Farrow's size enhanced the heavy ambience. He sat somber in a throne-sized black leather chair. A huge hunk of cherry wood desk separated the two men. One large photograph sat beside a much smaller one on the glass-covered surface. A hutch attached to one side contained what appeared to be a new computer, its components still wrapped in plastic.

Sterling looked closer. A woman with a mass of coiffed blue-tinted silver curls smiled from the big picture. The very small one appeared to be a family portrait. In it, the new mayor stood behind a sunken-faced woman in a wheelchair, his big paws on her shoulders. Around them, three sullen children stared into the camera.

Dan Farrow extended a fleshy hand. "Starlick! Good to meet you."

"Sterling. Myles Sterling." The reporter winced as he withdrew his crumpled fingers and sat in the proffered chair.

His smile chiseled in place, his eyes cutting like lasers, the mayor leaned back and stared at Sterling.

"Okay, Mr. Starlick."

Sterling wished he'd taken to Brendan's practice of wearing shades. He had never been in the same room before with a jacket so bright. It glared a mighty rude yellow and orange plaid, a combination in which pedestrians would feel safe walking unlit roads, especially wearing the complimentary red pants. Farrow's salmon-coloured hair gleamed slick but receded from the front of his head in two semi-circles. Beads of moisture sprinkled the bare patches. It took sweat to move a mountain.

The mayor looked at Sterling hard and steady, as if forming a war strategy. He said, "What do my good friends in the press want today?"

"I thought I'd take the opportunity to introduce myself. Mr. Farrow, Dan, which would you prefer?"

"Mr. Mayor would be best."

Was he joking? Sterling studied the inscrutable smile. He glanced at his watch to make a point. "You must be a very busy man, Mr. Mayor."

"The last hour's been quiet but otherwise yes." The mayor had just made his own point. "Your reputation precedes you, Starlick. After covering those wars, Candle Lake must seem pretty dull."

Sterling reached forward and placed a pocket-sized tape recorder on the desk between them.

"For the record." he said. "Actually, I find it quite intriguing here."

"Well, Starlick, shoot."

The politician's smile remained set in concrete. His restless eyes, however, flitted between Sterling and the little black recorder. Making Sterling wait, the name game — was Mr. Mayor's prickly attitude just natural bluster or a wariness of the media, or a bit of both? An idea struck Sterling. Give the man a pulpit.

"I'm doing a memorial piece on John McTaggart," Sterling said, reading from his research notes. "You and he had some heated exchanges. Most of them came over your proposal for a casino in exchange for the Minowukaw Band dropping Candle Lake from its land claim."

Farrow's posture tightened, ready for a low blow.

"I suppose," Sterling continued, "those spats now pale in the face of the colonel's tragic death?"

The mayor's eyes widened, surprised at the delightful tack the question had taken, then they became steady and bright. He seemed now to find Sterling a fine reporter fellow. A politician that had been around as long as Farrow knew the full value of praise for the hallowed dead, especially when the corpse can't talk back.

Sterling noted the time as Farrow began to speak. Once he launched into his cascade of words, his calm gaze levelled at his audience of one. The mayor's focus, however, never quite met Sterling's eyes but fell just to the side, the shoulder. It was an old trick.

Sterling considered what he knew about the big man while lending him half an ear. He ran a snowmobile and quad all-terrain vehicle dealership in town. Driving by the business earlier, it appeared Farrow also dabbled in used cars, a few old clunkers huddling on the front of the lot. The biography supplied to the *Sun* by the Committee to Elect Dan Farrow described the candidate as a "prominent Calgary businessman who has left the hustle and bustle to make the beauty of Candle Lake his home." The information, as slim as he was big, revealed little else. There had to be more to the man than that. A long time acquaintance at the *Calgary Herald* had promised to fill in the blanks.

Five minutes passed and the mayor showed no sign of slowing down. "While John McTaggart and I had a disagreement or two, we more often united in a common cause. The contentious issue of re-location of the garbage dump immediately comes to mind. When I got wind of the stink . . . "

"Mr. Mayor," Sterling interrupted.

Farrow's eyes, although steady, had dulled once his patter shifted into overdrive, an easy pace during which he leaned back in his chair and let his mouth steer. His mind, however, seemed to re-engage at the sound of another voice, once again looking back and forth between Sterling and the tape recorder.

"As you say," Sterling continued, "the world must go on, just as the colonel would have wanted. Are you still proposing a deal for a casino in Candle Lake?"

The mayor's jaw tightened. He grunted, the matterhorn shifting to the edge of his seat. "Our ratepayers are very concerned about the pending land claim and they want action. Many of us have given up everything for the calm and solitude of Candle Lake year round, not to mention the recreational enjoyment of our seasonal residents." He jammed a large digit in Sterling's face. "I've had hundreds of calls and letters and the people are scared. What's going to happen to our homes, our property? Just the other day, old Joe Yablonsky stopped me on the street and begged me not to let them take his home away, leave him in the snowbank to die."

"You, of course, reassured him something like that could never happen?" Sterling said.

Farrow fell back into the cushion of his stuffed chair and folded his bear paws on his desk. His mouth remained closed, grinning.

"Where was this concern during the election?" Sterling asked. "McTaggart campaigned against the casino unopposed?"

"Exactly," said the mayor. "He won by acclamation. We don't know what would have happened had a candidate in favour of progress run against him."

"Why didn't anyone? You for instance."

When the huge man shrugged, his whole body rumbled. "It's a small community. Many people don't have the time or the means to indulge in the fulfilling task of public office." He had picked up a momentary facial tic. "I, myself, have a business to run and am taking the mayor's chair only under these unfortunate circumstances. To help out, you know."

Farrow's chair squeaked under his great bulk. His twitch vanished, a satisfied glint in its place.

The man came across as a down home yokel but underneath he oozed slick. He used some slippery and inflammatory logic to lay open his way for the casino proposal. With the political instincts of any alley cat, he knew how his comments would play in a news story. They'd scare the hell out of people, make them easier to bend to his cause. The arrogant Mr. Mayor wielded a sharp mind.

"The Minowukaw Band hasn't shown much public interest in your proposal." Kevin Parenteau hadn't given away much. Perhaps Farrow would shed some light. Sterling let the statement hang.

The mayor remained silent then his face lit like he'd been thrown a piece of candy. "Public interest is the key phrase here, my friend. Since being tragically forced into taking office, it's been my duty to initiate talks in an effort to calm public fears. I can't say much before I bring it to my fellow councillors." He paused and narrowed his gaze at Sterling. "But believe me Mr. Sterling, we're talking." He nodded. "We're talking."

Sterling shut off his recorder. Farrow only got Sterling's name wrong off-tape, another cute trick. After a few photographs, the mayor rose from his chair, offered his hand — Goliath meeting David. The memory surfaced of seeing Farrow tower over Staff Sergeant Milburn, no runt himself, at the spot on the frozen lake where the colonel's body had surfaced. Up close, Goliath looked to be well over six feet and 300 pounds.

"I understand my name has been connected to some ugly suggestions about McTaggart's death," Farrow said, through clenched rows of yellow molars.

Pain shot through Sterling's limb, his hand crushed in a vise.

"The terrible tragedy has officially been declared an accident," Farrow stated.

Was that a knuckle cracking? Sterling squeezed back hard.

The mayor flinched.

"For your information," he said, "I was at a convention in Regina and McTaggart was already missing when I got back. I mention this in case you're planning on putting any of your speculation into print."

The men stared at each other, hands locked. At last, Farrow's grin widened and he released his grip. He laid his arm around Sterling's shoulder and steered him to the door. For the first time Farrow's face turned somber with earnest, solemn eyes.

"It's best for everyone that this sad episode be left to rest in peace." He winked. "What do you say?"

Late Afternoon March 5

"Every player gives me 110 per cent each and every shift or his ass warms the bench. When the going gets tough my guys reach down further into their hearts and overcome adversity. It's character that makes a team strong. I treat these men with respect and, in all humility, I'm proud to say they'd go to war for me. To answer your question, Myles, we're positioned well for the play-offs."

With those well-worn yet immortal words, the coach of the Candle Lake Teddy Bears rallied his team of eight year olds into this week's battle. Now alone in the wooden stands of the small arena, Sterling penned the last of the interview into his notebook. Only his editor's insatiable appetite for column inches could spawn a hard-hitting tete-a-tete with the coach of a hockey team mired in the middle of the Tadpole Division.

Sterling dug his hands into his pockets seeking warmth to soothe his numb fingers, wiggled his toes in his boots to get the blood pumping. Only a few ardent souls now hunkered in the three tiers of seats. Vestiges of the last crowd — crushed paper cups and wrappers — littered the concrete underfoot in muddy pools melted from hundreds of pairs of winter boots.

The scrape of steel on ice, the thud of hard rubber bouncing off wood and an open winger's frantic yell for a pass echoed in the empty building. A pickup game danced around the rink in cadences: darting, then floating and again rushing. A heavy crash of two bodies slamming into the boards punctuated the slow ballet. One player slid down, lay prone for several moments, cursed the broad back of his attacker rejoining the play.

The rules for recreation hockey spoke plainly from the signs posted at each players's bench: $10/hr./player (Pay At The Office BEFORE Each Game), NO raising the puck, NO bodychecking.

Someone didn't care, still saw himself as the first star on *Hockey Night in Canada*. Sterling watched the cyclone at the far end of the rink. The modern day Gordie Howe elbowed another opponent off the puck, stick-handled through four players and blasted the black disc bulging the top right-hand corner of the net. The slapshot sent the padless goalie diving.

The whirlwind could have been a star; he oozed talent. His hapless victims turned back, skated to their own end, not one complaint about the breach of gentlemen's rules.

Staccato clapping turned Sterling's head toward the far stands. A man stood alone, smacked his gloves together in vigorous approval. He bared one hand, raised two fingers to his mouth. A shrill, hard whistle pierced the air. The stocky form, the peaked cap worn backwards pinned the fan's identity. Sterling glanced back at the ice as the play approached him. Sure enough, one Braun twin reigned over the rink today, his brother cheering from the stands. Sterling headed toward the front lobby where a silver electric urn burbled "welcome."

"Some coffee?" Sterling asked, returning to the far side of the stands where he sidled up to the man in the cap.

Intent on the play, the eyes of the spectating twin narrowed, suspicious, as he turned toward the Styrofoam cup offered him. A paper napkin lay in the trucker's lap, a pen in his hand. Tracking his brother's goals, assists, penalty minutes? Why bother for a scrub game?

Sterling peered closer, saw a much more genuine tabulation of the action, a snapshot of sorts. A drawing portrayed in almost perfect likeness the moment his twin's slapshot rocketed the puck into the net. In the foreground, the player's body in full extension, the blade of his stick pointed at the exact spot in the goal where the

Scott Gregory Miller

binding bent, as if the black disc had exploded from the barrel of a rifle.

The faces drew Sterling's eyes. A few exact lines captured Braun's expression — the animal calmness of a predator whose natural instincts commanded his body and mind in perfect motion. In contrast, absolute fear twisted the features of his unprotected victim wearing only jeans and an Oiler's sweater, the eyes ballooning during the frantic dive from the deadly missile.

"Tinkertoy man," the trucker said at last, a smirk working its way across his lips. One black leather glove turned his cap forward then accepted the offering. The other hand flipped the napkin face down on the bench seat.

"Thanks for calling the tow truck the other day." Sterling sat and blew on his own steaming cup. Forget the game of cat and mouse the truckers played, let bygones be bygones. For the moment. "You saved me a long walk. As it happens, my cell was dead."

Braun nodded, his eyes keen on the ice three tiers below. Sterling watched also, let the silence between them become comfortable, two fans enjoying the game.

For a scrub affair, all the players glided fast and strong, their feet as much at home in a pair of skates as most people are in runners. Forwards and defencemen weaved and dipped, passes between them skimming crisp, at times, as if choreographed. Whatever these guys's day jobs, hockey had flowed in their blood from the cradle. How many dreams floated about the rink uncaptured? Still, as much skill as the others displayed, the Braun twin shone a star above.

"Your brother's a tornado out there," Sterling commented.

"That used to be his nickname, Tornado," the young man said, his eyes seeming beyond the play, in another world. "We were both scouted by the pros since we were fourteen. All Zeke ever talked about was playing in the NHL. I wasn't as crazy about the idea. I guess it showed. He always scored more, won most valuable player every year."

"You must be Zak. We were never introduced. I'm Myles Sterling."

The trucker stared at the offered hand as if its touch might injure. At last, he nodded, shook. "I know. My old man met you in Africa." He gestured with the java — thank you — seemed to relax, leaned back against the bench seat. "We had a dug-out on the farm filled with water. In winter when we were small, we'd scrape off a patch of snow and pretend we were Wayne Gretzky. The ice was bumpy and cracked but we didn't care." Zak chuckled. "But for Gramps, it wasn't good enough for us. In summer, he worked fifteen hours a day yet he still put in a front lawn exactly half the size of a real rink, graded it so it was perfectly level." Young Braun sipped his warm drink. "Late fall, as soon as it dipped below zero, he'd be out there hosing the grass. By December, that ice would be as smooth as glass." He glanced at Sterling, looked away. "Every chance Gramps had, he'd be out there with us, having fun, teaching us."

Zak drank more coffee, his eyes following the flow of play. From the seat between them, Sterling picked up the napkin, turned it face up.

"This is very good, "Sterling said. "Brendan Matheson isn't the only artist in town."

The trucker glanced down at the drawing, its simple, intricate lines. The lines of his mouth drew down, sad. What did he see there?

"I don't have as many trophies as Zeke but I beat Matheson in more than one art contest. Our teacher gave both of us special classes, told us if we applied ourselves we'd go a long way. Me and Zeke even hung around with Brendan." Zak paused, looked away. "He was my best friend. For awhile."

Braun emptied his cup, set it down on the puddled grey concrete floor, his eyes returning to the pickup game.

Sterling said, " So trucking for your dad is just spelling time until you and Zeke get to do what you want?"

The young man stared at the reporter, through him, for a long moment then said, "No, trucking is it."

"What about your art, your brother's hockey?"

A crash shook the rink boards, snapped both men's heads toward the corner. Zeke lay on the ice, moaning, a scarlet stream flowing from his nose down his chin. His earlier victim hovered over him, spat and skated away.

"What about it?" Zak said, grabbing the sketch, crushing it in his fist, winging the little ball through the air. The wad of paper landed in a pool of scum water and floated there. Scrambling over two tiers of seats to rink level, the trucker leaned over the boards and screamed at his brother, "Take off his head!"

The light for the fourth floor glowed under the touch of Sterling's finger and the elevator lifted, leaving a momentary hollow in his stomach. The antiseptic odour that seeped from hospitals always conjured the opposite of cleanliness. More than a battle against germs, the smell seemed to be a clumsy veil over the sickness and decay that stood as the building's *raison d'etre*. When it came time to take that thankful step outside again, it felt like one more escape from the inevitable.

When Sterling had called the newsroom, Joe said the meeting with the boss was off. Mrs. Lord had forgotten a hair appointment after skydiving that afternoon and the Annual Arts Board Dinner tonight. A head table guest, she'd plunked down her 300 dollars for a ticket. They'd have to get together some other time.

It was a bit of luck though, wasn't it, Joe had said. Since you're in town anyway, scoot over and find out what you can from the Milburn girl. She'll have to do for now. The anchorman, Larry Fredericks, has already been released.

Megan Milburn lay recovering in room 423, said she'd be up for an interview, up for the questions that had to be asked. She sounded like an aspiring scribe. In his younger days, Sterling would have spouted the same kind of bubbles.

Only the odd electronic beep pierced the quiet as Sterling walked past the nurse's station. A computer screen engrossed the woman seated there as her finger moved across the clipboard on her desk. She looked up then returned to her work.

Sterling decided against asking her to look at his bruised hand. His fingers tingled in an odd way, pained to the touch. Leave it be for now, let gangrene set in. The headline would be magnificent, his best ever:

"Reporter's arm amputated after handshake with mayor."

If that huge lump thought he could back off Sterling by breaking his bones then Mr. Mayor had another think coming. Legal action — now that talked a different story. The threat of it always got newspaper management changing its underwear. No bumpkin that Farrow, he operated smart.

The story about the weekend in Regina would be the first thing to confirm. Mrs. Dankewics had been very helpful on the way out. She had written down the name of the hotel and slipped the reporter the folded paper. "Checking up on his alibi, I'll bet," she'd said.

"By the way," Sterling had queried, "the big picture on his desk beside the little family portrait, who's the woman?"

"His mother. She's bonkers."

The door to 423 lay open. Patients occupied all four beds, three of them chatting with visitors. In the fourth by the window, a young woman sat alone.

"Miss Milburn?" Fresh lipstick painted her smile that wrinkled the freckles across her nose. Brown hair, shiny and soft, bounced over her shoulders as she nodded. She wore a white button-down sweater over her hospital-issue gown. "I hope you're feeling better."

"I'm getting out tomorrow," she beamed. "I'm so glad to meet you, Mr. Sterling."

One wouldn't call Staff Sergeant Milburn's daughter beautiful but her engaging sparkle and eagerness made her pretty. A youthful crackle bounced in her voice. "I read the announcement in the *Sun* when the paper hired you," she said. "Call me Megan."

"I'm Myles."

Megan almost burst, leaning forward. "What's it like?"

Sterling's line of questioning, just forming, evaporated. "What's what like?"

"Being a war correspondent, travelling every-where, meeting important people, everything."

Should he put his hands on her shoulders to stop her from bouncing? After all, she was supposed to be ill.

"I'll bet it's the most exciting job in the world! It's exactly what I'm going to do!" Megan's words flowed leaving no breach, nowhere to put one or two of his own. He leaned back and hoped her story would run where he wanted her to go.

"Stupid! Stupid! Stupid!" Her fists pounded the bed, an exclamation behind each word. No tears poured, just anger. "He spoke to our media studies class, big voice, Mr. Tall and Handsome. I couldn't believe it, I saw him on TV all the time. Larry Fredericks asking me out. When he crooked his finger for me to go over to him, Cindy was so mad. She thinks all the guys are after her. But it was me he wanted. And not just for coffee or a smoky old bar but for dinner at La Ristorante Italia. That's got to be the most expensive place in town."

Megan's cheeks glowed. Her release tomorrow wouldn't be any too soon. Her convalescence had dammed her stores of energy and now they over-flowed. It was easy to see what made her miser-able old man so protective.

"I didn't mean to but I guess I got a little drunk," she continued. "There were martinis, then wine with dinner and cognac after." She paused, gripped the bed sheet in her fists. "I'm lying. I don't guess, I know I got drunk and not just a little. Then we went to this party and that's when things get foggy. I remember thinking I was seeing double but I wasn't. These two guys came over and I thought it was the same guy. It was so weird. Zeke and Zak, those were their names. They were twins." She laughed. "One wore his baseball cap backwards, the other forwards. That's how I could tell them apart.

"Anyway, Larry pulls me into a bedroom about the same time I'm beginning to feel sick to my stomach. He lights a up joint and hands it to me. I'd never smoked before but I've smelled it. He said it would make me feel better." Megan became still for a moment and gazed at the floor. "I know it sounds dumb but I didn't want to seem uncool, like some small town chick who didn't know anything. And I hoped he was right, that it would make me feel better. It didn't and I told him I still felt lousy. He pulled out a little plastic bag of white powder and a tinfoil pipe and said this would do the trick for sure." She raised her head, blue eyes blazing. "After that he made his move." She cringed. "Or at least that's what I thought but I just pushed him away and he fell on the bed. He'd passed out. The last thing I remember was a burst of light as the door opened. I guess someone called the ambulance when they couldn't wake us." Megan paused, took a deep breath. "I just wanted to get that off my chest before the interview. I want my Dad to know I've owned up to the truth and that I've learned my lesson even though it probably means I've blown my chance to become a journalist." She shook her head, her voice small. "Stupid, stupid, stupid." She exhaled, smiled. "I'm ready now Mr. Sterling. Are you sure I can call you Myles?"

"Megan, would you like a job?"

Late Evening March 5

The junk heap wore a coat of patchy green paint, a big improvement on the pitted blue of the first one. The kid behind the counter at the car rental agency — all you do is drive, we do the rest — had rings on all his fingers, through his ears and nose. The pewter jewelry augmented his orange hair. He read from a printed card. "I'm sorry sir, customers are our first and only business. Please take this beautiful model . . . " he wagged his head at the one lonely car on the lot . . . "if you're not satisfied." He tossed the card on the table, pulled on his nose ring. "It's a Bumbler, man! Radical!"

The young leader of tomorrow knew of what he spoke. The Bumbler *was* radical. It rumbled, spit and coughed. It idled just like Grandad's 1947 Massey Ferguson, the tractor company that went bankrupt. Like the first rental, this rat trap also ran on three cylinders. However, it oozed potential. Unlike the original little four banger, a sophisticated V–6 hunkered under the hood. As Sterling let the engine warm, his heart leapt when a fourth or even fifth piston tried to get in on the action doomed only to disappointment as the poor things pooped out after a valiant few seconds.

Sterling glanced at the crate on the seat beside him, felt a surge of excitement. TR6 afficionados haunted the world over; he'd tracked down the parts he needed with a trip through the *Sun*'s want ads. A few all-nighters with the engine and his baby would be back on the road.

Sleep still came hard. Last night, Prokofiev and Rachmaninov kept the voices in the wind at bay while another couple of hours passed shaping the McTaggart memorial feature. The interview with Monique would round out the colonel's life in Candle Lake and then the piece could be shot into cyber-space to make a soft landing in Joe's hard drive at the *Sun* office.

Sterling punched his own number into the cell phone to pick up messages before heading back. Joe's desperate voice crackled and whined. A matter of life and death, he said. The third page loomed half empty. Two hot stories begged for ink: the junior boys jazz band concert at Louis Riel High School and the annual ladies auxiliary charity production of *Pygmalion* at St Joseph's Bingo Hall. Could Sterling cover one, or better still, both?

He shook his head. So sorry, as nice as it sounds, I'll have to miss the concert and play.

Great news, though Joe, help is on the way. At nine o'clock tomorrow morning the vivacious and enthusiastic Megan Milburn will walk into your office. Your gopher in angel wings has arrived.

Okay, Staff Sergeant Milburn, your daughter has graduated to the big time. Stick that up your — Sterling smiled — pipe and smoke it.

An edgy Ed Braun had left the final message:

"Myles! What's happening? All I read about in the newspaper is bad drugs. What about John's murder? I thought you were supposed to be this crackerjack journalist, get the cops off their duffs. Or has somebody got you scared? Give me a call."

His voice sounded ragged. The armour accumulated by twenty years in and out of war zones can dissolve when put against the death of a buddy. Sterling remembered the day McTaggart 's body turned up, Braun at his office seemingly composed, then in a flash, pounding his fist on the desk. Someone killed John! There's no other explanation!

Braun couldn't keep it all inside, needed someone's ear to bend or he'd explode. A compliment of sorts, Sterling had become that man.

He punched in the office and home numbers from the business card Ed had left him. Voice mail machines answered both calls. Sterling donned his dark shades and pointed the Bumbler toward Candle Lake.

The days had begun to lengthen, to beckon the spring sunshine with longer hours to wash away winter's snow and grime. A dirty grey blanket covered the fields on either side of the highway. There'd been no precipitation all month according to the *Sun* and farmers worried about another drought if the skies didn't open up in April or May. The attitude could be summed up as "expect the worst and if it doesn't arrive, there will always be something else to complain about."

By the time Sterling turned onto Highway 125 at Meath Park, the sun had been sleeping below the horizon for a good hour. Two pairs of bright lights approached in the distance, dimmed then grew larger as the silhouettes of a couple of B-trains materialized. Averting his eyes from the glare, he still managed a glance at the trucks as they passed. A coincidence, perhaps, the Braun and Sons units seemed headed on another road trip.

Megan Milburn had said that the twins mingled at the party at which Fredericks offered her the joint but she didn't see either of the boys smoke anything. Ed had circled the story in the *Sun* about the bad crystal meth, no doubt to show his sons, and probably it was not the first time he'd tried to make a point about drugs. Before settling into his desk job, their father, too, had driven the road life, the endless hours, the countless kilometres. He'd know his bull-headed progeny would want to relax after a long haul, would want to party. Weren't relaxing and partying the same thing at twenty years old? Just maybe the twins had heeded their old man, bowed to his experience. After all, surprises never ceased.

He slid a Rachmaninoff cassette into the player and turned up the volume. Nothing kept the night at bay like the string section of the London Philharmonic rolling over the mind in waves of stirring Russian melody. Bonnie had done the same for McTaggart — kept the night at bay. During the last telephone call from the Colonel on the fateful weekend, John had stated, "The fish are here for the taking and, maybe for you too Myles, some peace of mind."

Where was peace of mind without the truth about his death? Sterling didn't need to look in the mirror to see the darkening crescents under his hollow eyes, the lengthening furrows in his face. The voices still haunted. *Prenez mon bébé. Prenez lui s'il vous plait.*

John had offered Bonnie a generous love. He encouraged her to follow her dream, to sing the blues even if it meant they had to be apart while she travelled. Yet, with only Brendan left now, she sang more alone than ever. She, too, faced the torment of ghosts each dark night.

And the next time they met, which Bonnie would surprise the reporter? She seemed to be at least three different people — the sweet sad-eyed survivor, the volcano stage persona. And who was that third woman, so quick to anger? The warning flashed bright. Take a long step back from her, not only in respect for the colonel, but to avoid getting burnt. A little distance would be safer for everyone.

But where was Bonnie's beautiful fur coat? The frigid day cried out for the warmth of a full length mink. Worth a couple of grand, a woman kept a treasure like that in her clutches, not left somewhere forgotten. Just the way she melted into the fur, parting it from the touch of her skin seemed unimaginable.

The reporter had bowed to Brendan — no more nosing around, upsetting Bonnie. Sterling could still question others, though. Sure. Who was he kidding? The young woman wouldn't let him go.

The Bumbler thrashed and pinged and snorted in an admirable effort to maintain highway speed. Sterling's right hand rested light on the wheel. Any pressure or bumps shocked his fingers, burned the tendons of his right hand, courtesy of the Mayor of Candle Lake.

What more motivation did a reporter need to dig up all he could about the big jerk? But now an uglier question loomed. Were the police, in fact, satisfied the colonel's death was accidental or was Staff Sergeant Milburn stonewalling, protecting Farrow?

Megan couldn't be a more likeable young woman and something of her old man lingered in her. Sterling didn't find the mountie wholly despicable despite what he'd done. Still, a mayor and a town's chief cop can get close. Milburn had sported a big grin when he left Farrow's office. Was that the smile money can buy? It wouldn't be the first slimy deal to go down between men at the top.

Sterling slowed the Bumbler at the junction sign, made the turn onto Highway 125. He floored the accelerator which started the long, noisy, painful process of returning to 100 kmh.

The lights exploded out of nowhere. Blinking, he saw only flashes and stars and turned the rearview mirror away. Some idiot rode the rear bumper with a roof full of running lights, everything on bright. It was like driving with the sun flaring from your back seat. What the hell was the moron doing?

Sterling tapped the brake, signaling to back off. In the side mirror, a thousand flash bulbs reflected but a quick glance discerned a tall vehicle hunkering above the Bumbler's back window. The Braun boys back for more fun and hijinks? It had to be some kind of truck but it didn't look to be pulling a trailer.

Again and again, Sterling batted the pedal, flashing the brake lights. It only seemed to encourage the idiot. The blazing lamps inched closer becoming a wall of light burning into the interior, the windows flashing like mirrors. Squinting into the windshield, only white luminescence and black dots waltzed. Sterling drove blind. He eased off the accelerator; the little car slowed.

The impact snapped his head. A pause followed. A sickening crush of steel rammed the Bumbler again. No choice now, Sterling straightened his arms hard, squeezed the steering wheel and flattened the gas pedal against the floor. The Bumbler sputtered, then, as if fearing for its own life, roared, all six cylinders kicking.

The brilliant light cut like tiny knives, Sterling's eyes tearing, images fracturing through the liquid. The little mill whined in terror, its acceleration still pitiful. The attacker growled louder.

The road here was straight, wasn't it? It had to be. Sterling glimpsed the road sign. The turn, the bad camber sweeper where the TR6 had gone off, lay ahead.

The Bumbler did all it could, its pistons yipping and yapping as the huge iron carnivore once again nudged and prodded with its jaws, little love taps on the bumper just to show it still wanted to play.

The brightness overwhelmed him, forced his eyes closed. He had to see. He squinted and followed the solid white line down the centre of the blurred black highway. He stood on the gas, the tinny engine screaming. The needle of the speedometer wavered at swimming numbers, 130 it seemed, enough to make the car scrap metal in a head-on confrontation with the approaching guardrail.

The centre line blurred, vanished. Now only radiant flashes and spots swirled. He had to see the road. This was suicide. Or murder.

Leaning over, Sterling pushed the button on the glove compartment door. Nothing. Was it locked? He tried again. Still nothing. The key dangled from the ignition, useless. He balled his hand, smashed the knob with his fist. The little door fell open, the bulb lighting. Fumbling inside, his fingers crawled over the shape of his sunglasses.

The shades at least allowed tiny slits of smeared images to form. A silver band emerged — the guard rail at the bad camber curve. Sterling hit the brakes. His head whip-lashed as the Bumbler shuddered and cried, driven into the barrier in a long scream of steel pinching steel.

Sterling yanked the wheel, sliding the rear end in line, the passenger side now scraping flush. The Bumbler rode the rail through a firestorm of sparks. When the curve ended, he could only grip the wheel steady as the vehicle bounced down the ditch, ploughing through the snow to a stop. Like a sigh, a cloud of steam rose from the hood.

Sterling shook himself, heart pounding, breathing hard but no blood, no bones broken. He looked around, no wall of light, only a pair of red eyes, tail-lights, growing dimmer down the highway. The hunter had called it a day.

"You have a choice." The distorted voice had been muffled. "Leave the colonel be. Or join him."

Sterling raised his arm, signaling the waitress for another scotch. He'd taken an empty corner of the Wheelhouse where he could compose himself without an audience. As soon as she nodded, he pulled his hand back down, shaking.

He'd walked through killing fields before. The job demanded it. This, however, had turned personal. Did the threat prove the colonel was murdered? Was the man behind the voice his killer? If so, he seemed very capable of keeping his word. The colonel's flesh-eaten corpse demonstrated that. And not two hours before on Highway 125, did the same guy show he'd not lost any of his nasty disposition.

The tow truck Sterling summoned on his cell-phone arrived promptly and soon dragged the Bumbler out of the ditch. The little bucket of bolts proved to be a tough old soldier, the passenger side wounded, a little rumpled and bent. Despite all the noise and pyrotechnics during the ride along the rail, it took only a hammer and some muscle to pry the wallowing sheet metal away from the front wheel.

The chilling message waited for him at home on the answering machine. Some expert electronics had gone into the call. Even after playing it over and over, the altered voice remained unrecognizable.

Sterling fingered the tape now in his pocket. He pondered the wisdom of ordering another scotch as he sipped from the one that just arrived. Could there be any doubt now that McTaggart was murdered? Only hours after the mayor had threatened to sic a lawyer on Sterling, the highway had delivered an even more sinister message.

Not wanting to give the local law any more reason than necessary to see him as a deviant, Sterling had reported the accident. It seemed prudent to leave out the fact that he'd been given significant help in losing control in the corner. If Staff Sergeant Milburn and Mayor Farrow tangoed together, the less said the better. Either one of Candle Lake's leading citizens could have been behind the wheel. And after all, Sterling had only a wall of blinding light to offer as identification. That Sterling had fudged the report might just keep anyone who knew the truth guessing. Or it might suggest the job had been done — the nosy reporter scared off, his mouth shut.

A little breathing space wouldn't be a bad thing. Still, it couldn't hurt to let the lawyer in on the situation. Kevin might make for some needed insurance.

Sterling drained his glass. A third scotch would be the limit. He didn't want his nerves too calmed. Monique stood wiping glasses behind the bar and had agreed to talk to him on her break.

The young woman with the flowing auburn hair he'd seen working the other day walked to the table, except now she wore a pony-tail. Her long legs the colour of smooth pine, she looked down and clicked her gum.

"Another, please." The reporter managed to smile. "A double."

"You want something to eat, some peanuts?"

He shook his head. She blew a quick bubble, hard and small. It snapped as she walked away.

Moments later she returned with a glass full of ice smothering a hint of yellow liquid. Sterling scooped out most of the cubes with his fingers, shrugged as if to ask what do I do with these? She nodded at the floor and he reached out, opening his palm.

"You better eat something," she said, placing a basket of peanuts on the table.

Sterling's grin came easy this time. She wanted to mother him. That was nice. Some mothering would be good, especially tonight.

Just then, the door man, the young giant the Braun boys had bounced off the wall, ran up and swept the waitress off her feet. She squealed as he hauled her toward the bar, his feet crunching on butts, shells and ices cubes, her slender arms around his bull neck as if they crossed the threshold.

Sterling sipped his drink. He was busy tonight anyway.

The hands of the large Mickey Mouse clock that hung above the waitress station pointed to exactly twelve o'clock. From behind the bar, Monique emerged.

"Hey, you two!" she snapped. The waitress and bouncer tickled each other, laughing. "Knock it off, you'll wake up the customers."

She walked toward Sterling in the dark corner, a freshly lit smoke dangling from her lips, the forefinger of one hand looped through the handle of an over-size coffee cup emblazoned with the Aries zodiac sign. The other hand gripped a cigarette package and a yellow plastic lighter. A purse hung from her shoulder.

"Thanks for agreeing to talk to me," Sterling said, as she sank into a chair, sighing, a load off her feet.

Her shadowed eyes narrowed and painted mouth curled tight. "This is about John and not Dan Farrow, right?"

Sterling kept a straight face and tried not to show his surprise. Then it came back. At their last meeting, a coldness had descended over her at the mention of Farrow's name.

"If you wish," the reporter said. There was no point in pressing her. If she hid something, he'd discover it by some other means. Or, at least find some kind of lever with which to pry. "I was hoping you could tell me about the colonel when he first came to Candle Lake? Were you working here then?"

Monique nodded, drew on her cigarette, the end glowing tangerine. She held it over the ashtray, her finger still tapping after the ashes had fallen.

"I was just a waitress then. John was a very organized, thorough man but he didn't know much about running a bar. I've been waiting tables since I was nineteen and learned a few things along the way. I helped where I could and soon he made me assistant manager. He dropped the assistant part when he ran for mayor."

Sterling's pen stopped. He glanced up from his notepad. "Candle Lake is a small community. I wouldn't think its politics would keep a mayor away from his first job. Or did he just prefer to let someone else run the club?"

Monique stubbed out her smoke, sipped her coffee, then pulled another cigarette from her package, which she left spread open on the table. Sterling picked up the plastic lighter and, with a flick of his thumb, offered her the flame.

She steadied his hand with hers, grinned. "Nervous?"

"Always, when I'm with a beautiful woman." Sterling said.

Even as she released her grip she held his gaze for several moments, considering. "You are full of it, aren't you?"

He wished he were but what he said was true.

Her face lightened and her posture loosened. She leaned back in her chair, inhaled, exhaled, this time long and easy, rested the cigarette in the ashtray. "The reason there was a groundswell for him to run was because he was so involved in the community. He was always going to meetings, volunteering his time. But I also think he lost some interest in the Wheelhouse once it became routine. He was one of those people who always needed to be occupied. He seemed to get edgy when his hands were empty."

Sterling nodded. McTaggart had said that Bonnie helped to keep the voices at bay.

Monique tilted her head back and the tip of her tongue tasted her upper lip. Her eyes became hooded, tiny tears pooling in their corners. "My God, how I loved that man." She blinked, reached for her cigarette in the ashtray, the tail of smoke spiraling into thick air. "This isn't for the paper, you understand." Her eyes widened. "Can I trust you?"

Sterling sipped his drink before answering. "This isn't Toronto or Vancouver. The people I write about are my neighbours now. I'll see them on the street and have to answer to them. If I deceive them, nobody's going to talk to me and pretty soon I'm out of a job."

Monique studied him. "It's no secret. Before Bonnie came along, John and I were . . . " she paused and glanced at the floor, its gravel, "close." She looked back at Sterling, her eyes now bright. "We worked so well together getting the Wheel-house in shape after he bought it. It all seemed so natural. And David looked up to him so much."

Placing her cigarette in the ash tray, she opened the purse sitting on the table and pulled out an envelope. Fingering through its contents, she extracted a snapshot, handing it to Sterling. The picture showed a grinning dark-haired boy chest-high to McTaggart standing beside him. David held the reins of a beige mare behind the pair, its long snout raised in a whinny.

"My boy's at boarding school in Winnipeg. He couldn't wait to come home for holidays to see John. They'd go riding, to hockey games, you name it." She paused and smiled. "John was like a father to him." Monique's mouth twisted, her face flushed angry. "And then *she* came along."

Her hand ripped at the cardboard package on the table, thrusting a new cigarette into her mouth. "There's one who must have learned right out of the cradle. Bonnie had her hooks out for John from the very first minute she came to work." She snatched the lighter and lit her own damn smoke. "I curse the day I ever hired her. She had no shame. It was obvious he was with me but that didn't stop the little tart from chasing a man old enough to be her father."

The barrage of words came with its own cloud engulfing the table. A machine gun series of drags consumed most of her cigarette as the glowing ash drew closer and closer to her lips. She threw the butt on the floor, grinding it under her heel and fell back in her chair. Noticing that a half-finished smoke still smouldered in the ashtray, she looked away, ignoring it.

The outburst appeared to deflate Monique, the lines of her angular body softening, her arms falling to her sides. Her eyes looked red. She stared across the table at Sterling for several moments, lost, then seemed startled that he sat there.

After a pause, she said, "And now I don't even know if I have a job, if I can keep David at his school." Her shoulders shifted up and down. "Maybe I'll know tomorrow. The estate lawyer phoned to say he wants to discuss John's will. Mr. Parenteau said he'd tell me then who the new owners are."

Parenteau! Shark lawyers lurking in the waters everywhere.

Monique sipped her coffee while gazing at the table top, a long red fingernail scratching the surface as if some answer lay underneath. Then her eyes narrowed.

"I know I sound bitter but I'm telling you the truth. Some say they were a great couple but I knew different. Bonnie was no good for John. She didn't get the chance but she would have drained him, left him out to dry."

She raised her cup to the bar and gestured at Sterling. The waitress returned with a coffee pot and a scotch over ice.

Monique waited until her employee left before continuing. "I could see the unhappiness growing in him even as they announced their engagement. He should have given me that ring and it haunted him. I could see it in his eyes. He looked dazed like he did the first weeks after he arrived." Monique tapped herself on the breastbone with her forefinger, her voice rising. " I was the one who made him whole, put him back together. It was Bonnie who tore him apart again. The last couple of weeks before he went missing, John just wandered around lost. He began to miss staff meetings and appointments. He even forgot to sign our paycheques. When I reminded him he blew up." Monique shook her finger at Sterling. "He was the same distant, paranoid man who came to Candle Lake two years ago. John might have drowned but in her own way Bonnie killed him."

Monique fell back, spent.

"You're making a serious accusation without spelling it out," Sterling said. "What exactly was Bonnie doing?"

A lock of hair had fallen across Monique's forehead. With her fingers, she combed the tress away.

"I've said enough already." Monique shouldered her purse and picked up her coffee cup as she rose from her chair. She crushed the empty cigarette package and tossed it on the table. "Check out the Fox's Nose Casino in P.A. I expect you'll find your answer there."

Sterling watched her head back behind the bar and then hailed his waitress, ordering coffee. He had been the only customer in the back room of the club. Now a well dressed man wove his way to a table in the opposite corner. Handsome by

most standards and wearing a suit that probably
cost more than a Carribean vacation, the guy
slumped into a chair. Upon closer inspection,
Sterling noticed the man's hair flared uncombed
and his jacket hung misbuttoned and rumpled.
He sat, head in hands, eyes toward the door. At
least he wasn't going to be one of those annoying
friendly drunks.

Sterling's order arrived. He blew on his hot
coffee. Of course, Monique considered McTaggart
lost, taken away from her before he died and
she'd made no attempt to hide her bitterness. *In
her own way, it was Bonnie who killed him.* Or was
it all a ruse by a jilted lover? Could the
Wheelhouse manager have exacted some revenge
of her own and killed John? But then, why him
and not Bonnie?

Sterling studied the dark liquid. After too
many years of watching people, it wouldn't
surprise him if no clear answer emerged. A
jealous rage knew no logic. And it made one
question even more intriguing: why did Monique
refuse to talk about Dan Farrow? It would be
interesting to know her whereabouts the weekend
the colonel went missing. Was she familiar with
a truck and a roof rack of driving lights?

"More coffee?" One corner of the waitress's
mouth curled, a hint of a grin. Her eyes did a nice

dance, teasing. Or was it the scotch doing the number?

Sterling nodded. "Where's Tarzan?"

She had deep sea eyes and they studied him. "Oh, Lance. The beer truck's here. He likes to show off to the drivers, hauling in a keg on each shoulder."

"Good man to have around."

Her mouth pursed, thoughtful. "A beautiful body but even one that pretty can get tiring after awhile, if that's all there is. He's no Stephen Hawking, in every way."

How did she know about the brilliant and popular physicist confined to a wheelchair? It seemed she pined for intellectual stimulation, some delving into the theoretical. "Are you a college student?"

Flinching at the last word, she said, "I'm completing my Masters in English. The political feminization of George Eliot's early and middle works," she added for clarification.

Beautiful and smart, too, that deadly combination again. Sterling produced his most engaging smile. "I've read a few novels but never one of his."

An anguished moan came from the drunk at the other table. He mumbled something too marble-mouthed to understand.

The sparkle in the woman's eyes vanished. Was that a look of contempt? She looked at Sterling then at the drunk in the corner.

She looked down her pretty nose and said, "The literary definition of a tragedy is the fall of a great hero into sorrow and disrepute. Perhaps you two reporters should commiserate together. He's still recovering from his inelegant dismissal from CRBI for engaging in illegal substances."

She walked away. What had he done?

He sipped his coffee. It went down hard. Damn! George Eliot was a *woman*.

Sterling turned toward the slumped man. So they were about to meet at last. He stood, his short career as an intellectual over, time to go back to work.

"Larry Fredericks!" he exclaimed, sliding into a chair at the disgraced newscaster's table. "I watch you on the tube all the time, man! Let me buy you a drink!" He offered his hand. "My name's Myles Sterling." Fredericks still stared at the shell-butt gravel floor, his eyes vacant and blinking. Like a snake serenaded from a basket, his hand rose slow and jittery. Sterling gripped a lifeless and clammy palm. "We're in the same sort of business but I'm no star like you." Most of television's talking heads floated in equal doses of ambition, ego and coiffed hair. They made for easy stroking. "I'm with the P.A. *Sun*."

At last, Fredericks seemed to notice he'd been befriended. He raised his head. "The newspaper," Sterling added, hoping it would cut through the fog.

Fredericks mumbled, "Rye and cola. A double."

Even shamed newscasters have a price. Sterling waved at the server, ordered the drink and more coffee. The man across from him did have the chiseled features of a star. Even his slurred voice still flowed smooth and low. His insides had to be churning, though, disgraced from his job. His fingers began to rap the table top, his eyes darting about, never resting.

"So what brings you to this neck of the woods," Sterling said, adopting a familiar local lingo. "Do you have a cabin here or are you just socializing?"

Fredericks's unsettled eyes fell upon his questioner. "Socializing." He nodded. That's it." His laugh stirred low and bitter. "Socializing."

His hands and eyes resumed their machinations as the waitress arrived. While she poured Sterling's coffee, Fredericks downed his drink and gestured for another with the empty glass.

"Tough luck about that drug charge," the reporter sympathized. The *Sun* story put Frederick's age at thirty-seven, a bit old to be hunting college girls. "Will you be back on the tube soon? Man, you're the best."

"The best," the newscaster repeated, not answering the question. His eyes roamed back and forth across the room like radar.

"Have you talked to Megan Milburn since you were released from hospital?"

"Who?"

"Your date that night, the college girl. She got sick, too."

Fredericks didn't answer. A man not weighed down by the plight of others even by his doing. Still, something bothered him.

His jitters stopped for a moment. "You're the *Sun*, right? Your story stunk." The newscaster's second drink arrived. It disappeared as fast as the first. Words began to blend with each other. "It cost me my job."

Sterling watched the man waiting for the anger to erupt. After a pause, he said, "You pleaded guilty to the possession charge."

"I wanted to get it over with." Fredericks's head fell forward, shaking, his arms sprawling over the table. Both his empty glasses thudded to the floor and rolled, the booze-treated wood cushioning their fall. He looked up and grabbed Sterling's elbow. "You've got to help me!" The handsome man's fingers trembled as he squeezed. "He showed me what he would do to me."

"Who showed you?"

The newscaster's voice squirmed into a whimper, the words slurring over a thick tongue. "I swore I wouldn't say anything but he didn't believe me." The grasp on Sterling fell away. "He showed me the pictures." Fredericks hugged himself, shivering. "Horrible. Horrible."

"What pictures?" Sterling asked, confused.

Fredericks looked over Sterling's shoulder at the bar. Absolute fear wrenched the man's face. Sterling turned and saw only his waitress and Monique, smoking, talking, killing time. The sensation of a breeze whisked over his neck and he glimpsed Fredericks dashing across the room, disappearing around the corner.

Sterling gave chase but when he reached the lobby, it stood empty. He looked back, surveyed the whole club, but saw nothing unusual. The same few old dedicated patrons lounged at the same old bottle-laden tables, sipping and muttering.

Stepping through the main entrance doors, Sterling met the clear cold night. The artificial daylight of snow-reflected street lamps brightened the parking lot. A couple of quad all-terrain vehicles sat beside a snowmobile. The humble Bumbler shivered beside another import. All seemed quiet, calm, no sight of the spooked newscaster. Then two headlights shone from the road beyond. Emerging from the darkness, a big blue

189

GMC, its unlit rack of roof lights glinting, rolled down the road. As the pickup pulled away, its tail-lights blinked red through the trees like an animal of the night.

Sterling searched the blackness. Once again the stalker had vanished.

There was no sign of the troubled broadcaster. What or who frightened him so? His drunken outburst made no sense but by the horror in his eyes, he could have been fleeing the devil himself. Sterling hoped the next time he met Fredericks, he would be sober and able to explain his strange behavior.

Sterling had turned to rescue his parka and mitts from the carcinogenic haze of the Wheelhouse and head home when the doors opened before him. There stood Monique, now blossomed into a new woman. She stepped aside to allow him through the doorway.

"A bit nippy out there tonight," she said.

She smiled, her cheeks snuggling in the deep collar of a full length fur the colour of elm bark.

"Do you know what time it is?"

"Yes, I do."

"Hear that? The twins are crying. The phone woke them and now they'll be wailing all night."

"How old are they? I thought they wanted to be hockey players."

"Five. They'll grow out of it and become astronauts. Or medicine women."

"Doctors?"

"No, healers."

Sterling shifted the cellphone, no larger than his palm, from one ear to the other. "Like I said, Kevin, the guy ran me off the road, smashed my little rental. It's a Bumbler, reminds me of your Jag. I could have been killed."

"What do you want from me? Driving lessons?"

"Who is Edith Dolmage?"

"I told you, confidentiality. We're in negotiations. Dig deeper journalist."

"I'm a reporter. Journalists have perfect hair and smile for the camera."

"When you're ugly, you're ugly."

"Farrow threatened to sue me if I wrote that he had the most to gain by McTaggart's death."

"Now we're talking. Did you mention my name? I love litigation. We've got an easy payment plan. Speaking of which."

A silence followed.

"The cheque's in the mail," Sterling sighed.

"This call is going on the bill."

"Listen, Parenteau. The maniac on the highway, I didn't mention him in the accident report. I'm not so sure I can trust Milburn."

"Isn't that a criminal offence? I saw that on one of those real police shows once. Yes, I remember now. Lying to the cops is definitely a criminal offence."

"There was a message for me at home. Something nasty could happen if I keep nosing around."

"I get threatened all the time in my business."

"When you're ugly, you're ugly."

A lengthy pause held before Kevin's breath hissed through the line. "What you're telling me is that I'm your only friend on the planet."

"You're tight with Crown Counsel. I just wanted you to know what's happening."

"Okay, Myles. Be careful and keep in touch." A soft pause held for a moment. "During office hours, if possible," he whispered. "The girls have gone back to sleep."

The dial tone droned. Sterling switched off the phone and laid it on the desk. The orange and yellow flames of the fireplace crackled, spit up the chimney.

Sometimes it seemed they were kids again, the banter, the knowing each other's mind. What if Kevin *was* his only friend on the planet?

Sterling pushed the play button on his answering machine one more time. The electronic voice thrummed without emotion, disembodied: "You have a choice. Leave the colonel alone. Or join him."

Morning March 6

Sterling checked the address against the one in
his notebook a third time. It had been a long
night, voices crying to him whenever he closed
his eyes, soft winds of anguish leaving him
nowhere to hide. Little sleep and it seemed he
couldn't even get a street number right. This had
to be the place. The Pleasant Valley Seniors' Care
Complex just wasn't what he expected. Should
he even bother?

Leaning back on the headrest, he watched the
monotonous dance of the windshield wipers. If
this was a typical March in Saskatchewan these
days, what were the real winter months like?
Boyhood memories flashed of kicking along in
rubber boots through slushy puddles.

Today, however, an avalanche smothered the
Bumbler, the white stuff half way up the little
car's wheels. The weather woman joked she
could see no end in sight. The drive from Candle
Lake to Prince Albert had been a knuckle-
whitener. The view out the window might as well
have been that of a television with no reception.
Several cars and a couple of semi's wallowed in

the ditches. Fortunately for Ed, neither of the tractor-trailers sported the Braun and Sons logo.

The colonel's best friend hadn't returned any calls yet. He had sounded distraught in his original message. Ed wouldn't do anything crazy, would he? Sterling shook the thought from his head. How easily the mind can panic with little reason. Braun planted his feet on good firm earth. A little patience and, perhaps, another telephone call seemed best. He'd show up.

Sterling zippered his parka, exited the car. The storm had dragged out the fifty minute drive to a wearying three hours. Might as well make certain that the Pleasant Valley Senior Citizens Care Complex was a dead end, no offense to its residents.

The single story brick structure occupied one side of a full city block, the building entrance in the centre. Sterling wiped his feet in the lobby before entering a second set of glass doors into the large common area. On one side stretched a dining room and kitchen — the thick smell of roast beef hung in the air — while on the other sat the recreation room.

Several balding and white-haired men and women sat in chairs reading while the more active shot pool or played shuffleboard. The metal click of the closing door had the force of a gunshot, freezing everyone in place.

A short, stocky woman with a jolly face and dressed in a blue institutional pantsuit emerged from a side door marked "Activities Co-ordinator." Making her way past the residents, she stopped at one table, and said something that made its occupants laugh.

"Room?" she smiled, approaching Sterling. "Just for a half hour or will you be making a night of it? The girls are awaiting your choice." The co-ordinator jerked her thumb over her shoulder toward the table of blue-rinsed ladies playing bridge. The four resumed their game, looks shifting between their cards and Sterling. Bent over the pool table, a silver-haired man dressed for the game in black suit pants and matching vest guffawed just before his cue spit forward. The white ball rocketed into the eight which slammed into a corner pocket. His shot elicited a wolf whistle from the bridge table.

Laughing at the visitor's red face, his greeter offered her hand. "We love to have fun here at Pleasant Valley, keep our spirits high. Hi, I'm Mrs. Beddington. How can I help you?"

"Is there a Mrs. Edith Dolmage here? My name is Myles Sterling."

"You're not her son, then. Poor Mrs. Dolmage, she talks about him all the time but I've yet to see his face. That sweet Mrs. Dancewics is the only one who comes around to pay her respects, all the way from Candle Lake, every second Thursday evening, eight on the dot."

Why was Dan Farrow's secretary visiting here? Perhaps it wasn't a dead end.

The co-ordinator liked to talk. Her rapid speech seemed designed to cram in as many words as time allowed.

She gestured to the hallway on her right. "This way. Dear Mrs. Dolmage will be delighted to have a new visitor. Are you a friend or relative.?"

"I'm with the Prince Albert *Sun*."

"Oooh, is she going to be in the paper?" Mrs. Beddington gurgled, as they padded down the soft carpeting.

"You never know."

The curt answer didn't seem to bother his guide. She prattled on naming each resident as they passed his or her door relating his or her current health status. For the most part, the reports focused on bowel movements or lack thereof.

The fine neighbourhood welcome felt a little too fine. Sterling's stomach stirred, unsettled. He checked for an exit. Was she warming him up for the long stay? Would she ever let him out? If a gang of oldsters circled, he'd make a run for that door under the red light.

"Here we are," the co-ordinator said at last, stopping before room 125. She knocked and

Scott Gregory Miller

opened the door touching her finger to her lips
— shh. "Are you decent, dear?"

Mrs. Beddington poked in her head, beckoned
Sterling with her hand.

They entered a bright suite of two rooms. A
table and chairs and a small sink occupied the
kitchenette. It appeared Mrs. Dolmage had her
food brought in, the small area unencumbered by
a stove, any sign of dishes. The second room
contained a green paisley couch and two matching
padded chairs that surrounded a small television.
In the corner sat a bed and side table across from
the open door of a bathroom.

The compact apartment looked unused,
nothing out of place. With the exception of the
small area at the rear, they could have been on a
tour of a show suite, Mrs. Beddington the realtor.
His gaze settled on the bedside table. An army
of pill bottles, a virtual pharmacy occupied its
surface. Mrs. Dolmage, it seemed, spent most of
her time sleeping. The large silhouette formed by
the bedclothes stirred as the co-ordinator called
again.

"This is a reporter from the P.A. *Sun*," smiled
the jolly guide.

Sterling's lofty status didn't appear to impress
the bed-ridden woman much. She opened her
eyes but only to stare at the ceiling. Grabbing a
kitchen chair, he came near and sat down.

"Is it all right if I ask her some questions?" He waved over his shoulder at his guide.

"Oh certainly! Mrs. Dolmage loves to entertain. Don't you dear?" Mrs. Beddington bubbled. "I'll leave you two alone."

Positioning the door open just so, she waved and disappeared.

Sterling studied the poor woman, a victim of her years. Her eyes, the opaque grey of cataracts, stared heavenward, unflinching. Could she see?

"Mrs. Dolmage?" Not to startle her, Sterling whispered. "Mrs. Dolmage?" A frightening thought occurred. Was this another joke? Was she dead? Leaning closer, he heard a soft, shallow breath. It seemed pointless but he might as well finish. "Do you know anything about Dolmage Enterprises?" He waited. She stared, catatonic. "Do you know Dan Farrow?" Nothing. Oh well, he'd tried. Rising from his chair, he made a stab in the dark. "Do you own property in Candle Lake?"

Mrs. Dolmage remained still, her breathing even as if asleep. Sterling looked out the window in disgust. He'd come all the way for this colossal waste of time. A touch of skin grazed his wrist then a hand wrapped around his arm and tightened. He looked back at the bed as the old woman turned her head, rewarded him with a huge smile.

"Son! You've come! You've come to see your momma!"

Sterling blushed, sheepish, shook his head. He tried to pull his arm back but her grip hardened. He sat down again.

"My name is Myles Sterling. From the P.A. *Sun*, Mrs. Dolmage."

"That nurse, the others, they said you were always too busy but I knew you had to see your momma."

"No, I'm not your son. I'm a reporter."

"Oh, you're still angry, aren't you, dear? You were only four but you still remember when we left your first daddy. He was a big handsome brute all right. But dull, my goodness. I thought I'd go nuts. You liked the others, though, dear, didn't you? Remember Francois from Gay Paree? What a wonderful dancer. Oh, and what about Giovanni, those smoky dark eyes, that Latin soul. When he wanted a woman, how could she resist? You understand, don't you dear? And surely you liked Emile, the Cree chief whose last name meant clear water. Strong and silent, yes, but once he got behind closed doors." Mrs. Dolmage paused, frowned. "Was he number four or five?" Her voice took on a note of helplessness. "Six?" She looked at Sterling, her gray fragmented pupils pleading. "Please dear, don't be angry with your momma."

Sterling fell back in his chair, stopped trying to relieve her of his hand. "I'm not angry."

"Come a little closer, my eyes aren't what they used to be." Her pudgy fingers squeezed. "You were such a good boy. I know your trouble at school was because the kids gave you a hard time over me. But I was no floozy! I made sure each one of those men married me first." Mrs. Dolmage looked to be about ninety, her skin wrinkled, her hair thin and white. Even so, for a moment her face glowed. "Well, most of them."

"Yes, Momma," Sterling agreed.

Mrs. Dolmage studied her son. All of a sudden her eyes grew large. She pulled her hand away. Her fingers twisted at the sleeve of her sweater uncovering a gold spring-band watch.

"Two minutes to. Please, dear, you must go now. I'm sorry but please hurry."

Flustered, torn from the mode of a sleepy listener, Sterling had trouble finding his feet, rising from the chair.

"Of course, but," he mumbled, unable to finish his thought.

Now a mother who brooked no nonsense admonished, "I said right now, young man!" Her arm shot out, her finger the tip of a lance pointing to the door. "Go!"

"Yes, of course."

Stumbling, Sterling picked up his chair, deposited it at the kitchen table. He turned to say goodbye. The words never left his mouth. The partition opening framed Mrs. Dolmage intent on her hand mirror, her hair loosened to her shoulders, a brush stroking it free.

Sterling walked down the hall toward the lobby. Glancing at his own watch, it read 10 AM on the dot. A sound, a sixth sense, something made him stop, look around. At the door to 125, stood the well dressed pool player whose game drew a whistle from the table of card playing women. The tall man held himself erect, unstooped by age. The silver fox stepped inside, the door closing behind him.

Mid-morning March 6

Sterling closed his fist and clipped the steering wheel a good one under the chin. What a waste of time! A whole morning gone and all for nothing. He might as well have been talking to the wall. At least, Mrs. Dolmage knew how to have a good time, her and the silver fox. On second thought, perhaps he should call it quits, spend his waning years at Pleasant Valley. Would he be up to it, though, all that sex?

Now he had to plough through carnivorous snowdrifts back to Candle Lake. That morning when dialing into his voice mail, he'd received a message from an angry Mrs. Dankewics. She'd had enough of that mean, miserable man and had a few things to say about the new mayor. Could she meet Sterling as soon as possible?

Sterling kept a lid on his excitement. While a declaration from a political insider to spill the beans sounded like a journalist's wet dream, as often as not, the motive reeked of personal vengeance. Experience had shown that, what the wounded perceived to be a mountain of scandal, often turned out to be, in the greater scheme of things, more akin to an anthill. The story proved to be more smoke than fire and, after a few days, it all blew over and the colony got back to normal, minus one burnt worker.

Still, he could ask Mrs. Dankewics why she paid regular visits to Mrs. Dolmage. The lusty old lass did reside at the address listed for Dolmage Enterprises Limited. If nothing else, he'd confirmed that much.

Sterling unzipped his parka, retrieved his cell phone from an inside pocket. Even though he'd yet to step foot in the vertiginous confines of the Prince Albert *Sun* Building, a call still seemed more prudent than a visit. After the rush of morning ablutions, he'd jumped into his usual lake country winter wear — a heavy wool sweater and jeans. Halfway to the city, it had dawned on him that a jacket and tie would have been a wiser choice. Especially, if the threatened meeting with the publisher materialized.

His eyes drifted about the Bumbler's ratty interior. Puffs of yellow foam excreted from holes in the upholstery. A vicious crack snaked across the windshield at eye level, its wandering snakelets creating a kaleidoscope of oncoming headlights.

He'd steered the little battered ball of steel up to the rental agency's shack and the kid rushed outside.

"What's wrong this time?" he'd said, pulling at his orange hair. It seemed the lad had wearied of admitting to an inferior product. He was invited to make a tour of the vehicle. "Looks fine to me." Directed to the crumpled and wrenched fender, the kid pulled on his nose ring. "It's a Bumbler, man, they come out of the factory that way."

Sterling had slipped back behind the wheel and driven away. Why not hang onto the striving bolt bucket? It handled better since the accident anyway and had started to feel downright homey.

The automobile had evolved into the modern journalist's office, technology providing all the communication that the world required. Between his palm-size telephone, laptop computer, and the magic of satellite modem, he could talk to anyone and file stories to the newsroom until his keyboard fingers turned blue while travelling from location to location.

Sterling had realized this upon his return from Eastern Europe and Africa. Overseas, he had spent much time holed up in hotels deciphering the propaganda. The tedious regurgitation of fictitious numbers for the public soon forced the ambitious reporter to seek the real story, often by finding and counting the dead. In order not to join them, he employed the journalistic technique of hiding behind rocks and between buildings.

Whether the fire you ducked came from friend or foe seemed a moot point at best. Now back home, planting his rear end on the coil springs of a jalopy's bench seat most of the day and night seemed like a remarkable improvement. Or did it?

Sterling punched the numbers into his phone.

"Prince Albert *Sun*. Newsroom."

"Myles Sterling here."

"Oh, Mr. Sterling, I'm so glad you called. Megan Milburn's young voice bubbled. "I just had to thank you for the job. It's wonderful. Joe is such a sweetheart."

"We're working together now. Please, Megan, call me Myles. What about school?"

"I start on the night shift tomorrow. Community college during the day. It'll be perfect."

"It sounds like long hours."

"It'll be good training," she laughed.

"What does Staff Sergeant Milburn think of your new job?"

After a long pause, Megan's tone grew somber. "My dad is such a grouch sometimes. He blew up. We had a big fight."

Her words hit Sterling with a pang of guilt. More than his philanthropy had sent the young woman through the newsroom door. She did strike him as a good candidate for the job but, if at the same time he could stick it to her father and twist the blade a bit, that would be fine too. Megan was a good kid. In some ways she reminded Sterling of himself at that age, not the bright personality, perhaps, but the gung-ho attitude. The wound in her voice spoke of a close father and daughter and the reporter's little vengeance game hurt her too.

"He's just protecting his daughter."

The frustration in her voice mounted. "Why does he think I'm taking media studies? For my health?"

"Megan, you might not understand this now but even a tough cop like your old man can be afraid, afraid of his little girl leaving the nest."

More silence, then, "I'm not his little girl anymore." In a determined monotone, she asked, "Mom understands, why can't he?"

"He's just concerned, that's all. But you're right, he'll have to learn to live with what you're doing."

"Could you talk to him? Please! I hate it when we fight."

"I'm not really the best man for the job, Megan." Without getting into detail, honesty seemed to be the best bet. "The professional relationship between your father and me isn't what it could be. Anything I say will just make it worse."

"You've met him," she insisted. "You can see he's just a big stubborn teddy bear. You're a famous journalist, Mr. Sterling. He's got to listen to you."

"Myles. Call me Myles." His defences crumbling, defeat seemed inevitable. "I'm not famous." He had helped cause the problem.

"You've been all over the world. Everyone's heard of you. Please!"

His head fell back and he released a long breath. She didn't listen, wouldn't listen. "No promises. Okay?"

"You're the greatest!"

He'd never been anyone's hero before. Was he ready for this?

"I asked Joe to do some checks for me. Could you see if anything's come up?"

"All done. He gave the job to me." Pride bobbed in her voice. "Dan Farrow wasn't registered at the hotel in Regina that weekend in February or any other."

"Good work. How did you find that out?"

"I said I was Farrow's secretary trying to track down a coat the Mayor left behind at some convention. The hotel clerk sounded kind of interesting and we talked a bit. He invited me for coffee next time I'm in town."

"You're a natural," Sterling said, like a proud teacher, his judgement confirmed.

"You've also got a message from the *Calgary Herald*."

"My wayward editor friend. What's he got to say?"

"Dan Farrow ran a couple of used car lots in Cowtown until he was practically run out of the city."

"Used car salesman! I knew it!" Sterling grinned into the phone. He could spot them a mile away.

"Pardon?"

"Sorry, continue."

"Farrow was cited twenty-seven times alone for turning back odometers. There were several other infractions and he lost his business license. He disappeared somewhere in Saskatchewan, your friend thinks."

"Candle Lake to be exact." Sterling watched the snowflakes melt on his windshield, thicker, heavier than minutes before. "By the way, I ran across the name Veronica Milburn in the village land titles. Any relation?"

"Yes, she's my grandmother," she replied. "I spent many wonderful summers at her cottage. Are you doing a story on Mayor Farrow?"

A truck roared past, blanketing the Bumbler with grey slush. "Yes, I just finished here at Pleasant Valley Seniors. Came up flat."

"I used to volunteer there. Mrs. Dolmage is such a sweet old lady."

Sterling lowered the fist he'd shaken at the semi. "Mrs. Dolmage? She's the one I interviewed, for lack of a better word."

"She had some romantic stories about that place. Those seniors can get pretty frisky," Megan said, with an embarrassed laugh.

"Wait. How did you make a connection between Mrs. Dolmage and Farrow?

Now confusion steeped in the voice of Sterling's co-worker. "I assumed that's why you were at Pleasant Valley, to interview her for your story."

"What are you saying, Megan?"

"Mrs. Dolmage is Dan Farrow's mother, of course. Farrow is her first husband's name, Dan's father. Dolmage is the name of her last husband."

"Mother. His mother," Sterling repeated. "I could kiss you."

"I'm sorry, Mr. Sterling. I've had it with older men."

"The man is incorrigible, absolutely incorrigible."
Mrs. Dankewics's red, bony hands twisted the
paper tissue into knots. "I speak with the utmost
gravity, I assure you, Mr. Sterling."

Dan Farrow's secretary had been seated at a
corner table in the Candle Lake Café when the
reporter arrived. The blizzard had worsened on
the return trip from Prince Albert, the road like
a skating rink, visibility not much more than a
few car lengths. Worn by the drive, Sterling
savoured the hot coffee as he listened.

"I'm certain you do," he said. "Can I call you
Irene?"

The café overlooked Highway 265 as it ran
through town. Across the road, the vacant property owned by Dolmage Enterprises hid in a
copse of pine. Soft pastels, yellow curtains over
the windows rather than blinds, decorated the
small and homey restaurant. A girl of about high
school age served the steaming java, her strong
resemblance to the woman who poked her head
through the port from the kitchen to yell "order!"
suggested a mother and daughter team. The

aroma of Sunday cooking captured Sterling's stomach the second he walked through the door.

"Mrs. Dankewics will suffice." She gave the reporter a stern look before continuing. "How two men as different as day and night, dare I say as different as good and evil, could occupy the same office is beyond me."

The public deserves what it gets in a democracy. The simplistic reply passed without being voiced. It appeared Mrs. Dankewics had much to unburden and the fewer interruptions the sooner they could get to the heart of the matter. That would be, Sterling suspected, the thick manila envelope impaled under her sharp elbows.

Mrs. Dankewics sneezed, blew her nose into her crumpled and soggy paper hanky. "Candle Lake doesn't realize the true tragedy of John McTaggart's passing."

Just in time, she covered her mouth.

"*Gesundheit.*"

"Thank you." With some relief, Sterling watched her retrieve a new tissue from her purse. She began again: "Those darn renovations. Excuse my French. From his first day, Dan Farrow has had them tearing down walls, moving new furniture so his majesty would be living in a style to which he'd like to become accustomed." Once more she blew her nose. "The drafts blowing through there, my desk might as well be outside in a snowbank. I've been sick ever since that infernal man arrived. Nothing's too good for him but do you think Mr. Mayor cares about the secretary who has given twenty-two years of her life to the Candle Lake Village Office?" Sterling didn't have time to shake his head. "You're darn right he doesn't. He hasn't even touched his new computer. I've had the same one since 1984. My machine makes molasses in January look like a horse race. And what does Mr. High and Mighty say when I ask for a new one? He says we're in a period of fiscal restraint. Ha! Makes me laugh. There aren't enough notches on that man's belt to restrain his big fat belly!"

Leaning back, Mrs. Dankewics took a respite from her barrage. Sterling's notebook remained open, blank. No Watergate. He laid his pen down. Still, there would be a few questions when she finished. His eye kept catching on the thick yellow mailer on which her elbows perched. It beckoned with the allure of a present under the Christmas tree.

"Mayor McTaggart, bless his soul, knew we couldn't afford all these things and I didn't mind making do." Mrs. Dankewics had recovered her breath and headed down the back stretch. "We even shared my little computer. Whenever he needed to use it, he would always ask my permission."

Her drawn face lightened for a moment.

Sterling remembered watching the secretary dust the portraits of Candle Lake's mayors. She had embraced McTaggart's gold framed picture like a newborn. Farrow, as if taking him into the corner of the local hockey rink, she'd elbowed a couple of times leaving him cock-eyed and crooked. It brought to mind the sage advice of one of the country's prime ministers who always appeared suave and erudite in public but loved to wallow in the vernacular once he got to the backroom. He advised that once elected, don't piss off the hired hands. They'll make your life hell. Farrow would soon learn that very lesson.

"I don't mind being treated like dirt, regarded more as a slave than a human being," Mrs. Dankewics said, "because I'm proud of the job I've done for my community over the years. Besides, mayors come and go. I hoped the public would see a man who thinks he's Caesar has no place in charge of our village." Her gaze locked on Sterling to ensure he understood the magnitude of her words. "I admit I refused to call him Danny Boy as he requested. Imagine calling a grown man Danny Boy." Her eyebrows raised in exasperation. "However, I did many things for our Mr. Mayor in kindness wishing he'd return the same and make my job at least bearable again. I went out of my way to visit his mother in P.A.

because he asked me to. I even put up with telling his wife half-truths or even outright lies because he said she was a nervous woman who shouldn't be worried." She clenched her hands and leaned forward. "Then I saw what it was really about." Her fist hit the table. "I won't be in concert with cheating!" For a moment, the woman's head dropped and she twisted her bony fingers. "Mr. Dankewics and I pride ourselves on the fidelity of our union. It made me feel dirty when I saw what I'd been doing to poor Mrs. Farrow, believing that man's lies, passing them on to her."

Mrs. Dankewics turned towards the window where, outside, snow rippled across the highway in drifts. Her red eyes puffing, tears formed in the corners. Her thin face and pointed nose enhanced her bird-like countenance. It would be her inner strength that drew Mr. Dankewics, the reason for their proud fidelity. Or fear of relentless wrath.

"What did you see?" Sterling prompted.

"I saw them coming out of that woman's house on Lakeview Drive. She looks to be a barmaid by her clothes. I pass by on my way to and from church. He had his arm around her." Mrs. Dankewics's face pinched in disgust. "I should have known when I found this." From the envelope she withdrew a small piece of paper and handed it to Sterling. The receipt from the Prince Albert Inn listed a room for two nights.

"Room 224 Occupants — 2" had been high-lighted in felt pen. "That beastly man wanted the taxpayers to foot the bill for his dirty weekend." She shook her head, incredulous. "Does his lechery know no bounds?"

Sterling kept his disappointment inside. He'd hoped for a little more. Muckraking always left a bad taste and it should be avoided if possible. Where was some real news? He read the receipt again. The dates caught his eye — February 2nd and 3rd. On second thought, this mysterious woman deserved another look.

"Can I make a copy of this?" Sterling asked.

Mrs. Dankewics nodded before sneezing one more time.

"You said you visited Mrs. Dolmage every second Thursday," he said.

She glanced up from her clasped fists. "No, I didn't say when." She stared at the reporter, considering. "I suppose that's your job, snooping around other people's lives." Her eyes fell again to her white knuckles. "About the first week on the job I mentioned I went into the city every Thursday evening for shopping. Mr. High and Mighty asked if I would mind taking some papers for his mother to sign. I enjoyed her company so much I now make regular visits."

"Did you see what kind of papers?"

She shrugged. "Only that the company's letterhead had the same name as hers."

The page of Sterling's notebook began to fill. Mrs. Dolmage didn't even know she presided over what seemed to be a going concern in Candle Lake property development.

Eyeing the envelope so secure in his informant's keeping, Sterling asked, "Is there anything else you wanted to tell me, Mrs. Dankewics?"

The woman straightened her back, squared her shoulders. "I'm sure I've given you more than enough information to reveal to the public just how undeserving of the mayor's office is Dan Farrow. There's something else, though. It has to do with the casino development Mayor McTaggart was so against. From day one, it's the only thing which Dan Farrow has spent his time on."

She slid the package across the table. Sterling smiled, gripped it in both hands like a child on Christmas morning.

"In there, you'll find all the details. Notice that our current so-called mayor has signed the permits to proceed without council having voted on the matter." The twenty-two year civic employee sniffed. "That's just not right."

Sterling tapped the envelope. Documentation of the casino proposal, now they were talking. He held out his hand to shake hers.

"Thank you Mrs. Dankewics." Her strong grip surprised him. "I suppose you're kept busy with all the calls and letters from people afraid they will lose their homes to the Minowukaw land claim?"

Her face pinched harder. "Is that what Farrow told you?" Her scowl could unnerve a statue. "He started it all."

Early Hours March 7

The noose looked good closing around Dan Farrow's fat neck. Sterling massaged his hand still tender from the mayor's grip.

The papers spread on the carpet in front of the fireplace said it all. Mrs. Dankewics hadn't missed a thing. The village council had approved nothing, had no idea how far the whole business had been taken. Farrow alone had authorized a rezoning for the Dolmage Enterprises property from residential to commercial. He'd also signed the development permit for a ten storey hotel and casino complex on the eight acres.

No doubt he expected the other councillors would be quick to fall in line once such a major project took off. No politician wants to stand in the way of progress and the mayor would be seen as oiling the ever creaky civic bureaucracy, clearing away obstacles to ensure the success of the largest development in Candle Lake's history. Farrow would come out of it looking like the hero. The fears of residents that their land verged on being scooped from under their feet by the

Minowukaw First Nation would be allayed. All this, as they say, would put the place on the map.

It would be a neat trick, too, because the paranoia had been planted by the mayor. Of course, as a result, the real owner of the company, Dan Farrow, would see a nice little bulge in his bank account.

By the same token, the value of the Milburn property next door would skyrocket once rezoned to commercial use and who would want to live next door to a casino? Was the staff sergeant in on the game?

From where he sat on the floor, Sterling leaned over, parted the fireplace screen, tossed in another log. The sweet smell of pine and a comforting blanket of heat wafted across his face.

He hovered on the precipice, he could feel it. No one could bring the colonel back but perhaps justice could be served. Closure they called it, as if there could ever be such a thing.

The evidence so far provided more than enough motive for a man with Farrow's shady past. It showed that he'd pocket upwards of a million dollars if he took the next step and committed murder. Many had done it for much less. But was he that ambitious?

Sterling stared at the twists of orange and yellow flame. The driver of the big blue GMC didn't play games, his telephone threat had been no joke. Next time, it wouldn't be a ride along the guard rail, Sterling would end up blowing bubbles under the ice.

How did Staff Sergeant Milburn tie into all this? Was the rude reception he gave Sterling simply blind vengance against the first reporter he saw after what had happened to his daughter? Or was there more to it than that? Milburn, too, stood to gain if the casino went through. For Megan's sake, Sterling hoped the stink of corruption hadn't seeped that far.

Sterling studied John McTaggart staring back from the front page of the Prince Albert *Sun*. The memorial story came off as a sharp little piece. It covered the colonel's life from his boyhood in small town Ontario through his career in the army. Sterling still seethed over how a moribund United Nations, its controlling Security Council with interests elsewhere, left McTaggart and his troops helpless. The blood of almost a million Rwandans flowed before their eyes. The story told of how only the bravest and strongest of men like John McTaggart and Ed Braun could not only survive the horrendous experience but also be among Candle Lake's leading citizens. Braun and Sons, for instance, now stood as one of Saskatchewan's biggest trucking firms. Its owner, like the late Mayor McTaggart, could be described as nothing other than a hero.

Sterling turned to the wooden coffee table where the telephone sat, silent. Ed had still not returned any of the calls. Tomorrow would be a good time to stop by the yard just to see what was up.

He halted at another headline: "Toxic methamphetamine sending users to hospital in Saskatchewan and Manitoba." The story said samples of the tainted crystal meth had turned up in Winnipeg, Brandon, Portage La Prairie, Yorkton, Regina and Saskatoon, and also mentioned the Larry Fredericks case in Prince Albert. So far, twenty-three people had been sent to hospital.

The case must have rubbed the yellow-striped trousers of Staff Sergeant Milburn raw. What father wouldn't react the same way — roust some stranger, some scumbag reporter like the creep who sent Megan to hospital and left her lying there catatonic from bad dope. No doubt, among the sickened, many would be kids, their families torn apart in the same way.

The clock read just after midnight, a few hours before sleep would come and time enough to get at the Triumph's cylinder heads. The cloud that erupted like Mount St. Helens from the exhaust pipes four days before had screamed blown engine. The motor apart, though, revealed only a burnt valve and scoring on two cylinder walls.

The replating done, it wouldn't be long before the precious thing rode the highway once more.

The TR6, still a joy, seemed in some slow and sly way to be separating itself from Joanne, her image fading. Lately Sterling noticed that the memory of her scent had dulled, that distinctive smell a loved one imprints on the mind. And for the first time that he could remember, that morning her face had blurred and it took him a moment of concentration before her features returned. He knew, though, the phantom weight of her lifeless head on his shoulder would never leave him.

Was this a good sign? Kevin would think so. He saw the little car as a morbid connection with a dead fiancée and a never born child. He just didn't get it. A classic, the Triumph would already fetch twice what Sterling paid. He would be crazy to sell it now. Even though heating bills for the garage would be astronomical, payback would come. Parenteau had a right to his opinion but he just didn't understand. No sir. Not a clue.

The reporter reached over the mess on the floor and retrieved the box of files he'd carted from Ontario. From the stories around the world, he pulled the thick file marked "Rwanda." Inside, smudged pages, bent corners spoke of a trail of eyes worn thin. How could you let go when you keep going back again and again? Was it ever possible to make sense of genocide?

The slaughter had haunted McTaggart's mind, and like Sterling, left him wandering and searching. Only Candle Lake quelled the human screams cresting from the mountains and the insidious sweet stench of blood. Had Sterling been blind or just afraid of the whisperings of ghosts? The reporter could avoid the obvious no longer. One way or another, the birth of John McTaggart's death took place in Rwanda.

Sterling held his breath, prepared to have his heart stopped as it always did when he gazed upon her face. Turning the page, he studied the photograph of the Tutsi woman and her child. *Prenez mon bébé. Prenez lui s'il vous plait.* The paper here became dog-eared, from being read over and over. This incident spoke loudest among the almost one million deaths, more so than the dogs, more so than even accompanying the colonel to the front door of an adobe house in Rwanda to find 132 bodies stacked inside. The Hutu regular army, McTaggart had said, can afford bullets.

Even that scene didn't stalk Sterling's mind, track him everywhere as if a sharp blade had etched the picture into his brain. The woman and her baby did. Her brown doe eyes that stared at him in silence. The mother crouched and sobbed on the ground, the rich, red Rwandan earth staining her white robe — this blazed in Sterling's skull.

His hand followed the words of the newspaper clipping to the point where fingerprints no longer smeared the page, the ink now clear to the end of the story. At this point, he wouldn't read further. The place ahead, he visited only in unbidden dreams.

Tonight he ventured to the end. The woman had remained sitting at the side of the road, swaying as if singing a lullaby to the baby swaddled in her arms. She'd stopped crying, her head down, her long brown neck bare. The folds of her *pagne* protected the child from the heat, the white material fluttering in the wind like wings. Sterling had been transfixed, reminded of an angel, as he burned against the seat of the U.N. four-by-four. He did not see the *Interhamwe* until a machete glinted in the sun, flashing down. Her head toppled to her shoulder still connected by a strand of muscle and skin, a geyser of blood filling the air, raining down to soak her gown crimson.

This wasn't regular army but one of many gangs recruited to rid the land of the *inyenzi*, the cockroaches — the Tutsi and their Hutu sympathizers. The ragged, drunk and stoned *genocidaires* carried no guns. They wielded machetes and crude spikehammers — clubs from which long nails protruded. The motley death squad hovered around the mother and baby slashing and stabbing, stabbing and slashing like frenzied dogs. After awhile, the two victims became a red mass, slaughtered animals unrecognizable as human beings.

The Land Rover had pulled away when Captain Braun said, "You can't let it get to you or you'll go insane."

Had his eyes not glanced away from the rearview mirror as he spoke? Had he not seen the murder taking place a few short steps behind the truck?

Sterling still didn't know for certain. Did it matter? He walked over to the coffee table where he poured himself a couple of fingers of single malt. He swallowed, let it burn. Braun was the survivor, the strong one. Not in his world did silence invite the dead year after year, night after night. *Prenez mon bébé. Prenez s'il vous plait.*

Returning to his place by the fire, the reporter filed the article back in the cardboard box, paper memories oozing over its sides. Fanned by a breeze from the flames as if needing special attention, the hotel receipt courtesy of Mrs. Dankewics fluttered on the carpet. Farrow had lied. He didn't stay in Regina the weekend the colonel went missing. The big fat mayor cavorted at the

P.A. Inn doing, no doubt, a little gambling next door at the casino.

Mrs. Dankewics had jotted down the address of the house from which the mayor and the mystery woman emerged. Candle Lake's thousand population translated into about a third as many residences. Sterling began to thumb through the small section of the Prince Albert telephone book dedicated to the village. Tracking Lakeview Drive homes, it didn't take long to find the name. He shook his head. He was surprised. More to the point, why was he disappointed? She had seemed like someone with a good head on her shoulders. Yet who can say why people do what they do? Whatever she saw in a corrupt piece of work like Dan Farrow, only Monique Tremblay, the Wheelhouse Bar manager, would know.

Morning March 7

"You need a lawyer to go fishing, Noel?"

"If we don't catch anything, Myles," the elder Parenteau said, nudging his son, "I might sue you for defamation of character, the damage it would do to my reputation."

"Slow at the office," Kevin grinned. "I thought I'd take the opportunity to throw a line in and catch a walleye supper. I'm a little tired of Dad gloating over his life up here."

The three men walked out onto the surface of Candle Lake.

"Do you think you'll be able to tell if the ice in McTaggart's shack is recent or from the beginning of the season?" Sterling asked.

"Stranger things have happened," Noel smiled.

Brendan had discovered the colonel's body 300 metres from where his tackle box sunk directly under the fishing hole. To Sterling's eye, all the ice that comprised the floor of the fishing side of the shack looked new, not just what would be needed for a small opening. If a larger hole had been chainsawed, Noel's seventy-years-plus fishing wisdom could find it.

The underwater camera found in McTaggart's shack swayed from Sterling's shoulder. It would illustrate another bit of confusion Kevin's father may be able to clarify. Noel mentioned that the colonel had revelled in the angling pot of gold — a depression in the lake bottom teeming with shy pickerel. Yet the camera revealed a hunting ground only the voracious jackfish would patrol.

Sterling turned to Kevin as the three sets of boots crunched on the ice-crusted snow path. "You could have just told me Farrow owns the property in the hotel-casino proposal without playing games."

The lawyer replied with a deadpan look. "I told you, I work for the Minowukaw Band. Any dealings we have with the mayor are confidential. Besides, we had to dig for ourselves. Why make it easy for you?" Kevin said, his white teeth a sharp contrast against his brown skin. "I knew once I put the bit in your mouth you wouldn't let go."

Sterling didn't try to hide his chagrin. They were supposed to be friends. Why the run around?

Noel glanced at the two younger men. "Just like old times, you two fighting again."

Raising his eyebrows at his father in a mock glare for butting in, Kevin said, "Look, Myles, Farrow is a slime ball. He thinks we haven't found out what he's up to. We're just dumb Indians." The lawyer paused, considered his words. "First Nations casinos have had some problems in the past. The Minowukaw Band insists everything be above board. To honour that, I can't leak information to anyone, even you."

Sterling looked at him. Even as a kid, Kevin had this strange sense of morality. He thought rules were made to be obeyed, at least most of them. "I'm not going to sit on this."

"I would hope not. Corruption in high places is important news." Kevin dropped his voice and spoke with the authority of the suppertime news: "The people of Candle Lake have a right to know."

What was Parenteau up to now? Sterling eyed his friend. "But a story like that could derail the whole project."

"Not our proposal." Kevin said, as the three men stopped in front of the colonel's fishing shack, the gun metal grey padlock barring entrance. "Give Dad the key."

Sterling dug deep in his parka pocket. Riddles, riddles, riddles. Not our proposal. What did that mean?

Once unlocked, the door swung open. Everything appeared untouched, still in its place except for the spikes strewn on the floor.

"Farrow's secretary put him on a plane to Winnipeg," Sterling said, as the men peered into the grey-lit interior. "When he gets back tomorrow, I give him a chance to answer some questions. Then the story goes to the editorial desk."

Two windows provided enough light to dispense with the propane lantern but Sterling lit the gas heater, clapped himself for warmth and sat beside Kevin on the bench.

Noel took a flashlight from his pocket, kneeled and shone it on the ice-covered fishing hole. Sterling reached up to the particle board wall where a pickaxe hung by its head from two protruding nails. The hole had last been augered on his visit to the shack a few days before and the nights had dwelled in the minus thirties.

"You'll probably need this," Sterling said.

Noel swept snow particles away with his fingers, glanced up at his two companions. "It's all new ice, very new," he said, gesturing over the open side of the floor. "Not just the fishing hole." He stared down again.

Perhaps Noel hadn't heard. Sterling rose and hoisted the axe to his shoulders ready to smash through the frozen lake. Kevin's father, his hood down, lowered his head to the ice and raised his arm. The reporter let the tool fall to his side as Noel looked up, his eyes now two brown full moons. He closed his hand into a fist and drove it through ice as thin as a pane of glass.

It took a moment to recognize the head that floated there. A rope tied to a spike in the ice wall of the fishing hole looped around the neck holding the body in place. The razor-cut hair washed against the skull, the sculptured features of the face bloated, the fearful eyes now closed forever. There would be no more newscasts for Larry Fredericks.

Mid-morning March 7

"No arms or legs," Kevin said, as he approached, "they were hacked off."

Sterling and Noel stood by the rusting fender of the elder Parenteau's old Toyota Land Cruiser. McTaggart's shack bustled with the men and women in uniform.

"The police say the clothes were drenched in blood," the younger Parenteau continued. A phone call had made him Crown Counsel liaison in the case after the police took their statements. "Whoever the killer is, he didn't bother with a saw." Kevin zippered his jacket having spent the last ten minutes in an RCMP cruiser. "He just hacked the limbs away."

Sterling's throat constricted. He leaned against the truck. The stench of Rwanda's river of blood, the Akagera, flooded his nostrils, flowed before his eyes. After a moment, the ice white expanse of Candle Lake reappeared. Be careful for what you wish. He had hoped the next time he met Fredericks, the newscaster would be stone cold sober.

The reporter had to swallow before his tongue would move. "Do they know how long he's been dead?"

"The coroner says not more than eight hours."

Sterling's saliva gland didn't seem to work. Fredericks had bought it not long after he fled from the bar.

Sterling pressed off the truck, stood straight. "He saw it coming," he said, at last. "The poor guy was at the Wheelhouse last night." He paused, remembered the man's carved features contorted in panic. "His killer told him exactly how he would die and let him stew about it."

Noel's eyes became hooded. He let out a long-breath, a cloud streaming in the cold air. "What kind of man would do such a thing?"

Sterling pursed his lips, remained silent. He'd pondered the same question for many years. Friend and neighbours infected with hate in Rwanda carved each other's children with machetes, stabbed their babies with spike clubs. Madness descended upon a whole country. What had happened to Fredericks showed that evil could touch anywhere.

"A calculating, vengeful one," said Kevin. "Probably insane." He pulled off his cap, combed his fingers through his hair, replaced the cap. He nodded at his friend. "This goes a long way to putting credence to your theory that McTaggart was murdered."

Sterling cursed. All the evidence so far had pointed to Farrow. Sterling had the big arrogant jerk by the neck, squeezing. Now the mayor waltzed free sending the investigation back to square one.

"If there is any good to come of this," Kevin said, "it's that there is reason now to re-examine the colonel's death." The lawyer wore big Kodiaks laced ankle-high. He tapped one boot then the other trying to keep his feet warm. "If Staff Milburn doesn't agree, I'll get Crown Counsel on his back."

"One murderer then?" Sterling tried to stem an involuntary shiver.

"What's left of Fredericks was anchored to the fishing hole of another man who also died mysteriously." Kevin's pointed forefinger jabbed Sterling's shoulder. "Someone's taunting someone."

"And you're saying that person killed both of them," the reporter continued.

"It's a working theory, at least until the autopsy tells us different."

"I thought I had the answer." Sterling retorted. "It was Farrow. This blows it out of the water. Unless Farrow parachuted out of a passenger jet at twenty thousand feet, we know he's been in

Winnipeg. He couldn't have killed Fredericks. If there's only one murderer, it isn't our mayor."

"Now you have a new theory."

Noel had slipped away as the two men debated. Sterling's eyes followed the elder Parenteau into the colonel's shack which, for the moment, stood unguarded.

"And the new one stinks," Sterling said. "For one thing, McTaggart's body wasn't savaged. One trauma to the back of the skull is all the coroner found."

"Serial killers, if that is what we have here," the lawyer conjectured, "have their own egos. The investigation was going nowhere. The murderer wasn't getting his due, the publicity he craves. He raised the stakes, rubbed our noses in it by leaving Frederick's body in the colonel's fishing hole."

Sterling felt the frustration smoulder. "What did they have in common to make them victims? They didn't know each other." The reporter's voice grew harsh. "Fredericks was never in Rwanda, never in the army. There's nothing to put them together."

"Take it easy, Myles," Kevin said, his hand gripping his friend's shoulder.

The reporter jerked away. "You haven't heard a word I said! What if Milburn and Farrow are in this together? There's a lot of money up for grabs here. It wasn't you who was rousted by the cops for no reason, run off the road for nosing around a corrupt mayor."

Kevin stepped closer, looked down his hawk nose. "And that's why I can see this thing clearer than you do. You're after vengeance, not facts." The faces of the two men glowered inches apart, their breaths mixing in clouds in the frigid air. "You want Milburn but you've got nothing on him and the only thing you have on Farrow is that he's a greedy fool." Neither gave an inch. "You're being sloppy here and it's helping no one find out how McTaggart died."

Sterling raised his arm to his shoulder, fist closed.

Noel stepped between them, said, "Just like the old days, isn't it boys?"

He slapped both of them on the back. Sterling dropped his scowl and looked away but only after Parenteau did the same. How many times had Noel parted the two grunting kids in the dirt wrestling over whether the last goal counted or not?

The tin racket of a chainsaw rattled the air, then another. Two men who had emerged from a plain white van parked near the fish shack cut a hole in the ice several metres in circumference. The aperture complete, the vehicle's side doors slid apart and two frogmen flopped out. The figures looked more amphibious than human with their heavy thermal rubber suits, masks, oxygen tanks and flippers. The slap, slap, slap of their enlarged feet preceded their silent disappearance into the lapping black liquid.

"Hell of way to make a living." Colour had returned to Noel's dark face since discovering Fredericks mutilated torso. Kevin's father looked at Sterling, gestured at the fish shack. "In all the excitement, it slipped my mind. There's something not quite right in there, on the floor in the corner under the bench."

Police and emergency service personnel milled about while an intent circle of onlookers stood back from the open water in which the divers had disappeared. The radios crackled and barked in vehicles parked haphazardly on the white expanse of parking lot.

"You mean the four spikes that seemed to have been just tossed in?" Sterling asked. "Are those to anchor the shack?"

Noel nodded. "The spikes should have been hammered through the loops at each outside corner and into the ice. Now nothing holds the building in place. What if a strong wind came up or even just kids fooling around, playing pranks." He gestured with his head toward the main group of huts. "Or some fisherman trying to get at the pickerel hole." He pulled off his bright red tuque, rubbed his hair with his knuckles. "It's like I said. I helped John with his little project and I'd never seen a man so meticulous. He was army through and through." He scratched his beard with the thumb of his tan leather mitt. "John would never have left his little house unanchored."

A note of disapproval slipped into Noel's voice, no stranger to order in his own work. As a boy, Sterling had strolled into the carpentry workshop in the Parenteau basement. Wipe your feet and don't touch anything, his buddy had warned as they breathed in the sweet sawdust, watched the craftsman create.

"Do you have a VCR?" Sterling said, turning to Kevin. It didn't seem a high priority before but perhaps the tape from McTaggart's camera held some clues.

"About four. One should work. I hope."

"I'll be over tonight."

"Dirty movies?"

"I suppose pornography would be a good word for what's happening in Candle Lake."

Sterling's eyes roved across a growing crowd. News of the grisly discovery had spread like fire. He gestured for the Parenteaus to wait and walked over to a group of gawkers hovering just beyond the police tape perimeter.

"How are you doing, Ed?"

Braun seemed startled. He broke off his conversation with a couple of men and stepped over to Sterling.

"I was beginning to worry when you didn't get back to me," Sterling said.

The former army captain looked tired and drawn and a little worse for wear. A bandage covered his right brow and dried brown blood traced a cut healing on his cheek. Tiny worms of red flecked the whites of his eyes; his gaze stirred restless.

"I've been okay," Braun replied.

"Fall under another bale?"

"Bale?"

"Like the one that put you and the boys in hospital."

The confusion on the injured man's square faced cleared, his finger tracing his wound. He laughed, embarrassed. "I should stay behind the desk. Getting too old, I guess." He flattened his hand, swooped it through the air. "Tripped off the top of a trailer, fell face first into the gravel."

The spit 'n' shine soldier never missed a beat, not a guy one would expect to become accident prone. A proud man had been made to look foolish.

"Just some bad luck," Sterling commented.

"Bad luck," Braun agreed.

He didn't appear to be resting very easy, however, his body ramrod straight, his eyes still wandering.

"Are you sure you're okay, Ed?"

Braun focused on Sterling as if seeing him for the first time. He smiled and said, "Great article in the paper. John is probably cutting it out of heaven's *Times* right now." His eyes seemed to mist. "You said some nice things. Thanks."

Was that a tear? The tough soldier and hard businessman had never before shown any pious notions or even much sentimentality. He kept it all inside.

"I meant every word," Sterling said.

Again Braun peered up at the sky, composing himself. He turned back to Sterling.

"Another murder. What did I tell you?" Braun said. "Instead of playing around with this drug thing, the cops should have been trying to nail the colonel's killer, not stonewalling, calling it an accident."

He eyed Sterlng.

"This wouldn't have happened if everyone had done their job," Braun said.

"Take it easy, Ed." Sterling put his hand on Braun's shoulder. "I'm on your side."

"Side? It's everyone for himself in this man's army." The colonel's best friend whipped his arm from Sterling's grasp. "Your feature never

241

mentioned a thing about John being murdered but half the paper these days is filled with stories about those damn drugs. What are you guys, the new women's temperance movement?"

Taken aback, the reporter studied Braun. His temples pulsed and his eyes locked open, the blue iris surrounded by white.

"What about you? Are you wired?" Sterling could feel the lid on his anger toppling. "One second you're maudlin, telling me how much my story means and the next thing I'm some jerk covering up the truth!" He paused, slowed his hard breathing. "That's why I phoned. I thought I had something until Frederick's body was found." His voice trailed to nothing. He looked away in disgust. "Maybe I still do, I don't know."

Braun eyes seemed lost somewhere out over the ice. Then, as if he'd been pierced, all that was bottled up rushed out. His shoulders slumped and, for a moment, he appeared to shrink in his clothes.

After several moments, he said, "Look, I'm sorry." He seemed to search for words. "It's been rough lately, too many hours, too many things to take care of." He looked away. "The boys."

Both men looked over to see a diver emerge from the sloshing black hole onto the snow-packed ice. A long brown object protruded from his thick rubber-gloved hand. A closer look revealed, at one end, a brogue wing-tip crusted with ice, the kind of shoe Fredericks had worn at the Wheelhouse. The diver handed the severed leg to a uniformed cop, slipped back underwater. The mountie dropped the evidence into a plastic bag.

"Come and see me." Braun began to walk away. Over his shoulder, he said, "We'll talk."

Sterling felt sick, swallowed and looked away. What could he do for Braun to help him get through this? The man looked bad, his emotions amok: one moment furious, the next, teary and melancholy. He'd gone through the horror of Rwanda standing straight, walking tall. Was he now crumbling under the death of his lifelong friend?

Sterling took his time strolling back to where the Parenteaus stood. The news of Frederick's death, his hacked body, would move like a shot through the whole P.A. area. Was that the simple end to which the killer designed his viciousness, to monger fear and titillation? Or was there more to it? Kevin spoke the truth in one sense. The newscaster's execution formed a connection between McTaggart and Fredericks, his body slaughtered like those in Rwanda, found in the colonel's fishing hole.

The way the big cop appeared just before the reporter reached Kevin and Noel felt like an ambush.

"I don't understand your thinking," Staff Sergeant Milburn said. He glared down at Sterling, trying to burn holes in his head. "Do you want to spend more time in a stinking jail cell? I told you to back off and the next thing you're turning up another body." Milburn's nostrils flared, his nose hairs black, worm-like. "Or should I say body parts."

"Good morning, Staff." Sterling stepped back, attempted to regain some personal space. "I gave the constable a full statement."

Milburn stepped forward, closer than before. "And where do you find the corpse? In McTaggart's shack, no less."

Sterling gestured toward the lawyer and his father. "Of course, we're all glad to co-operate with the authorities."

"I could charge you with disturbing a crime scene," the cop said, moving back, allowing some breathing room.

Sterling stared, thinking. But you're not going to, are you? Was there something other than bluster in that red face?

"The shack wasn't taped off," he noted. "Are you going to charge the Crown Counsel's man, too?"

Milburn's eyes remained trained on Sterling but they didn't have the same fire. The mountie stayed silent. What was he trying to say? It dawned at last. "McTaggart 's death is now a murder investigation, isn't it?"

"If anything happens to Megan you'll be swimming in more than drunk tank vomit." The policeman surveyed the white frozen waters of Candle Lake. "Anything."

Sterling watched the cop amble to where the divers had submerged. He stood on the edge of the black hole, staring.

"This is getting ugly."

Sterling turned toward the voice and looked at his lifelong friend whose eyes darkened as they always did when things became serious. Kevin pulled his tuque down over his ears. "Milburn will be over his head on this one. You can expect the major crimes unit out of P.A. pretty quick." He clamped his hand on Sterling's arm. "Take it easy, Myles and watch yourself. If this was your road rage man, he's serious."

"Do you want to stay with me for awhile?" Noel asked. "The wife will be away for another week. I could use the company."

Kevin's father, as generous as ever, willing to put his own life in danger.

"I've got a sports car to fix," Sterling said. "But thanks."

The Parenteaus walked toward their vehicles — Noel's ancient four-by-four and Kevin's sleek Jaguar. The growl of the Jeep and the purr of the X-100 mellowed into the distance as they disappeared into a mountain of ice fog rolling across the lake. Sterling walked closer to the break in the ice. He knelt near the steaming edge as the divers surfaced and plunged again into the darkness.

The last item discovered in the frigid waters had frozen into an immediate lump when exposed to the air. The diver dropped the ball into the hands of the officer documenting evidence. The mountie placed the hard wad into a plastic bag which he labelled. Sterling, however, would have known that gentle shade of blue anywhere. John McTaggart's beret had been rescued from the deep of Candle Lake.

The search called off for the day, Sterling rose. His feet and hands felt numb. He headed toward his own vehicle in a soup of milky air. The divers had found nothing else on the lake bottom. Having completed the gruesome task of recovering all of Frederick's body, they'd uncovered no evidence that would lead to his killer, below or above ice. Only one other item, a fishing rod, most likely the colonel's, made it to the surface. When asked about anything that looked like a spud, McTaggart's heavy chisel-ended walking stick, the frogmen shook their heads.

Sterling flexed his fingers to warm them, clapped his mitts together every few steps. Could there be any other connection between McTaggart and the television announcer other than the obvious that Kevin had suggested? Sterling shuddered as if the cold had fused his spine. The nightmares lived.

The ice fog had settled, erasing Candle Lake, leaving a blank canvas. The Bumbler sat a few hundred metres away, invisible behind the pure white wall.

Fog had shrouded the morning of April 1993, too. The haze had just begun to lift as cool air drifted down from the mountains tempering the blazing African sun. McTaggart was hunkered behind the wheel of the only Land Rover still working — under its own power only because three other wrecks had been scavenged for their parts.

Both men, their nostrils stuffed with wads of toilet paper, kept their eyes trained on the road ahead avoiding glances at the Akagera alongside. Water swept its banks, the flow diverted by dams of bloated corpses, a sewage of human bodies. The stench blanketed the air, insidious.

Ahead, a fallen tree beside a mound of burning tires blocked the highway, black acrid smoke pouring into the sky. Several men dressed in ragged civilian garb — dirtied, bloodied pants and shirts —guarded the barrier. Bottles of banana beer slopped among them and some of the motley sentries staggered as they milled about. Even at a distance, the Land Rover's motor did not drown their shouts — tense, angry, soaked in adrenalin.

The weapons in the hands of volunteer militia, the *genocidaires*, drew the sweat onto Sterling's forehead, chilled his spine despite the morning sun. Could there be a death worse than the slow and painstaking one administered by machetes and spike hammers? The reporter tasted blood. With the tip of his tongue, he feathered the wound where he'd bitten through his lip. Trained for war, McTaggart wore a face of stone.

The colonel braked to a stop as the vehicle reached the roadblock. He pointed to the U.N. insignia on his door, to his blue beret and waved at the militia to clear the way. At the same time, out of sight behind the dash, he unbuttoned his holster, his fingers resting on the butt of his sidearm.

The men stared, unmoving. One laughed and walked towards the vehicle. Others followed surrounding the U.N. patrol unit. In a moment of calm, grins rolled across their faces. Then fell the terrifying hell of homemade weapons battering the Land Rover, smashing headlights, tail-lights, mirrors, hammering the sheet metal.

Sterling's stomach roiled as the Land Rover rocked side to side. The Hutus fed on their own anger, grew more enraged by the second. A thunderous crash inches from his face had the reporter cowering behind his arms. The windshield wallowed, spider-webbed. The militiaman raised his club to strike again, to shatter the glass when three quick cracks of gunfire exploded. The mob froze.

Sterling turned to see the colonel's arm out his window, aiming at the sky. He lowered his handgun, pointed it at the attackers, then gestured at the tree.

"Now!" he barked. "Move!"

No one moved. Sterling found himself not breathing. His heart pounded, a drum deafening in the silence. The attack had stopped, freeze-framed as if the slightest noise, movement would trip the terror's wrath again.

The sea parted. The *genocidaires* opened a path among themselves. Along it strolled a man tall by Hutu standards wearing khaki combat fatigues. He brandished an AK 47.

"Regular army," McTaggart whispered. "This must be his post." He gripped Sterling's forearm. "Whatever you do, don't get out of this vehicle." The colonel nodded at the soldier with the Kalashnikov sub-machine gun. "Or he'll kill you."

The mob's leader walked to the Land Rover and smiled, several of his front teeth missing. He stood relaxed, his feet apart, his weapon cradled across his chest.

The colonel withdrew his sidearm inside the window. He spoke first, his voice harsh, asserting authority: "Colonel John McTaggart, U.N.

The soldier's lopsided grin widened. Authority would be a delicate matter.

"Drugs first," he said, in accented English. "Then you pass."

McTaggart's eyes held firm. "I have no drugs."

A frown tugged at the Hutu's face. This U.N. colonel wasn't listening. "Morphine for our injured." The African's smile returned. "Other drugs for fun."

"I have no drugs," McTaggart repeated, his tone flat, controlled.

The mob's leader lost his humour. Now his few blackened teeth revealed themselves in glances as he spoke: "Rwanda is our country. Foreigners are alive only because we say so. We told the other blue berets before. Drugs or die."

Once more the colonel shook his head. "No drugs."

The soldier's fingers tightened around his rifle. He walked around the Land Rover to the passenger side, as if more success could be found there.

As he passed before the windshield, McTaggart whispered, "Don't open your door, whatever you do."

With a gentle push of the gearshift, the transmission snicked into first.

The Hutu peered through Sterling's window. The sight angered him. He raised his Kalashnikov. "Who are you?"

As if holding a shield to the deadly weapon, the reporter displayed the media identification card that hung around his neck.

"Out!" the soldier shouted, shooting into the ground. Automatic weapon fire shattered the tense calm, the ground spitting red dust.

The engine roared and McTaggart wrenched the wheel hard right. The Land Rover forced the Hutu into a backpedaling dive then roared through its U-turn and back the way it had come. Both men ducked in their seats as bullets smashed glass and punched through metal. Soon the shouting became distant and the gunfire sporadic until it ceased.

The colonel cursed. "Captain Braun came to me with rumours of dope dealing. I guess they're not rumours."

By the time Sterling dared look through the gaping rear window, the enraged *genocidaires* stood small in the distance. Even six years later, the brush with death endured, still vivid in his mind, unlike the location of the Bumbler, for instance.

Sterling peered about. The car had to be here somewhere. Had he passed by without seeing it? The noise of a small engine on the lake grew louder, either a snowmobile or a quad all-terrain vehicle. The frigid air magnified and deflected sound making it difficult to pinpoint.

The next moment, Sterling bit a mouthful of snowbank. A second crack of rifle fire, the sight of snow spitting at his feet sent him rolling. Another shot kicked ice in his eyes. He tumbled the other way but had nowhere to go, nowhere to hide. Flat on his stomach, arms over his head, Sterling waited for the inevitable. He just hadn't expected it to come so soon.

A very large man at the controls of a quad skidded the little vehicle to a stop beside him. Sterling raised his head, eyed what appeared to be a thirty-thirty gripped by a huge mitt.

"Mayor Farrow."

"Darn, I'm sorry. A bear's been reported wandering around here." The shooter grinned. "Lucky I missed. Your miserable hide wouldn't look like much hanging over my fireplace."

Sterling rose to his feet, brushed the snow from his clothes. "Your secretary said you were in Winnipeg. I had a few questions for you."

"Just flew in not two hours ago." Farrow looked warm and comfortable in a blue snowmobile suit, the peak on his cap protruding from under the hood. A rifle holster hung on the side of the quad but he seemed to prefer to cradle the weapon in his arms.

He shook his head. "Gosh, what is it about reporters that I mistake them for wild animals that should be shot for the good of everyone."

"Is that another threat, Mr Mayor?"

"Heck no," Farrow said, in his down home drawl. "This is as good a place as any. Ask away."

Sterling studied the fleshy face. Do all these guys go to the same slippery smile school? He wouldn't dare kill somebody out in the open, would he?

"This casino that will save all the good people of Candle Lake from being thrown into the street," the reporter said, watching the big man, "is proposed for three parcels of land on Highway 265. That land is owned by Dolmage Enterprises. The president and signing officer of Dolmage Enterprises is Mrs. Edith Dolmage of the Pleasant Valley Senior Citizens Care Complex. Mrs. Dolmage's name by her first marriage was Farrow. She is your mother."

The mayor of Candle Lake didn't blink, didn't lose his grin. "My, you've been a busy little boy."

This was one cool, fat cucumber. Sterling couldn't help but return the sarcasm. "If that's a compliment, thank you."

"You're welcome. I'm wondering, though, what you think you've proven."

"That you stand to make a lot of money if the project goes through. I'd call that a breach of trust of your beloved community."

Farrow laughed. "You would, would you? Well, Mr. Globetrotting War Correspondent, I don't suppose you've had time to read anything as mundane as the law governing our municipality. There is nothing illegal going on."

Sterling kept his face inscrutable. The fat man had to be bluffing. He had to be. "I don't think your electorate will think much of the deal."

"When I explain how I saved their cottages and homes, the voters will understand perfectly."

The fires of hell wouldn't raise a bead of sweat on this guy. "I'm going to make certain we find out."

"I'm sure you will. You're not a journalist unless you sling mud."

"A statement for the record, Mr. Mayor. What is your reaction to the discovery in your lake of a second body, this one mutilated."

It seemed to be second nature for Farrow. The question straightened his spine, opened a pool of sincerity in his face, as if the lights had flashed on and the cameras rolled.

"The loss of another prominent citizen is a horrible tragedy for everyone. The criminal death of Larry Fredericks is a shock and loss for both Candle Lake and the whole Prince Albert area. I give my personal pledge that the authorities will not rest until the perpetrator of this horrendous crime is brought to justice."

Sterling's hands still rested in the pockets of his parka. He had not even pen and paper in his possession, let alone a television crew.

"Thank you, Mr. Mayor, for officially releasing the name of the deceased. RCMP policy, of course, is to wait until the next of kin have been notified. I'm not sure what Fredericks's relatives and the police will think of your little speech."

Farrow glared for a moment. Then that grin crawled across his face. "There is one good thing about what's happened."

The reporter waited. What could that be?

"There's one fewer reporter around."

Sterling held the big man's gaze. In one sense the mayor had to be admired. He didn't back down. Farrow slid the rifle into the quad's side holster and started the engine.

"Oh, one last thing," Sterling said. "You weren't at the convention in Regina the weekend McTaggart went missing."

The mayor's head shook in exasperation. "You're like a leech in the water, clinging to an ankle, sucking blood anywhere you can get it. Half-truths aren't good enough anymore. Now you're going for out and out lies."

"You spent that Friday night and Saturday night at the P.A. Inn, room 124." He paused. "With a woman."

The politician's glove fell away from the wheel onto the dash. He switched off the key and the motor died. His eyes drifted down to the rifle. Leaning over, he rested his arm on the butt of fine-grained wood. He looked up with unadulterated hate.

"My wife shouldn't have to read about this in the paper. It's a private matter." He looked across the lake, searching. "The shame would kill her."

"You should have thought of that before."

The big man's leather glove caressed the stock of the thirty-thirty as he pondered. After several moments, however, he sat back placing his hands in his lap.

"What are you going to do now?" he said.

"I'm not with the *National Enquirer*. Your affair interests me only as far as it puts you within easy driving of Candle Lake and the man who stood in the way of your casino deal."

"I warned you about playing that tired tune of yours."

Sterling became irritated, his tone harsh. "Look! In court, truth is the best defense. Why did you lie?"

The big man seemed to deflate, cast his eyes down. Was it another act of a consummate politician?

When he spoke, his voice stalled for a moment. "It really would kill her. My wife has been frail for years." He stared at Sterling. "Do I have to spell it out for you?"

Sincerity dripped from the mayor's eyes as they pleaded the role of the loyal husband of an invalid. He dallied only because of his overwhelming needs as a man. In his own mind, he fought life as a hero.

"What did you do that weekend?"

"We stayed in the hotel, played the Fox's Nose, a little blackjack, mostly the VLT's."

"Monique Tremblay will confirm that?"

Farrow flinched. Speaking the name nailed the final proof he'd been found out. He nodded.

"You don't happen to know anything about a blue three-quarter-ton pickup with a rack of running lights on the roof?" Sterling continued.

The mayor shook his head. After a moment, that smile once again wrinkled his face. "She sounds like a babe, though. I'd like to have a jewel like that on my lot. Say, that's an awful wreck you're driving. A Bumbler, right? They're a joke."

A pitch coming down the pike, Sterling stepped back in case the used car pedlar tried to slap a beefy arm around his shoulders.

"Come around the shop. I'm sure we can get you into a pre-owned unit that will make you very happy." Farrow extended his glove. "To show my appreciation that my private matters are staying private."

The fog had lifted, the view across the white expanse sparkled. Sterling kept his hands in his pockets, turned away and began to walk toward his rental. He hadn't been getting much sleep lately. Why should the fat man?

He stopped, turned around. "Mr. Mayor, you better read tomorrow's paper before you start offering sweet deals."

Sterling flexed his right hand. All of a sudden, it felt much better.

Evening PM *March 7*

"We need a clown," Kevin said, returning from the telephone in the hallway. "For the children's play day at the community hall on Sunday. I'd completely forgotten."

"Don't you have enough of those at Crown Counsel?" Sterling said.

"The only funny man I know doesn't pay his bills."

Sterling chose to ignore his friend and toyed with drawing up a nation-wide petition demanding a time limit on old debts. If you can dodge them for twenty years, you're free. Millions would sign.

The very second he stepped into the Parenteau house, Sterling had felt at home. It nestled in the north end of Prince Albert, across the North Saskatchewan River from the main part of the city. The two storey Cambridge Street home spoke for the middle class neighbourhood, neither humble nor pretentious.

In one swift movement, Sterling twisted and peered behind the black leather chesterfield on which he sat. Giggles and screams blurted from a pair of little mouths, both with two front teeth missing. The twins scampered across the maple-wood floor of the spacious living room to safety behind the couch's mate, a large plush black leather chair.

"That was Gloria," Parenteau continued. "Her meeting is running late. She says hi."

"Hi to her."

"Our clown quit. You remember my cousin Emil Cuthand?"

Sterling bent to the floor, his head upside down, and looked through the legs of the coffee table. This sent the girls out of sight, snickering through the doorway to the kitchen. Settling into the sumptuous couch, he breathed the aroma of dark coffee from the cup in his fingers. "You mean that little runt that used to tag along with us, his dad rode broncs in the rodeo?

Parenteau chuckled. "That's the last you remember of him?"

The reporter's forehead wrinkled at the question. "Why?"

"No reason."

Sterling's eyes narrowed. What mischief did Kevin stir now? "Your cousin was a funny little guy, would've made a good clown."

Parenteau's voice sombered. "After high school, he headed for Mexico and took up deep sea diving. Then he came back and rode the circuit in his father's place, bulls, horses, anything that moved. Until he got kicked through a fence, never entered a competition again." The lawyer sighed. "That's when the trouble started. He couldn't leave the horses alone, betted on them instead. Lost his truck, his house, his wife and daughter."

Sterling whistled then said, "How is he doing now?"

Parenteau's eyes trained on his friend. "And you remember him only as a little kid?"

Impatience lined Sterling's voice: "Yes, I said."

Kevin eyes twinkled. "Emil joined a group for problem gamblers, turned things around. He's doing well now, got his fingers," he sputtered, an explosion of laughter halting his words. After a few moments, he continued, "in a few different things."

The hilarious joke, whatever it was, hung Parenteau over the side of his armchair, chest heaving in guffaws. At last, his convulsions subsided.

Sterling watched, unimpressed, at last said, "What's so damn funny?"

The jokester ran his sleeve over his tearing eyes, held up his hand waving off the question.

"Obviously, you have all the attributes of a good clown," Sterling continued, puzzled. Never before did he rank a sense of humour among

Kevin's qualities. "Anyway, you'd look great in face paint and big red ball nose."

"I can't, I'm running the ring toss." Parenteau burst again. "Little Emil and the Constable Cuthand who conducted your body search are one and the same." Parenteau grabbed a handful of tissues from the box on the coffee table, wiped his face, blew his nose.

He paused, eyed the kitchen. It was silent, too silent.

At last, a squeaky duet of voices floated back into the living room: "Daddy, can we have a cookie?"

"No," he replied, sternly.

The girls did a high tip-toe, a goose step, from the kitchen, to emphasize how quiet and unobtrusive they could be and, perhaps, to obscure their stuffed mouths. Stopping at the leather chair, they turned their backs and together jumped into the seat. Arms crossed, they chewed without a sound.

"I said no cookies."

Two heads nodded, each twin wiping her mouth with the back of her hand.

Kevin sighed, reached for the television remote control. "Wait till your mother gets home."

"Rewind McTaggart's tape to the beginning. He must have shot some underwater video himself," Sterling explained. "The camera's counter showed a few minutes running time before I started recording." He leaned back, sipped his coffee. "I don't know if this is going to tell us anything or not."

As soon as the tape rolled, however, he knew it would. The lake bottom carved into a hole, its depth reading on the screen seven metres. Gauging by the size of the circling school of pickerel, the circumference of the depression looked to be about five metres. Its sandy banks began as a gradual valley then became a steep descent.

The screen jiggled, the camera bumped by dorsal fins, plump bodies or the wall-eyed snouts of milling pickerel. Despite their natural shyness, these fish had decided that the red-eyed globe posed no threat. At times, however, they scattered amongst the sparse vegetation as if an alarm had sounded that danger lurked above. Moments later, they'd drift into the open again heeding some kind of "all clear." Always, they stayed well below the lip of the crater. This, indeed, was McTaggart's pickerel hole.

The view began to rise, the screen displaying more of the same: weeds, rocks, the occasional log and darting, shy pickerel. Then it all stopped leaving only a barren underwater desert. The camera had been reeled out of the depression.

Rotating 360 degrees, as far as the lense could see the lake bed spread flat. In the distance, above a solitary log a large fish glided, its tell-tale flat snout marking it as a bony pike on the hunt.

Once again the camera descended and the sandy banks of the rift skimmed past. Sterling turned to his friend. Both men laughed. A minnow punctured with a hook drifted into view. McTaggart had recorded himself fishing.

The plump pickerel seemed uninterested, however. They swam about ignoring the little morsel except for one that drifted by and, with its tail, swatted the bait. All of a sudden in a flash of silver wriggling, the school vanished. No pretense of hiding in winter wisps of weeds, this time the fish had fled.

The reason floated into view. Like the jaws of a steel trap, the gaping maw of an ugly jack filled the screen. It must have been the one circling earlier in no man's land. Beside the pike dangled a bare twisted string of metal. The predator had swallowed the minnow, spit out the hook like a piece of spaghetti caught between its teeth. With a shake of its razor-hook tail, the big fish vanished. The screen went black.

The armchair fishermen shook their heads, laughed at the bad luck of a fellow angler. For a short time, the colonel had seemed alive. Sterling found himself imagining the look on McTaggart's face when he felt the tug on his line, the disappointment a moment later when his rod became weightless and he saw the pike spit out his mangled hook. This would be followed by the patient shrug of the angler as he reeled in and set new bait. There were more fish from where that one came.

In an instant, the reporter's coffee tasted stale. McTaggart lay in a morgue, his face devoured to the skull. And Fredericks may have been tortured before he was killed and mutilated. Sterling hoped it had been in that order.

Somber now, Sterling said, "The next part is what I recorded."

Once again, the television became alive with the rouge-tinted marine-scape seen through the infra-red eye. The flat underwater desert sat motionless: no weeds, no rocks, no fish. Only a solitary sunken log, half-immersed, rose from the sand.

"This is what I saw, why I was confused," Sterling said. "There was no pickerel hole." He studied the dead tree. "Roll the tape back to where we first see the jack."

A few seconds later, McTaggart's video played again. Rocks and weeds and pickerel glided past as the camera reeled over them to the rim of the crater. There, vague but visible across the flat lake bed, the log sprouted from the sand, the jack patrolling above.

"Pause it," the reporter whispered. He studied the television. "Forward to my part." He leaned over the coffee table, peering closer. "Do you see?"

"The log," Parenteau said. "It didn't move. It's stuck in the bottom."

"Exactly. Between the time John shot his tape and I shot mine, the shack had been moved. That's why I couldn't find the pickerel hole."

"But why? No sane fisherman would leave a spot like that."

Sterling stood, paced the maple wood floor then sat again. "The first time I was there, it looked like the new ice covering the hole had a different texture from the older area surrounding it. That's what I wanted Noel to look at. There was too much new ice just for fishing." Sterling nodded. Things began to make sense. "It covered an opening big enough for a man to fall through."

"At night, some snow," the lawyer nodded. "He wouldn't see it."

Sterling rose again, walked the length of the living room. The twins's wide eyes followed his every step. His words came fast: "Your father was awakened in the middle of the night. He figured the colonel knew better than to make such a racket. But McTaggart hadn't arrived yet. It was

Scott Gregory Miller

the murderer chainsawing the ice." Sterling halted, looked up at the ceiling, painting the scene in his mind. "He'd taken a chance on the noise because he knew that everyone back in the main group of shacks would believe, just like Noel did, that it was the colonel out there." He began to pace again. "Whoever it was waited inside the shack or John would have seen him. The killer had to be close to make sure his victim didn't climb out of the water. Afterward, the guy pulled the anchors out of the ice, tossed them under the bench and moved the shack over the new opening. The real fishing hole left behind would be small enough to cover with snow."

Sterling stopped, turned toward Kevin and waited.

"Could be," Parenteau said, at last. "How did the murderer get inside? You found the lock intact, no sign of a break-in."

The reporter returned to his seat at the far end of the chesterfield, picked up his coffee cup.

"Yes," he said, "it had to be someone close enough to John to get access to his keys."

"They could have been stolen," the lawyer pointed out. "There was the engagement party that Saturday night." He looked across at the plush chair where his daughters sat, staring, mouths open. "How do you know it was a 'he'?"

"I just," Sterling replied, his voice trailing to nothing. "Assumed." He sat back down on the chesterfield. "But a woman could have done all that, killed the colonel. Except that our mayor keeps popping into the picture. After you and Noel left this afternoon, he paid me a visit out on the lake. He rode his quad, hunting bear, thought I was one and took a few shots at me."

This turned Parenteau's head. "Did he threaten you?"

A tinge of sarcasm brittled Sterling's voice: "Nothing he couldn't dance around in court." His dig in, he evened his tone. "More to the point, he admitted lying about the weekend McTaggart went missing. The mayor wasn't in Regina, he was at the P.A. Inn shacked up with a woman." He frowned, reminded of his disappointment. "Her name is Monique Tremblay. I'll see if she confirms the story about their affair."

"Monique Tremblay!" Parenteau exclaimed. Sterling nodded. "She now owns fifity-one percent of the Wheelhouse Bar. I read the will this afternoon. Two daughters down east get the minority share. Bonnie Matheson receives the rest including a nice little savings account."

Did the bar manager know the colonel had written her into his inheritance? Was she afraid she would be crossed out again, replaced by

Bonnie? "Did Monique seem surprised?" Sterling asked.

"Very. She wept and laughed, then became embarrassed." The lawyer studied his friend. He said, "It could have been an act, I suppose. Both Farrow and her *She* could be lying, providing each other with alibis."

Sterling leaned back. If Monique knew about the will, that would provide a motive for expediting its provisions, especially after being dumped for another, younger woman. The bar manager just seemed so sincere in her love for John. The reporter closed his eyes. Why should he care if Monique messed her life up with a man like Farrow?

"I know," Sterling said, at last. "I know."

"Even if there was no bear, if Farrow was playing mind games, it's still not proof he killed McTaggart."

Sterling looked heavenward. He could see another legal lecture coming down the line.

"The mayor may be just trying to scare you off from making an issue of his property in the casino proposal. But," Parenteau said, "there's a lot of circumstantial evidence here, more than just a gut feeling."

Sterling tried to keep the surprise out of his voice: "Well, thank you, Mr. Justice."

"Daddy," the twins spoke in chorus. Two chubby forefingers pointed to the picture window covered by beige floor-to-ceiling drapes as a pair of lights streaked across the material.

"Someone's parking in the driveway," Parenteau said, rising. As he walked toward the entrance foyer, the headlights reversed their path across the curtains and vanished. He peered through the window of the front door. His voice tensed: "Blue GMC three-quarter-ton, a rack of roof lights, right?"

It took a moment for the reporter to comprehend.

"Right?" the lawyer barked, turning his head back toward the living room. His face flushed, angry.

The reference connected. The truck that ran Sterling off the road. "Yes," he said, scrambling off the couch.

Parting the drapes, he watched the red flash and twinkle of tail-lights disappear down the street. He stepped back, looked at his friend.

Rage vibrated Parenteau's body, his eyes sparking. "How dare he come here."

The twins, seeing the sudden alarm in their father, jumped off the chair and ran to him.

Sterling started toward his coat, his car keys, then stopped. By the time he got the Bumbler moving, the truck would be long gone.

He shook his head. "He's like a ghost. He's done that to me a couple of times, evaporates into thin air."

Each girl had her arms wrapped around one her father's pant legs. Kevin looked down at the small faces, black hair swept across their shoulders as wide eyes stared back.

"It wasn't you I was worried about," he said.

Late Evening March 7

Lights blinked and flashed everywhere in the huge cavern, a space age anthill. White tobacco smoke hung in a cloud from the three storey high ceiling of the Fox's Nose. The giant enclosure made insects of the people packed inside. The Saskatchewan Tribal Council boasted its casino offered over 2000 video lottery terminals as well as gaming tables on two acres of floor space.

The twang of country music serenaded through ceiling loudspeakers. Although most patrons sat like statues before their VLT's, action buzzed around them. Money changers, drink servers and gamblers searching for better luck moved between row upon row upon row of little bandits, these days without one arm. The horde of VLT's just kept pace with demand. A vacant machine often gave only an unoccupied appearance. One of the thousands of grey plastic folding chairs tilted against a favourite terminal signified its player would return in a moment from a quick bathroom break.

Sterling ambled down the countless aisles, patted his wallet as if to reassure the money inside. Casinos wielded hypnotic power over loose cash, attracted it like the faithful to an altar. The two hundred bucks he had withdrawn earlier had to stretch until pay day. The withdrawal had dwindled his account down to mere cents. Tonight, he'd keep the money in his pants.

Canada's European descendants outnumbered First Nations people about two-to-one. While everyone wore simple, casual attire, the parking lot had illustrated that the gamblers crossed all classes. The middle class dominated — sedans, vans and station wagons. A fair share of BMW's, Cadillacs and the odd Lexus, as well, consented to mingle with the masses but insisted upon wide margins between themselves and rusty bolt buckets like the Bumbler. Anyone could enjoy the past-time of gambling.

Sterling didn't see much joy, though, no smiles. Hypnotic beams emitted from the revolving fruit, bars or lucky sevens on the screens captured intent faces.

Even when a lucky player hit the jackpot, red light atop the VLT flashing like an ambulance at a roadside accident, the winner's glee disappeared after a moment. A look of impatience followed as loonies poured from the machine's bottom mouth. The last coin jangled out only to be inserted into the terminal's top slot, the much more used and lucrative orifice.

The strained focus common to all the faces lit by the coloured lights of two thousand electronic screens forced Sterling to look twice. Sardined among the crowd, blonde hair uncombed, flat against her face, Bonnie sat with a plastic pail almost empty of loonies in her lap. She fed a VLT as if it were a baby.

Sterling stood behind her, watching over her shoulder. The first time he had seen her at the Wheelhouse, the terminal reminded him of a computerized wizard that had eaten her mind. She'd been angry at the interruption, ignored him until no money remained. She'd kicked some paper coin wrappers out of sight under a table. Now he recognized their significance. They would have contained more than one hundred dollars, gone in minutes. The loss didn't surprise her. Some liked shopping, she said. She plunked herself in front of a VLT once in a while.

Sterling remained motionless, watching. How much of this kind of shopping did she do? Another man stood a few metres away, staring as well.

She dropped the final dollar from her pail into the slot. In quick succession, two oranges appeared in a line, a flicker of hope, dashed when a cherry twirled into the third space. Bonnie's shoulders sagged and she slumped back in her chair. For several moments, she didn't seem to breathe.

The stranger beside Sterling walked up to her. "Hey, lady, you finished with this one?" Determined to land his favourite? Bonnie looked up, eyes blank. He crowded her chair. "If you're done, move so I can sit down."

Bonnie rose, pulled the felt cloth coat from the back of her chair and trudged past Sterling without a glance. Her slow pace made her easy to follow. She seemed in a trance, head down, each foot a burden to lift. People brushed past, knocking her shoulders. She didn't notice.

In the lobby, the crowd thinned. Bonnie stopped at the two large entrance doors, stared through the glass. Pushing one open, she stepped into the frigid night, her coat still under her arm.

Sterling followed, stepping beside her as she reached the parking lot entrance.

"Bonnie."

The young woman's head turned. Her eyes took a few seconds to focus. She jumped back.

"Stay away from me," she said. She headed between two rows of vehicles.

Sterling hurried behind, called out again, unsure, "Bonnie, it's me. Myles."

She stopped, swirled about, closed her eyes and, from the bottom of her lungs, screamed, *"STAY AWAY FROM ME!"*

Her screech froze Sterling on the spot. He watched as she ran to her little Mazda. From a distance, however, it looked odd, slumped. Bonnie's hand rose, covered her mouth. Her whole body crumpled to the pavement.

Sterling scrambled to her side, held her in his arms as she wept. Smashed glass covered the rust-pocked vehicle, sparkled in the snow. Every window in her car had been broken, the four tires slashed.

Sterling pried away the piece of paper she squeezed in her hand. Unfolding it, he read: "At times like these, it's best to keep your head. Arms. Legs."

Before Midnight March 7

The drive back took forever, every flash of head-lights in the rearview mirror tightening Sterling's throat. By the time he'd turned into the driveway of the Matheson house, he closed his eyes and exhaled a long breath.

The P.A. police treated the Mazda's smashed windows and slashed tires as a case of vandal-ism. Some kid's idea of a good time, the officer had said. Pretty vicious, this one, though. Bonnie told him she had no idea who it could be.

Sterling had slipped the note into his shirt pocket. He had a hunch that the written threat would be better passed along to the Crown Counsel Office rather than some beat cop. Who knew what connections led where? At this point, Sterling trusted only one person in authority — Parenteau. On the phone, Kevin had said he knew someone at the Meath Park detachment, Cousin Emil, it so happened, who would patrol on the sly by her house. Still, he said, it would be better if Sterling could stay with her.

Bonnie invited Sterling in without prompting. "For the awful way I've treated you," she said, looking down at her white knuckles, hands clenched. Inside the cold, dark house, they walked into the sitting room where a couple of coal oil lamps raised a soft light. Low flames flickered in the fireplace. "Brendan must have gone upstairs to work. Excuse me."

Sterling wandered about the dark room, squinted in bad light at her brother's paintings. The light switches yielded nothing, the telephone no dial tone. Sterling plunged into a large padded chair, every muscle weary, and realized something. When he was in the house last to interview Brendan, the bathroom and front lobby lights didn't work, either. At the time, he'd assumed faulty bulbs.

"I hope you like yours strong," Bonnie said, walking into the sitting room. She placed a tray of coffee settings on a low teak table, its smoky face shining under a protective sheet of contour glass.

She'd changed into jeans and a baby blue lamb's wool sweater, and brushed out her hair, long and shining.

Holding up an almost full bottle of brandy, she smiled, "I found this."

She wasn't wearing lipstick before, was she? Her face glowed in the flickering orange of the fireplace.

Her long slim fingers patted the bearskin rug. "It's warmer over here."

Sterling rose from his chair and joined her on the floor, the coffee table between them.

"I'd like to thank you again. If it weren't for you, I'd still be in that parking lot."

He felt his face warm at her words. "It strikes me that you're a pretty strong woman." He topped his coffee with an inch of brandy, gestured to do the same for her. "You've recovered well from tonight, your car, the note."

She shrugged, held up a thumb and forefinger slightly apart.

He poured. "If I'd received that threat, I'm not sure I'd be as composed. Not with Larry Fredericks being found the way he was."

"That was awful, just awful." Redness no longer rimmed Bonnie's eyes. "But why would anyone want to hurt me?" The fire danced in her pupils. "Like the policeman said, tonight was just some dumb kid's idea of a horrible joke."

The reporter took a swallow of coffee, let the liquor burn down his throat. The cop didn't see the note — 'it's best to keep one's head. Arms. Legs.' Was she blind to the obvious or putting up a brave front?

"Just in case, though," he said, "you should be careful. Watch for anything strange."

"That's sweet of you to worry."

She lifted a strand of hair from her cheek. Joanne used to do that. Sometimes, she seemed foolhardy, too. Under attack at the hotel in Sarajevo, his fiancée had hammered away at her laptop, shell fire rocking the building, showering her in plaster and glass. Nothing else mattered; she'd meet her deadline. Was it dangerous that every time he looked at Bonnie she revived memories?

"I'd say call me if you see anything but your phone is dead." Sterling swept his arm at the darkness. "No lights, power."

Bonnie stared into the flames, poured herself another shot from the brandy bottle. "I don't usually drink," she said, raising her cup. "Here's to monkeys on our backs." She sipped, wrinkled her nose. "I owe you an apology." Her eyes again settled on the glowing, crackling wood. "I've made a terrible, terrible mess of things." She rose to her knees, pulled a crumpled paper from the back pocket of her jeans and sat down again. "I'm back at step one, have been since John went missing," she said, handing over the pamphlet.

Unfolding it, Sterling read: "12 Steps of Gamblers' Anonymous." At the bottom of the list, a handwritten note said, "Emil — Call Anytime." A telephone number followed.

Bonnie's voice dropped to a whisper: "We're assigned a buddy, someone who has already been to hell and back, someone who will be there when we feel we're falling off the edge." She played with the hem of her sweater, knotting an errant thread with her fingers. When she stopped, her hands quivered. "I guess I should have called."

She paused finding strength. "I promised John I would get help after he caught me stealing from the Wheelhouse. When Mom and Dad were killed in the car accident, it was as if I were thrown in a black hole. For months, everything seemed meaningless. All the reasons I'd given myself for going to university were gone. I spent most of the time in my room, sleeping, trying not to think about anything. Through it all, Brendan was wonderful, serving me meals, getting me anything I needed. One day, though, I took a long look at his face. He'd aged twenty years worrying himself sick over me. I had to get out of the house, do something to make it look as if I was returning to normal. The summer before, I sang at jam sessions, afternoons for amateurs at the Wheelhouse. I heard the bar needed a waitress so I applied." Bonnie closed her eyes for a moment, opened them as if seeing a flood of memories. "I was early for the interview so I sat in front of a VLT and inserted a quarter. From that very moment, I was hooked, soon onto the loonie and toonie machines. It was better than any high I'd ever gotten from singing, or anything else. When those cherries, lemons began to tumble, I was swept into another world. The first jackpot I hit made me delirious. Nothing else in the world mattered. And the next big score always called to me from just around the corner. All I had to do was keep plugging."

Bonnie's eyes looked far away. Sterling picked up the carafe, poured more coffee, added brandy. The first time he'd met her at the Wheelhouse, she was playing a VLT. She'd kicked a pile of coin wrappers under the table. He'd missed the signs.

"For me, it's a drug," Bonnie took a swallow from her freshened drink. It seemed to be going down easier. "I needed more and more. I had to play. After awhile, the highs grew harder and harder to get but, at the same time, I needed them more. It got to the point where I could go only so long without action or I'd get sick. I'd actually throw up. And when I lost, had no money left to play, I'd go into a rage." Waves of darkness and light played across her face changing her profile one moment to the next just as gambling had done — one time sweet, the next vicious.

"It was awful some of the things I did to get money. One time, I even sold marijuana to a couple of kids from college. And believe me, I considered worse. By the time John caught me dipping into the till, I'd hit bottom. The insurance left to me and my brother had been cleaned out, the power cut off, the telephone. Worst of all, I'd missed mortgage payments and the bank threatened to take away the house. Brendan couldn't help much. You'd be surprised how little artists make." For the first time, a tear welled in the corner of her eye. "My god, I miss John so much! Such a sweet man. The shame of stealing from my own fiancé was awful. If it weren't for him, I may have done myself in. But he helped me see there was a way out of the hole. He got me to counseling and Gamblers' Anonymous. He paid off the debts, the mortgage arrears, the utilities. Brendan and I still had our house." There was a long pause. Bonnie chewed on her thumbnail, shook her head. "It's my fault, I guess. I mean we were about to get married. It was natural John move in. With him in the same house each day, though, it didn't take long for me to realize I wasn't ready. I hadn't sorted my feelings about my parents's deaths, about what I wanted to do, about anything. I loved John very much but it was just too soon. When I told him, he said just be patient. But I could see I'd hurt him deeply. I waited but it just got worse. And John became a different man, moody, dark."

Sterling refilled their cups one more time. Monique had said the same thing. She knew about the gambling and, even if she was unaware of Bonnie's reticence about the marriage, the manager of McTaggart's nightclub saw her former lover fall apart before her eyes. What did she say? Bonnie turned John back into the same paranoid man who first came to Candle Lake.

"All I think about is the last night," Bonnie said, her voice cracking. "After our engagement party, I told him I couldn't get married, not now anyway. We argued and he walked out the door. I never saw him again." Bonnie put her head in her hands and sobbed. She lifted her face to Sterling. "Those weeks he was missing, I blamed myself. When his body was found, it was as if I'd sent him to his death."

The slim fingers of both Bonnie's hands were wrapped around her coffee cup. The shadows of the flames flickered across her face lighting and darkening her eyes.

"Someone struck John with a weapon, cracked his skull," Sterling said. "You didn't do that, did you?"

She seemed lost in the fire. Her eyes widened as she understood the question. "No, of course not," she replied, looking hard at Sterling.

"Then you didn't kill him." He put his hand on her forearm, the lamb's wool so soft it might melt. "You've got enough hanging over your head as it is. Don't beat yourself up over that, too."

She looked at him, thoughtful. "That's kind."

"You said you're back to step one. Is that why Monique Tremblay is wearing your mink?" Bonne bit her lip. "You've been losing again." She nodded, turned away. "You sold it to her."

"Such a pretty coat," she whispered. Both sat silent for a moment listening to the burning logs hiss and snap. "I feel I've lost everything but at the meetings they tell you that you've always got more to lose. Step one is admitting you have a problem, stop rationalizing it away." Bonnie's eyelids looked heavy. "I've tried to be honest or there's no point, no step two." She stifled a yawn. "I really needed someone to listen, someone to hear me talk it out." She crossed her arms on the coffee table, laid her head down. "I must have bored you to death."

"No, not at all."

"The brandy," Bonnie mumbled.

"I should be going."

"I'm cold."

Sterling reached for the Hudson Bay blanket on the chesterfield behind them. He leaned over, covered her shoulders. Hunched that way, she'd wake stiff as a pretzel. Guiding her to the rug, all of a sudden, her cheek nestled against his chest, his arms fell around her. For a few moments, only the spit and crackle of the wood spoke to the silence.

"Bonnie?"

She snuggled closer. He listened to the soft breath of sleep.

Bonnie's blue eyes flicked open. She slipped to her feet. Myles's arms held a sudden emptiness, a cold vacuum.

She held out her hand. "We'll be more comfortable in my room."

Bonnie's mouth burned, seared his lips. Their tongues slithered together like writhing snakes. Electricity flashed over Myles's skin where their naked flesh touched. She wrapped her legs around his waist so he could enter, pierce unimaginable softness.

Her saucer-wide eyes locked on his. Sharp cries issued with each panting intake of breath. Forgotten strength flooded his limbs, muscles, a tide rising, rushing. He stared into her face. Slowly, her eyes, mouth, hair merged into those of Joanne, a red circle where the bullet had punctured his fiancée's skull. He squeezed his eyes shut. Her skin darkened into black. Blood smeared the long, flowing ivory *pagne* where she swaddled her babe on her shoulder. The desperate pleas of the Tutsi princess shot icicles up his spine: *"Prenez mon bébé. Prenez lui s'il vous plait."*

No! No! Myles shrank back.

Bonnie's soft voice melted into his brain, caressed his ears. He opened his eyes.

"Naughty boy," she said, touching his nose with her fingertip. She slipped from under Myles, laid him on his back. "Don't think of anything else but me." Her lips brushed his neck. "Think only of now, these feelings."

Her tongue traced a wet trail down the gulley of his chest, his stomach. A thought danced into his mind: Bonnie had been with a man before whose nightmares unbidden ripped at his mind any moment day or night. She knew. If Myles could only trust her, she would wrestle him away from his ghosts.

Her mouth, teeth pulled at the hair below his navel. He grew large. A sudden, sweet hotness engulfed him, became the very centre of his being. He shouted, his whole body about to burst. She straddled him, rode him hard, her moans stabbing the air. Inside, he drove closer to a yielding core, stronger than ever before.

Drawing her mouth down to his, he rolled them over together, she now on her back. Her nipples rose stiff and dark. He suckled, bit. She twisted, spread even further to take him deeper. He licked saltwater. Tears rolled down her cheeks, her neck, her breasts. She, too, tasted absolution, forgiveness.

He thrust harder; she carried him deeper. Together they shed their bodies, their pain, became two people in one skin.

Morning March 8

> *Thank you for being such a wonderful listener.*
> *I'm off to the hairdresser.*
> *XXX*
> *Bonnie*

Sterling lifted the note from the coffee table, held it under his nose. The paper carried her scent — sweet and bright. He smiled, tucked it into his pocket. He'd awakened with the delicate smell of her in his nostrils, as if the storm of her golden hair lying in waves across his chest still caressed his skin.

A burst of energy, a strange lightness surged through his body. He hadn't slept that long, that well since he couldn't remember when. Yes, he could. He'd rested fine before Joanne was cut down by a Serbian sniper.

Was it wrong to feel this good about nothing really? He'd spent a single night with a beautiful woman who had spilled her soul to him as they lounged on a bearskin rug in front of a fire. One night. Kevin had called Sterling's obsession with the TR6, his investing the car with Joanne's spirit, morbid. Let her go. Yet, was this any better, whatever this was? John's fish-eaten body lay cold in the morgue, not even its final resting place, and here his so-called friend lounged in the bed of the bereaved fiancée. Some friend. Could he find nothing pure, nothing without ugly nuances?

Sterling stretched, rose to his feet. His breath exhaled in clouds as he dressed. Only a tiny wisp of smoke rose from the ashes in the fireplace. Draping his parka over his shoulders, he headed for the kitchen. His smile returned. His body hadn't been this recharged in years.

Bonnie had slipped away. The whine of a chainsaw in the backyard had been the first sound to enter Sterling's conscious. He'd lain there listening as the hard thud of an axe assaulting soft wood followed the tinny racket. Now a quiet clatter and the hiss of a frying pan led him to the large room where Brendan stood at an island counter breaking eggs into a shiny glass bowl.

"Omelet?" Brendan asked.

Sterling shook his head, took a chair at the kitchen table. "Coffee's good."

The young man's wispy pony tail swung as he worked. The morning sun had forced him to don sunglasses. The shades gave him an urbane look that contrasted with his casual attire of a plaid shirt and blue jeans.

"It's more like lunch for me." Brendan grated some cheese over the bowl, tossed in a handful of green onion bits. "I've been up since three." After stirring, he poured the egg mix into a frying pan. "Beautiful out there this time of year. You can see the sleeping forest ready to nudge awake for spring"

A delicious aroma stirred Sterling's nostrils. It still amazed him that Brendan's walks in the dark or under heavy grey clouds gave birth to the painter's rainbow of kaleidoscope-filled works. The onset of his migraines gave him the colours.

The crackle of bacon frying drew Sterling's eyes. Another pan sat over the delicate blue flame of a propane camp stove. Brendan placed his omelet on the second burner. This is how the Mathesons managed hot meals without power and, of course, last night's coffee.

"Bonnie says you'll soon have your lights and telephone again," Sterling commented.

Brendan nodded. "The Montreal show sold a couple of pieces and a few more look good." With a smooth, gentle movement, he scooped and flipped the omelet. "Bonnie said she told you everything. I'm glad." He glanced at his visitor. "She needs someone to talk to. The gambling is out of hand again."

"She's been through an awful lot." The delicious smells rumbled Sterling's stomach. "Seems like it was her way of escape."

"It isn't a good way," Brendan said, lowering the flame under the bacon. "She needs help."

"I'd like to do what I can."

The young painter didn't look up. "She likes you."

At the rear of the kitchen, a large window overlooking the lakeshore brightened the room. Bits of the odd looking metal sculptures decorating the yard shone where the morning sun had melted away their snow cover. Sterling hadn't often found himself captured by art but Brendan's steel figures created a life of their own, moved in their stillness. There were deer, bear, beaver, wolves but his eye always returned to the speared fish he'd noticed on his first visit. The lines flowed both abstract and real.

"Any of those for sale?"

Brendan looked toward the focus of Sterling's gaze. "The animals, yes, the fish, no. It's special."

Sterling waited but Brendan didn't elaborate. The aroma of the eggs and bacon overwhelmed, started his stomach talking.

"About that breakfast?"

Brendan said, "Say no more."

Within the minute, the two of them were digging into their meals with gusto. Sterling's appetite surprised him. A good night's sleep cured all ills.

"Did you know this Larry Fredericks fellow?" the young artist asked. "You being in the same kind of business."

The reporter swallowed. "Television stars and grubby newspaper grunts don't mix much."

"Does that mean we have a serial killer roaming Candle Lake?" Brendan asked. "That's scary. At least he had the decency to leave John's body alone."

Sterling wiped his mouth with his sleeve, forked in more omelet. "The police seem to think it's the same killer."

"I was going to stay another few days in Montreal but now I'm glad I got back last night." Brendan matched his breakfast partner mouthful for mouthful. "I wouldn't like to think of Bonnie here alone."

Sterling studied the young man for a moment, his pink, almost translucent skin, his long flimsy white hair. "She didn't tell you?"

"She said some kids vandalized our car. That's why she caught a ride to the hairdresser."

Sterling reached into his shirt pocket, pulled out the plastic baggie in which the note was flattened. "This was on her dash."

No doubt she hadn't revealed the threat to Brendan to save her brother worry. But what else might she have held back?

Brendan read the note: "At times like these, it best to keep your head. Arms. Legs."

Brendan's pale skin blanched even more. He dropped his knife and fork on the table, pushed away his plate.

After several moments, he said. "Did Bonnie tell you she sold marijuana?"

Sterling nodded. "Just that she did it only once to get some gambling cash."

"Did she say her suppliers were Zeke and Zak Braun?"

Sterling's face showed his surprise.

Brendan said, "You know them then?"

"I know their father." This on top of the colonel's death could break Ed Braun's heart.

"The twins and I were friends in school until their old man came back from Africa. Then they got mean, started picking on me, beat me up good a couple of times."

At the rink, Zak had said Brendan was his best friend once. Sterling asked, "What happened after their father came back?"

"They came to class with fat lips, black eyes. That had never happened before."

"You think Zeke and Zak trashed Bonnie's car?"

"She told them she wouldn't sell any more drugs but they kept after her. They said she was asking for trouble."

In the Wheelhouse, one of the twins had hovered over Bonnie like an animal. She screamed at him to get away.

Brendan rose from his chair, walked to the window. He studied his sculptures in the yard.

After a long pause, he said, "Do you think they could have killed John and Larry Fredericks?"

Sterling shrugged. "The twins were in hospital the weekend the colonel went missing. Their dad said a round bale rolled over the three of them." Was that round bale Ed? Had he lied? "I'll try and find out where they were when Fredericks was killed."

Brendan stood silent, a silhouette in the clouded light. He opened his tight fists, flexed long fingers. They wouldn't stop shaking.

Afternoon March 8

At noon, the dank and dark Wheelhouse Bar stank of beer and cigarettes stale from the night before. Butts, peanut shells and the odd broken bottle or glass littered the floor. Sterling stepped with care making his way to the long oak bar. At the back of the room, the bouncer raised dust with a push broom, made slow progress gathering the mess into a pile.

The place could dampen any appetite but a wonderful bouquet teased the air. Above the mirror reflecting row upon row of chromatic liquor bottles, a blackboard advertised — Wing Wednesday. By evening, plates piled high with hot chicken wings would fly from the kitchen. Gallons of beer at packed tables would flow to douse the spicy flames.

Monique, her hair pinned in a bun, stood at a sink. Wiping a shot glass with a towel, she turned her head as Sterling climbed onto a stool.

"Mr. Reporter," she said, her voice a happy lilt. "What can I get for you? Beer? Coffee?"

"Coffee would be good."

She placed the glass in its row and walked over to Sterling. "John's memorial in the paper, that was nice. People appreciate it."

"Congratulations, I hear you've got a job for as long as you want."

Monique beamed. "When that good looking lawyer told me I was in the will, I couldn't believe it. Me, the owner of the Wheelhouse!" She stopped. Her face grew red. "John was such a generous man. He didn't forget me, after all. I feel bad that it's made me happy but I know he did it for my boy."

"I was hoping you could give me some more information."

Monique made an abrupt turn, stepped back to her place by the sink. She buffed a beer mug to a high sheen, studied it. "Look, I just don't want to ruin anything."

"I know about you and the mayor." Her slim hands froze, her nails scarlet spots on the glass. She set it down, tossed the towel on the counter. "Farrow admitted you're having an affair," Sterling continued.

Monique cursed, shook her head. "That fat no-good creep."

"He didn't have much choice."

"A man like that always has choices. He makes them by using people." The handsome woman pulled out a stool from under the bar and sat. Opening a package by the sink, she put a cigarette to her lips, lit it and exhaled a long white plume. "Okay, Mr. Reporter, what do you want for your scandal story? If he's going to talk about me, I certainly have a few things to say about him."

"Farrow said you and he spent two nights at the P.A. Inn on the weekend of February 2nd."

"Two pretty boring nights," she replied. "It wasn't a fiery thing between us, if you know what I mean. But he was paying the shot and I had some luck at blackjack."

"Did you go to John and Bonnie's engagement party that Saturday night?"

The nervous tapping of Monique's cigarette on the ashtray ceased. "That was here in Candle. What are you getting at?"

"I'd just like to know where you and Farrow were when McTaggart went missing."

Her tone incredulous, she said, "You think I had something to do with John's death?"

"I expect the police won't be far behind with the same questions. You and the mayor each had a lot to gain."

"You're crazy!" Monique's voice quivered between fear and anger. She covered her face with her hands. "John didn't say anything about leaving me the club." After a moment, her arms dropped to her sides. "I'd never do anything to hurt him."

Sterling studied the tiny furrows across her forehead, the laugh lines around her mouth. "The party?"

"I went for an hour or so but only because John asked me. But I couldn't stand seeing him there, holding hands with that little witch. I should have just gone home but I was so angry I drove back to the P.A. Inn. More than three hours later and Dan still sat at the same VLT."

"You and Farrow were there for the rest of the weekend?"

Monique nodded. "I thought about leaving but changed my mind."

Sterling leaned over the bar, close. "Can you prove neither of you left the hotel again?"

Monique turned to a table at the back of the club where the young auburn-haired waitress sat smoking a cigarette, drinking coffee. Monique waved, crooked her finger at the waitress. The George Eliot scholar of the long shiny legs rose from her chair.

Monique gestured toward the approaching woman then pointed toward the other side of the room where the bouncer worked the push broom. "The reason I changed my mind is that we ran into these two." She touched her employee's arm.

"Giselle, remember the weekend at the Fox's Nose?"

The English Master's student wrinkled her nose. "I'd like to forget."

"Would you tell this gentleman about it."

Giselle eyed her boss, silent.

"Please," Monique reassured her. "Everything."

"Well." Giselle paused, gathered her thoughts. "Lance and I were just about to leave the casino when we saw Monique and her friend, Dan Farrow. We ended up going back to his room for a poker party." She looked at her boss. "It wasn't any of our business if they were together. Monique asked me to go along as a favour. She said she didn't want to be alone with Danny Boy. That's what he told us to call him. We drank as much as played cards, I guess. Finally, Danny Boy passed out drunk and the rest of us crashed on the other bed and couch."

Giselle noticed Sterling's look. "Believe me, everyone was too beat to do anything but sleep." She accepted a cigarette from Monique, allowed her to light it before continuing. "He wasn't much of a poker player but I can see why the man's a politician. He bought us all breakfast the next morning and somehow convinced us to stay. Just long enough to win his money back, he had said. Lance had taken Big Dan for close to four hundred dollars. So the party continued, the casino, the bar, more poker in the room." Giselle turned to Monique. "Okay?"

"Yes, thank you."

"You were never out of each other's sight the whole time?" the reporter asked. "In the casino, perhaps."

Giselle thought for a moment. "Not for more than a few minutes at a time. The Sunday, we all hit the blackjack table."

A cold draft swept the club as the front door opened. Two couples entered, laughing.

"Is that all?" Giselle asked.

"Thanks," Sterling said.

The waitress stubbed her smoke in the ashtray, picked up her serving tray and sauntered over to her first customers of the day.

"Satisfied Mr. Reporter?" Monique asked.

From his jacket, Sterling fetched his wallet peeked inside and frowned.

She waved him off. "The coffee's on me."

"It's none of my business but are you still seeing the mayor?"

The question seemed to surprise Monique. She gazed back for several moments. "I came to love John and when he went with Bonnie I was devastated. It was like I went out to punish myself. I blush when I think about it now, scraping the bottom of the barrel like that."

After the interview, Sterling walked outside, pondering, the wooden doors of the Wheelhouse slamming shut behind him. Again, he peered into his billfold, searched the pockets. Nothing but worn leather stared back.

Where was his 200 dollars? The answer taunted Sterling, mocked his brief escape from nightmares, the sunshine that had lit his mind all day. The age old lesson thrown in his face one more time: never let your guard down. Bonnie had stolen money from her own fiancé. Why not from a little one night stand? For all the reporter knew, he stood at the rear of a long queue of her victims. Would a woman who stooped to those levels hesitate to kill the colonel if it were to her benefit?

Sterling paced the garage beside his TR6. He took a deep breath, let his mind settle and punched the *Sun*'s number into his telephone.

"Newsroom." Over the receiver, her voice sounded listless, without its usual bubble.

"Megan, it's Myles."

"Oh hi, Mr. Sterling."

"How are you?"

"Okay, I guess."

Something was bothering her. He'd ask, but first things first. "Did you get a chance to check with P.A. General?"

"Yes." Paper shuffled. "The hospital confirms that all three Brauns, Ed the father and Zeke and Zak the sons, were admitted the evening of February second and released February fouth." Meagan's tone became all business. "I got through to the duty nurse who worked that weekend and she says she remembers them. They were kept for observation because all three were pretty beaten up around the head. She wondered what kind of hay bale could do that."

"She was suspicious?" Sterling asked.

"Off the record, she said the injuries didn't seem consistent."

"Good work."

"I'm still trying to get through to someone at Braun Trucking who can tell me the whereabouts of the two brothers the day Fredericks died."

"Keep at it, please, this is important. I'll go by there myself, as well."

"And I tracked down the night manager at the P.A. Inn. As it happens, she does remember Mayor Farrow, "Danny Boy" he called himself. He made such a fuss about opening the kitchen at three in the morning that the desk clerk ordered pizza delivery for him. It seems he threw around a lot of "do you realize who you are talking to?" lines at the staff. The manager also fielded complaints about noise from the room. His behaviour didn't improve on the Saturday so they kept an eye on the party. The manager didn't say as much but it seems they didn't want to throw him out because he spent some pretty good money. Anyway, everyone sighed with relief when he checked out Sunday morning."

Sterling cursed, wrong again. That confirmed it. Farrow had been in Winnipeg the day the broadcaster had died and now he and Monique had solid alibis in the death of McTaggart. The mayor, however, would still make a tasty story.

Megan's voice crackled into his thoughts: "Bad news?"

"Back to square one, that's all. Thanks Megan, you're going to be a good one."

"Sure." Her voice fell again. "Whatever."

Where had the eager cub reporter gone? Of course, anyone can get hit by a bad day. "How's Joe?"

Concern about your boss's welfare never hurt in the minefield of office politics, a game, Sterling admitted, he played very well.

"He's pretty miffed you've never shown your face in the office."

A man in need of stroking, that's all. "Tell him I'll be in as soon as I can. Has he said anything about the stories I've filed on the McTaggart and Fredericks murders?"

"He says they're more colour than details."

Sterling exhaled. "My leads keep going nowhere."

"The same on this end. I can't get anyone from the major crimes unit to speak to me on the phone."

Perhaps this budding superstar didn't shine so bright after all. "Megan, you've got an inside line to the Meath Park detachment NCO."

A muffled sound, like a sob, followed the silence. "I think Dad's missing."

"What's happened?"

"Mom says he hasn't been home for two nights. He often works overtime but always calls. She phoned the office and all anyone would say is that he told them he had a couple of under-cover jobs to do."

"Try not to worry, Megan. You know how police work can be."

"It's these murders," she said, her voice tight-ening. "It keeps going through my head that it's cases like these where cops get hurt. Or worse."

"Try not to think that way. You only beat your-self up."

"I know." It was a little girl's voice. "I can't help it."

"Just be patient. He'll show up, ugly as ever."

Small and half-hearted, still it was a laugh. "I'll try," she said.

"My cell will be on. Call if you need to."

"Thanks." She paused. "Myles."

Sterling placed the phone beside him on the work bench. The bonnet of the TR6 hung open, gaping like a hungry mouth. So after Fredericks's death, the major crimes unit had descended on Candle Lake and Staff Sergeant Milburn had disappeared. Or had he?

The elements of the electric wall heater pulsed orange heat waves that brushed Sterling's skin. Still, a shiver slid up his back. Farrow had an alibi for both murders, Megan's father didn't. Had Milburn done the dirty work, now frightened onto the next desperate level, abandoned his family, his job, gone into hiding? Poor Megan, she loved her old dad. It would kill her.

And what about Bonnie? The fiancée. The lover. The thief. A poison ate at her mind. How far did it drive her?

Sterling walked over to the tool chest, wrapped his fingers around a crescent wrench. Dwelling on the absolute worst promised to make a wreck of Megan. He could feel pieces of his own mind falling apart.

He wiped his hands on his coveralls and leaned into the engine compartment, adjusting the tool's jaws to seize the fastening nuts of the inline six's manifold cover. An hour or two's work would get his pet running again, perhaps quell this creeping chill that the evil from which he fled on the other side of the world had followed him to Candle Lake.

Not until the second ring did Sterling realize the sound came from his cell phone. Setting down the wrench, he walked to the work bench, sat down.

"Hello."

"We read your McTaggart memorial story. What you said about Ed Braun is so much crap it's almost funny."

"Who is this?"

"He's no hero, he's a piece of shit."

"If you don't identify yourself, I'm hanging up."

"If you want the real story, you won't."

"I'll only ask you one more time. What's your name?"

"That old fart should go to jail for a long time. He's made a lot of people sick."

"I don't do anonymous. Goodbye."

"Wait! Wait!"

"Who are you?"

"Okay, we'll tell you. We want to meet."

"Not until you tell me your name."

"Somewhere that we won't be seen. We've got proof that will put that asshole away."

"You've got two seconds."

"Eight tonight. The picnic grounds at Fisher Creek."

Evening March 8

The headlights shone through the trees that appeared like lean, black figures in the darkness. Beyond the forest onto the frozen lake, about kilometre away, huddled the hamlet of ice fishing shacks. Off to the west, glints of yellow reflected from the thin band of police crime tape that surrounded McTaggart's hut, the scene of two murders.

Sterling wiggled the stick shift, made certain it was in neutral before lifting his foot from the clutch. The satisfaction of getting the Triumph back on the road dulled under the gloom and quiet menace of the meeting place. As the TR6 idled, his eyes scanned the snow-mounded tables and benches, a picnic ground in deep freeze. A lonely stretch of Highway 265 bordered the area to the north and, to the south, Candle Lake at the head of Fisher Creek. A couple of acres of aspen and pine separated the grounds from the nearest cabin. No one clambaked in the dark on a twenty below March evening. They would be alone.

Sterling killed the headlights, left the park lights as his beacon and rolled down his window.

Nothing moved. The silence of a winter night hung heavy in the blackness the same way noise carried over snow and ice in frigid temperatures. Quiet had reigned, Noel Parenteau said, just before a chainsaw had shaken the fisherman from his sleep.

Later, the colonel would have strolled along with his spud walking stick poking the lake's surface for soft spots. The hole, cut large enough through which a person could fall, must have been very near his shack, an area in which McTaggart was familiar and confident — in front of the door, perhaps? His attention distracted by his argument with Bonnie, minding his keys and the lock, he'd have stepped into the anesthetizing liquid below. The shack would have been slid back over the opening, the frozen lake would have been tranquil once again.

Larry Fredericks's death wouldn't have been quiet, however. In his mind, Sterling could see the newscaster at the Wheelhouse, eyes wild, words slurred, downing doubles. The grisly job would have been done elsewhere, too much blood, too much noise. After the killer transported the victim to McTaggart's fishing shack, he or she had hung the the body parts in the black water of the fishing hole.

Sterling peered through the windshield into the carbon night, the stillness. Was it the twins who were setting him up for more than the real story? They had an alibi in the colonel's death. The Braun family had spent that weekend in P.A. General. Megan, however, hadn't been able to trace the twins whereabouts at the time Fredericks met his end. The brothers raised hell, dealt dope according to Brendan. How far did the young and the wild go?

Sterling looked at his watch — 8:34 —more than half an hour after the appointed time. Was the phone call a hoax? It could have been anyone. Was whoever called out there watching, waiting for something, playing a game? Sterling drummed the steering wheel with his gloved fingers, nervous, mouth dry. Was it wise to have come out here without telling anyone? Perhaps not, but Ed Braun had survived more than most men. Such crazy accusations couldn't be ignored. The reporter owed the army vet that much.

The night seemed to be thickening, the lights of the village dim as if a blanket had been thrown over the forest.

The reporter's throat tightened. Why hadn't he remembered? There may not have been a connection between the colonel and Fredericks but the Braun boys had known the broadcaster. They'd spoken at the party where he and Megan became sick. Was the toxic crystal meth from the twins? Had a deal gone sour and Fredericks been made an example?

Sterling kicked in the clutch, snapped the shift into reverse. It looked as if the sky had fallen, no stars. Heavy ice fog engulfed the trees. Out on the lake, the mist rolled in waves. He sat in a perfect ambush. Flicking a toggle switch on the walnut dash, the headlights shone. They illuminated nothing but a white soup, the Triumph's bumpers shrouded in haze.

It didn't matter, he had to get out of there. He leaned out the open window to back down his own tracks to the highway.

The kiss of ice cold on his neck felt like a shot.

"Where do you think you're going, tinker toy man?"

Sterling turned, his eyes following the burnished grey of a rifle barrel back to one of the Braun boys, peaked cap backwards.

"Zeke or Zak?" the reporter asked. Together, they looked identical. Which one was the artist, which the hockey star? Megan had used their hats to tell them apart.

The other brother, headwear on frontwards, stood behind, smiling.

He said, "What does it matter?" Even the dim light and mist didn't mask that each twin sported a shiner and cuts healing on their faces. "You don't like it out here?"

Their foolish little games irritated. Animals could smell fear and they looked to be enjoying themselves.

"Either use that thing or get it out of my ear," Sterling snapped. "I don't do anonymous and I don't do stories at the end of a gun." The young trucker chewed a piece of gum. After a few moments, he stepped back. The pressure of the steel on the reporter's skin disappeared. "You're late. I don't have time for hoaxes."

The armed brother cradled his weapon in his arms. He slouched, shifting from foot to foot, chewing like it was his cud. No soldier, this kid; Ed would be ashamed.

The other one said, "We wanted to make sure you were alone."

Sterling opened his door, rose from the driver's seat. Now he didn't have to look up at the two young truckers. He studied the speaker, his brother, their wounds. Neither looked as if he'd won the fight.

"Why the gun?" the reporter asked.

Both men lost their smiles, glanced at each other.

Proper-like cap said, "If the old man was with you, we thought we might shoot him."

Ed, the last time Sterling had seen him, didn't appear in much better shape than his sons. The reporter said, "The two of you together still can't take the old soldier?"

Each brother, in identical gestures, looked down at his feet for a moment, up again.

The unarmed one, who seemed to do the talking, said, "The next time will be different." No bravado now, his eyes blazed pure anger. "And it'll be the last time."

The kid didn't look like a kidder. Sterling said, "You wanted to tell me the real story."

"Zak." The one twin turned to his armed brother. He shouldered his rifle, pulled a letter-sized envelope from his parka pocket.

"What's this?" Sterling asked.

"A set of keys and a map of the truck compound," Zeke explained. "Go there tomorrow night after ten. You'll have all the proof you need that the great Captain Braun is a piece of shit. And a criminal."

With his fingers, Sterling traced the form of the three pieces of metal enclosed by paper. "Even with these, it would still be an illegal break-in. I don't do that either."

A little lie never hurt anyone.

"I should have known," Zeke snorted. "You and the old man go back too far. You don't want the truth."

"You boys are known to be trouble-makers."

Zak stopped chewing, gripped his shotgun and raised the barrel. Sterling ignored him and, waving the keys and map, turned to Zeke. "This could just as easily be a set-up, a joke. Before I know it, I'm in jail."

For the first time, Zeke looked flustered. He ground his teeth, his eyes darting toward the forest. After a few moments, he looked at his twin and said, "We have to get the pictures."

Zak nodded.

Sterling studied the two men. The cuts and bruises on their worked-over faces, the fear in their darting eyes made them pathetic as much as mean.

Zeke decided he had something to say: "If you were fourteen, living on the farm with your gramps and gramma and one day some stranger came around calling himself your father, then once a week, just for the hell of it, beat you so bad you couldn't walk, you'd do the same as us."

Sitting in the arena the other day, Zak had said at fourteen, he had harboured dreams of becoming an artist, Zeke an NHLer. Then something had happened.

Ed Braun's two sons whirled about and walked into the fog.

Zeke turned back, reversed his cap as his brother switched his forward and said, "How will you feel when you find out your hero deals poison, puts kids in hospital?"

Morning March 9

Sterling steered the TR6 through the open gate. Atop the entrance sat a large wooden sign: "Braun and Sons Trucking." Below, a small sign secured to the chain link fence read: "Beware! Electrified during off hours."

Sterling's eyes swept the yard, its buildings. The morning sun, still reluctant to rise at this time of year, hid under the treeline. Electric lights shone from several windows. Again it struck Sterling how much the truckyard resembled the Canadian compound in Kigali. Here, though, lines of tractors and their single and double trailers instead of armoured personnel carriers, Hum Vees and Land Rovers lined the grounds in rows. That was, of course, before the civil war and genocide destroyed all order and any sense of humanity, allowing dogs to fatten on human flesh.

Ed Braun had always been the strong one. When the beautiful Tutsi woman and her little boy became a bath of blood and meat under the flash of silver blades and rusty nails, the captain warned that a soldier had to do his own job or he couldn't help anyone. Sterling remembered his words: "You can't let it get to you or you'll go insane."

It had overwhelmed Sterling and McTaggart, though, almost driven them crazy. Had Ed's sons paid the price for their father's special grasp of sanity? A piece of shit. A criminal. Their words spewed profound hatred.

Sterling got out of the Triumph, gravel grating under his feet, and headed toward the office door. Trying the handle, he peeked through the window. The office was locked. At one end of the building, the huge overhead doors to the repair bays hung open. A welder's torch flashed sparks, snapped and crackled.

Sterling began to walk in the opposite direction. Fresh light settled on the compound as the sun emerged. A row of semi's and their trailers hunkered at the rear of the yard. The map and its instructions indicated it might be interesting to inspect the second trailer of unit seven's B-train tonight after loading.

Open for business now, Braun and Sons Trucking buzzed with activity. The gate unlocked, men toiled at their craft, the boss off somewhere on an errand. Sterling had never taken a close gander at a grain truck before. The present moment offered the bonus of a legal peek-about.

He strolled along the front of the huge vehicles reading the numbers on each door until he came upon the designated tractor. Looking around, he slipped down the aisle to the rear of the trailer and bounded up the ladder. A canvas cover filmed with grain dust lay scrolled across the top of the box.

He looked inside. Only a few husks and seeds littered the empty floor. Down the corrugated wall, submerged had there been a full load, a limp hockey bag dangled from a steel hook. Reaching in, the reporter unzipped the top. His fingers searched inside but only touched what seemed to be more detritus. He scraped a handful to inspect. Among the husks, seeds and dust sprouted tiny curled green leaf buds, soft to the touch. Close to his nose, they whiffed a sweet aroma. Alfalfa, this was not. Pulling out the plastic baggie from his pocket, the sample joined the threatening note to Bonnie.

The growl rumbled up Sterling's spine. Blood drained from his face, stopped solid in his veins. He couldn't breathe. Turning, he stared down into a pair of large brown eyes, two rows of urine-coloured incisors from which saliva dripped, pooled on the ground. The Rottweiler began to bark, it's black fur rippling. The wall of noise hit like a cannon, clenching the reporter's fingers around the ladder. He hugged the steel close to

319

his chest and closed his eyes as the world shrunk and expanded in waves.

Kigali again, but this time the flesh devoured would be his. The dizziness grew. His arms deadened, his fingers slipping from the rungs as his body swayed out from its perch. Sensing weakness, the animal lunged, jaws snapping.

"Now I've got you, you mutt!" Like the staccato of a machine gun, the words filtered through the hound's attack. Sterling opened his eyes, pulled himself back against the trailer.

Ed Braun attached the animal to a heavy gauge chain. "Shut up!" The command did nothing to settle the dog. Its bull neck cracked the iron leash like a whip as the animal strained, bucked, furious at the loss of easy blood. Braun laughed. "My little pup scared you up there, did he?"

It was a tug-of-war between man and beast as they wrestled toward a kennel at the rear of the main building.

One step, one breath at a time, Sterling descended. At the bottom of the ladder, legs crumpling, he spilled to the ground. Rolling over, he raised himself to his knees, vomited. He didn't stop until his gut churned only dry heaves.

"Are you all right?" Braun leaned across his desk and placed a Styrofoam cup of coffee in front of his visitor. "You look pale."

"Your dog has some bark to him, could freeze a freight train."

"I was looking for Babe to put him in his cage for the day when I spotted your little sports car. Sorry, I didn't get him before he caught your scent."

"No harm done. I was looking around the yard for you when I saw him coming. Luckily, I was able to jump up on the truck."

"Lucky is right. I'm training him as an attack dog."

Sterling sipped his coffee spilling some on his chin. He returned the cup to the desk, dropped his hand out of sight. Squeezing his fingers into a fist, he spread them again. They still shook.

He swallowed. "I'm putting together a memoir on Africa. I was hoping you could help me with a small detail."

Braun's face brightened, expectant. "I think about those days a lot."

"The colonel suspected there was some drug dealing by his own men. He detailed you to investigate. Did you find anything?"

The army veteran pursed his lips, shook his head. "There's much that goes on in a war that's best left unsaid. Drugs were the only currency that worked at the *Interhamwe* roadblocks." He paused, looked hard at his friend. "But no, I didn't find anything."

The reporter stared back, silent. Was that an admission of some sort? Had McTaggart sent a fox to look after the hens?

"Did our office call, a Megan Milburn?"

Braun nodded. "Must be a city girl. Something about a survey on how much grain was being moved out of the area this week. I told her some but not a lot, not at this time of year." He studied Sterling for several moments. Suspicious? "Then she asked if that meant Zeke and Zak were staying in town this week, she said she knew them. I told her they'd been in the back working maintenance. She said she'd drop by as a surprise. Haven't seen her, though."

The wonder kid learned by the second. She'd established that the twins were in town when Fredericks was murdered. Sterling chanced another sip. The hot liquid soothed. Ed's black eye shone shades of yellow and green. A single bandage ran down his temple.

"I ran into your boys. They look a little worse for wear."

Braun didn't blink. "Those two are out of control, won't listen to a word I say."

"You have to get pretty tough to keep them in line?"

The father exhaled a long breath, exasperated. "Do you have any kids?"

"No." Sterling looked away. None that lived.

"You wouldn't know then," Braun said.

To mention the twins threat against their father would only stir what seemed to be an already boiling pot. By the looks of it, Ed would pay them back in kind. The scrapings in the baggie were evidence of nothing until under laboratory scrutiny. And who were the dealers here? Were the boys setting up their old man for a fall?

"I suppose not," the reporter replied.

Braun crushed his coffee cup in his powerful fist, gazed into the window's morning sunshine. After several moments, he looked back at Sterling.

"I sometimes wonder what would have happened if Susan had lived." The army veteran's voice softened. "What would the twins be like if their mother hadn't died giving them life." Rising from his chair, he strolled over to the window. "When I left the service, I thought I was finally over her, that I could be a good father to a couple of teenagers. But when I saw them again, I saw her eyes in theirs." He stopped and turned. Even though the room felt comfortable, a bead of sweat rolled down his temple. He smiled. "You know, I really miss Africa."

Sterling stared, silent, unable to believe his friend's words.

Braun gestured to the door. "Let me walk you to your car."

As they passed the service bays, Sterling realized the truck compound covered a huge area, the hangar-sized building alone home to an untold labyrinth of nooks and crannies, lost rooms where anything could hide.

They came upon an open door from which voices he recognized and the aroma of coffee floated. He wanted to see the twins's reaction at the sight of him and their father and stepped inside.

"We have no choice. We have to do it." The words came to an abrupt halt, the heads of the boys whipping around at Sterling's entrance. Zeke's mouth opened, about to speak, but shut again as his father followed through the door.

A large electrical coffee urn stood on a sink counter beside a fridge in the company's bare lunch room, its walls unfinished plaster, the floor plank wood. Zeke sat on a bench at a long table littered with coffee cups, a pencil in his hand, his head hovering over a drawing pad. Zak stood nearby taping the blade of a hockey stick with the care one might apply to medical surgery.

Rows and rows of glimmering trophies, each topped with the statuette of a hockey player, lined the shelves of a cabinet. On the walls surrounding the hardware, several beautiful ink and pencil drawings captured action on the ice. Seeing Sterling's appreciation, hints of smiles tugged at the twins unable to hide their pride. Despite all he knew about the two young men, at that moment, Sterling's heart softened at all the hope in their eyes.

"I told you to get rid of that crap!" Their father lunged toward his sons, his fists balled. "This is a workplace, not your damn bedroom!" He drew a breath, eyed one then the other. "Besides, if you two losers were any good at anything except dreaming, you'd be out in the world doing it by now."

Ed Braun wheeled about, marched out of the room. The eyes of Zeke and Zak pierced him goodbye with looks that could kill.

Early Afternoon March 9

Sterling shivered. The afternoon sun flooded his cabin's living room. The flames high in the fireplace, waves of heat emanated from the chimney's mortared rocks. Yet, ice layered the core of his body.

'I really miss Africa.' What was there to miss about the slaughter of almost a million people, rivers turned blood, their flow dammed by bloated corpses? Were those the experiences Captain Braun reminisced about?

Sterling admitted to knowing little about parenting but the way Ed had slashed the twins's obvious dreams could do nothing other than engender bitterness. Should it be any surprise his sons turned to dealing drugs or went as far as accusing their father of the same, peddling it across the country under the cover of Braun and Sons Trucking?

A hero? Zeke and Zak had laughed. How brave was the man who beat twelve-year-old boys until they couldn't stand? Held it as a point of pride that he could still do the same when they grew into men? Or were these the vicious lies of two addled brains that 'had gone out of control?'

Sterling hugged himself. The feeling that the world shook, its wobbly foundations crumbling, gripped him like cold fingers. Were the heroes who had come to Candle Lake to rebuild their lives after the horror of Rwanda miserable failures? John McTaggart had died the same paranoid man who'd arrived, rejected by his fiancée, still haunted by cries of the dead floating in the wind. And, the strongest of men, the colonel's aide and best friend, was he mired in the actions of the lowest? What chance then did that leave a reporter, a mere voyeur of the world's real actors?

Was he imagining the worst? The Braun boys could be hanging their old man out to dry, settling a score. Or, just as bad, setting up a mild mannered journalist for a B and E sting, not to mention another frolic with Babe.

Sterling reached for the cell phone lying on the coffee table. He'd some calls to make, get the evidence — the threatening note, the scrapings from the bottom of the hockey bag — to Kevin and under a microscope. Tonight, loaded B-train or not, he would wait.

The flames now dying, what remained of the burnt logs in the fireplace glowed darker and darker. A cold draft sent icicles up the reporter's spine. But to stew alone like this? Despite what she'd done, a hint of Bonnie's perfume, the scent of her golden storm of hair, the touch of her warm, soft skin still clung to him. She'd bestowed a night without dreams, sleep without nightmares. Sterling watched the few embers on the ashstrewn grate smoke, as if choking for air.

Sterling pushed through the huge double doors of the Fox's Nose Casino. The large afternoon crowd milled about in a grey haze shot through with slashes of red, blue and green VLT lights. The smoky cloud seemed to feast on its human captives. He paced down endless row upon row of somber gamblers intent on jackpots sure to land in their laps at any moment.

Sterling didn't see who bowled into him, knocked him sideways.

"Sorry," the man said.

Shaking his head, Sterling looked up. "Brendan!"

"I didn't see you."

Despite his dark glasses hiding his eyes, Bonnie's brother looked stricken somehow, the lines of his face cringing, head down.

"Something wrong?"

Brendan looked at Sterling as if deciding what to say. "I've lost her again."

"Bonnie?"

"When she gets like this, she's not the same person. I can't even talk to her."

"She is here, then."

"I'm not sure she ever left this place." Brendan said. "In her mind."

"Where?"

His fingers massaged circles over his temples and grimaced. "I can't stay here any longer." He pointed down the long row of VLT's. "Maybe she'll listen to you." He gazed down the endless aisle of faces then began to walk away. "Before she ruins everything."

Bonnie's silhouette drew Sterling's eyes from across the vast room. He watched other men snatch glances of her while pausing to light a smoke, sip a coffee or beer. As he approached her he saw a new, vivacious woman in the place of the defeated loser he'd followed out the doors only the night before.

An upswept hive of blonde curls had emerged from her trip to the hairdresser that morning. She sat cross-legged wearing a golden silk blouse and black jeans tucked into fancy-stitched, silver-toed cowboy boots, her foot tapping time to the country song serenading the crowd. Draped over her lap, the luxurious mink fur, the colour of elm bark don't you think, rested.

What should Sterling think? Brendan said she needed help but at that moment she looked fine, happy even. She had admitted to being addicted as if in the clutches of some powerful drug. Still, that gave her no excuse to lift the money from Sterling's pants.

He could still feel her breath on his neck as she slept, the touch of her hair in his fingers. He could still hear the hope in her voice when she said she wanted out of her black hole.

Next to Bonnie, a plump silver-haired matron stood and walked away clutching a plastic pail brimming with loonies. Sterling slid into her chair.

Bonnie's eyes shone. They now belonged to a new lover, one whose own eyes danced in dizzying circles. Her face brightened even more. Three cherries settled in a row. A siren wailed from within the bowels of the machine and, on top, a pulsating red light twirled alerting the world that yet another patron had won her due. The VLT's mouth vomited a stream of coins into the plastic vessel she held in her long slim fingers.

After the last bronze coin landed, Bonnie scooped a handful and plugged them back into her new flame's hungry slot as if she feared he'd starve without her constant doting.

"Congratulations," Sterling said.

Bonnie glanced over at him, her sweet fate glistening her smile. "Oh, it's you."

"You're a winner."

"Third time tonight."

Sterling studied the face of the woman with whom he'd imagined, for a few blissful moments, he'd shared the same skin, the same soul; the woman who the next morning rifled two hundred bucks from his jeans. Her bright eyes revealed nothing; he and the beautiful chanteuse might as well have been strangers meeting for the first time.

"You left without saying goodbye."

"I left a note," Bonnie replied, her tone flat, no hint they'd touched not so long before.

Sterling eyed her for several more moments, then said, "Thanks for leaving my wallet behind."

She whipped around to her VLT, punched in more coins. "I don't know what you mean?"

"Don't lie!" he snapped. "I'd just gone to the bank."

Her thumb rapid-fired the button triggering one nervous revolution after another of oranges, lemons and cherries, rolling, rolling, rolling.

Her face darkened. "I don't know what you're talking about."

"Perhaps we should tell the cops our stories, see who they believe."

Bonnie's skin flushed for a few moments then she looked hard at Sterling. "You mean talk to Staff Sergeant Milburn? Lover, you told me what he thinks about you." She leaned back in her chair. "I wonder who he would believe if I told him you'd been stalking me, harassing Brendan over John's death."

Anger rose like a flame, flared from Sterling's tongue: "Stealing that money was nothing but a cheap whore's trick!"

Bonnie jerked, flinched as if she'd been slapped, held her palm to her cheek. After a moment, however, she forced a smile. "Look, I'm winning, that's all that counts." She dropped her hand. "I'll pay you back tomorrow."

The reporter played a hunch. "You've spent the utility money Brendan gave you from his Montreal show."

"Listen to me! It doesn't matter!" Her own scream startled her. She stopped, breathed deeply. "I'll pay him back, too." Her eyes large, pleading, her fingers fluttered like a bird to Sterling's shoulder. "Tomorrow I'll give you $400. I'll double what I owe Brendan, too. I'm almost there already. Just one more jackpot and we'll all be making money." Her face beamed with the glow of the self-righteous, the blessed. "Tonight I've got it. I can just feel it."

Hoisting her money pail under her arm, her purse over her shoulder, Bonnie rose. Sterling watched as she left the vast banks of VLT's for the gaming tables. She sat down and tossed a playful grin to the blackjack dealer, a powerful man who could pile your winnings bigger, higher, faster. Or he could bury you.

Late afternoon March 9

The TR6 slid to a stop in the driveway bare inches from ramming the garage door. Hands still on the steering wheel, Sterling sat motionless, staring through the windshield.

Bonnie had turned from him in the worship of her god. A vision of her genuflecting before the lottery terminal seared his mind. The two hundred dollars stood as a lesson hard learned. He'd never see it again but that mattered little. It didn't mean nearly as much as the fact that he'd opened to Bonnie's touch, that she'd held back the night, allowed him a calm he'd never thought would be his again. She'd given him peace. Now she'd floated away.

Still, all this paled before another now obvious fact: Bonnie swam in sea of sickness beyond her control. She admitted that her relationship with McTaggart had stood on a rocky precipice, that she hadn't been ready to share her life with him. She needed money, though, to feed her VLT's, her blackjack dealers. Bonnie admitted selling dope to kids from university, said she'd considered worse. The colonel's will afforded her a tidy sum.

Broke and desperate, did she take the next step and kill her fiancé?

All of a sudden weary, Sterling stepped out of the Triumph and ambled down the path to the house. The outside screen door hung ajar. A delivery lay on the floor jamb. Envelopes had played an inordinate role in his life of late. Retrieving the package, he keyed open the lock, walked over to the counter where he dumped out the contents: a single photograph.

He stared, breathless, as if an iron fist had been driven into his solar plexus. The signs had hinted at ill omen but he'd never imagined this. On the back, the words chilled: "He liked to call this 'Fun in Africa.'" Sterling studied the picture again, dropped it on the table. He could almost hear the cries in the night.

Once off the telephone, Sterling walked to the bathroom and opened the medicine cabinet. He spotted his sleeping pills, unused of late, in the corner. The prescription just left him groggy all day, did nothing to still the moaning of the wind, the snarl of scavenging hounds. He grabbed the bottle and made his way to the kitchen where he found a mortar and pestle and began to prepare a marinade for the juicy t-bone in the refrigerator. He ground the pills into powder and mixed in steak juice but insistent knocking interrupted his task. Wiping his hands on a towel, he crossed the front room and opened the door to Constable Cuthand in his street clothes.

"So it's you." Sterling couldn't contain his smile. Now he recognized the source of Kevin's long belly laugh at the reporter's expense. "Little Emil" stood well over six feet. "I didn't realize we were all so intimate," the reporter said.

Cuthand looked away, brown skin flushing just as it had when Staff Sergeant Milburn gave the order for a full drug body search of Sterling. This time Sterling wanted to borrow the constable's gloves. "I imagine diving in Mexico beats what you face here. Grisly work these days."

For someone who retrieved body parts from the bottom of a lake at twenty-five below, Cuthand embarrassed easily. He rubbed his hand across his brush cut, relaxed. He opened the bag in his hand. "Cousin said you needed these."

Sterling accepted the diving gloves, squeezed the heavy thermal rubber. "Better safe than sorry."

"You have a delivery for me?"

"Tell Kevin to check the note for prints." The reporter handed over the plastic baggie. "Find out if those leaves are marijuana."

The policeman unbuttoned his topcoat, slipped the evidence into an inside pocket.

"Cousin said you better not be up to something stupid, perfectly legal or not."

"Thank him for his concern."

The young mountie looked down at his feet, up again. "Sorry about the other day."

"You were just following orders," Sterling reassured him. Constable Cuthand turned and stepped along the snow path to his car. "Any word on Staff Milburn?" Sterling called.

The policeman halted, peered at the reporter, surprised.

"His daughter works for the paper," the reporter explained.

Cuthand nodded then shrugged. "He's been out of touch. We're worried."

Sterling closed the door and turned back into the living room. He picked up the photograph left at his door. Captain Ed Braun stood with his arm around an *Interhamwe* militiaman. Both men grinned. Before them sat a pile of bones, about waist high, topped with the a few human skulls bleaching in the sun.

Floodlights blazed from atop the three metre high fence, the arching gateway, and the concrete block bunker of hangar-sized buildings which lay beyond. Babe's paw prints traced a path along the barricade's perimeter toward the rear of the compound.

Snow swirled in blankets. The office, the maintenance bays, all the windows mirrored only darkness. A sentry of Western Star, Freightliner and elephant bone-white Volvo tractors and their trailers stood at ease along the rear of the compound. Ed's pup would be back.

The Triumph's hot air vents blasted Sterling's face. Frost decorated the windshield as if it were a cake.

His stomach churned. He lowered his side window, gulped the ice wind. The odour of raw beef, the human images it stirred, mingled with the cockpit's leather. On the passenger seat sat a plastic grocery bag containing the meat.

Sterling got out of the car, sleet pelting his face. The keening of the wind smothered the crunch of his Kodiaks against the icy ground. He scanned the yard, the buildings. The bag arced over the fence, landed inside the gate.

Returning to the driver's seat, the reporter stepped on the clutch, flicked the stick shift from neutral into first. The TR6 rolled back into the night.

He signalled Giselle for a coffee.

The waitress waved and said, "I'll get the boss."

Sterling sat at a quiet table in the rear of the Wheelhouse. He had an hour or so to kill, enough time for the dog to discover his treat, digest it. Then Sterling would need all his wits about him.

The photograph of Ed Braun turned a worsening situation real ugly fast. Set-up or not, Sterling faced no choice. He had to take the twins up on their offer to get inside the truck compound.

A steaming cup on her tray, the Masters of English student trailed Monique. Sterling looked twice. The bar manager wore the mink fur that had been draped over Bonnie's lap only hours before. Monique pursed her lips, tapped her foot while Giselle served the reporter.

"I was just about to head out the door," Monique said, her waitress walking away. "I've been phoning around for you for the last hour." She slid into a chair and stuffed a yellow plastic lighter and a cigarette package back into her pocket, a newly lit smoke hanging from her mouth. She stared at Sterling, took a few drags before she spoke: "Bonnie's in the games room. She's lost it. Just sits there leaning against the VLT, catatonic-like but won't let anyone help her."

Sterling thought for a moment, somehow not surprised. "I saw her a few hours ago at the Fox's Nose." His eyes travelled the luscious fur. "With her coat. Now you're wearing it."

"Just after supper, she burst into my office, demanded I give her $500 for it again. As if I'm her personal pawn broker."

"You don't seem to refuse."

Monique's fingers burrowed into the fur, caressed it, brushed away specks of mud spotting the hem. "This time she threatened me. I've never seen her this bad. She ranted she was up ten thousand dollars, started crying, said she lost it all but just needed a stake to get started again." Monique's eyes widened at the thought. "She threatened to scratch my eyes out if I didn't give her the money." Her voice chilled as Sterling rose, walked toward the games room. "This is what killed my poor John."

The solitary figure sagged against the VLT. The closer he came, the more Bonnie unravelled. Some of the golden waves atop her head had fallen and now straggled her cheeks in loose strands. Blotches of black mud soiled her jeans

341

and her fancy stitched, silver-toed cowboy boots as if, in the final steps to the Wheelhouse, she had slogged through a dirty trail. She stared into the glass as the video invited her to play again and again, her thumb pressing the useless button over and over and over.

Sterling stepped beside the VLT into her line of sight. "Bonnie?"

Her eyes half-lidded, blank, she gazed into Sterling's chest. After a long moment, she raised her hand, opened her clenched fist. Sterling recognized the crumpled paper in her palm, the "12 Steps of Gambler's Anonymous" she'd shown him.

"Call Emil for me. Please," she whispered, her voice dying.

The chain link fence sparked, crackled, electric blue streams embracing the rock. After a moment, the stone Sterling had tossed fell into the snow, hissing.

Was this part of the Braun boys's sense of humour? The map instructions had lied after all. At 10 PM, power to the fence would be killed, the dog chained. Sometimes it paid to be a cynic. Sterling pulled on the diving gloves.

The thick rubber squeaked as his fingers inserted the key into the metal box. There was a click and silence. He turned the key again. Nothing. Again. Nothing. He cursed. Was the whole thing a hoax? One more time. A quiet click sounded. The gates parted.

Sterling slipped into the compound. His eyes traced the area where he'd tossed the bag. Only a few tiny shreds of white plastic fluttered there, almost invisible against their icy background.

Sterling peered about, his mitt shading his eyes against the brilliance, the blizzard's sting. He could see only blurred structures, the endless yard. In the open, he might as well have presented himself on centre stage. He dashed to the main building, flattened against the corrugated steel wall. Here, too, floodlights ate all shadow, left nowhere to hide. At least hard metal covered his back. His breath produced visible clouds in the cold air; the trick was to keep moving.

The row of parked semis stretched over the rear of the compound. Darkness beckoned. Even though under surveillance of fence-mounted floodlights, inky aisles separated the tall trailers. Sterling sprinted the never-ending fifty metres, each step a small drum roll of gravel under his boots.

Crouched at last beside the safety of a massive tire, his lungs heaved, breath seared his chest. No one had ever accused him of being an athlete. The years hadn't helped. As his breathing abated, his eyes travelled the compound. Low snowdrifts sloped against walls, rolled in motionless waves across the yard. Nothing moved.

In the afternoon, number seven had been parked midway down the row. Sterling made his way ducking below the trailer undercarriages, checking numbers on tractor doors. He poked his head around the final truck. Had he been sent on a fool's errand, after all? Where did #7 hide?

The map committed to memory, he surveyed the yard once more. From this distance, the far side of the maintenance and repair building wavered in white eddies. Once inside, a long hallway lead to an unused area at the rear. There, behind double locked doors, according to the map, Sterling would find all the evidence he needed.

Sterling's breathing quickened. Only Babe's home at the rear of the office stood between him and the maintenance building. Brisk steps brought him around to the side adjacent to the kennel. Back against the wall; despite the cold, a bead of sweat rolled down his nose.

He peeked around the corner. The gate hung open but the mutt could be inside his house. Trained to attack, the beast's fangs would be in an intruder's throat in seconds at the slightest sound. The taste of bile touched Sterling's tongue wrenching back the memory of his body, his brain seizing at the snarl of the rottweiler. Until he saw the dog peaceful and asleep, he couldn't be sure the meat had done its job.

The gate summoned him ten interminable strides away. If only he could shut the door on Babe. Sleep mutt, sleep.

Sterling's legs felt like petrified oak, his boots, bass drums crashing on the gravel. Step after ear-splitting step, his eyes were glued on the doghouse. At last his glove grasped the latch, lifted it from its slot and slammed the gate. Leaning against the steel fence, Sterling peered into Babe's empty home. The monster still wandered out there somewhere.

Hidden before by the angles of the buildings, the compound's rear loading ramp now played into view. A B-train sat in front. Was it number seven?

Sterling kept his back to the steel-ribbed wall as he stepped his way to the semi. From his line of sight through the driver's side window, the cab looked empty. Somehow, the area seemed darker. A desolate lifelessness palled over the truck, the building.

He approached. Glass littered the ramp from the shattered bulb above the door.

Peering about once more, Sterling slipped up the ladder of the rear trailer. At the top, the canvas cover scrolled part way across a cargo of wheat, as if loading had been interrupted. On top of the grain lay the same hockey equipment bag he'd seen earlier, unzipped and bulging. He reached inside and retrieved one of the small bales wrapped in clear plastic, sniffed and studied the compressed leaves and buds.

Sterling set the marijuana back in the bag and, with his hand, slid along a rope tethered to the handle then disappearing into the wheat. He sunk his arm into the seeds and traced the line for about a metre before hitting something solid.

Heaving up in a cloud of dust, another hockey bag broke the surface. Expecting more cannabis, Sterling's eyes widened as he opened the zipper to find plastic bags of white powder.

When the trailer had been empty, he had seen a row of hooks set across the bare wall. It would be from these that the secret cargo hung.

By the end of the rope, another three satchels of marijuana sat on top of the load. Just by the feel of them, they held at least a hundred pounds of marijuana, no mere delivery, a major shipment. But what had interrupted the loading?

Sterling descended the ladder. Wheat trickled from a hole in the wall of the trailer, a mound growing in the snow. He'd missed it in his rush. He fit his thumb in the opening: concave, about the size of a bullet hole.

Jumping to the ground, he hid behind the rear tires, looked about. The wind keened, bit his ears. A tarpaulin roped over a stack of wooden shipping crates snapped and whipped. Around the buildings, snow piled in corners, crept up walls.

Sterling rose, snow stinging his face, squinting his eyes. He edged his way alongside the rear trailer, past the forward unit and stopped at the elephant bone-white Volvo tractor. The passenger door hung ajar but not enough to trigger the interior light. Inside, nothing moved.

Sterling stepped onto the running board, leaned into the cab. Keys dangled from the ignition. Nothing else appeared out of order. About to jump down, his glove felt wet. The palm now dark, he sniffed, peered down where he'd steadied himself with his hand. A crimson pool soaked through the cloth of the passenger seat.

What was he getting himself into? Zeke's words chilled: "If the old man was with you, we thought we might shoot him." Their father's obscene smile floated into Sterling's mind as Captain Braun stood with the *Interhamwe* before the pile of bones and skulls.

Sterling's Kodiaks hit the ground running. Crouching as he sprinted, the maintenance and repair building looked to be about twenty-five metres away. Inside there would be a moment to ponder, plan the next move. Out in the open, he might as well paint a bull's eye on his back.

The snarl froze Sterling's lungs, stopped his feet dead. The rottweiler trotted out of the sleet-veiled shadows left by the smashed loading dock light and halted. Babe's brown eyes blinked, jaws snapping open, closed. The beast's lips curled back, yellow fangs bared.

The reporter's gut seized, his mind whirling. Behind the dog, a white mound rose streaked with heavy red swatches. The storm moaned, cried. Sterling peered through the sleet.

Prenez mon bébé! Prenez lui s'il vous plait!

The Tutsi princess beckoned. The woman lived! Somehow, she'd escaped.

She crouched in a snowdrift. Blood soaked through her long white *pagne*. In her lap, her baby, a slab of meat, dripped red, cried. The mother had no arms to hold her child, no head with pink lips to kiss him.

"Don't move!"

The voice, low and hard, jerked into Sterling's consciousness. He whirled about and saw the steel double barrels of a shotgun glint. He shut his eyes, opened them and turned back toward the animal.

Babe's muscled legs rippled one step closer, then another.

Behind the dog, the princess, her flowing gown, her baby, became a snowdrift from which jagged spars of a broken shipping crate protruded.

The animal's huge jaws widened, neck tensed. It's back arching, the black fur rippled. The lunge waited a moment away.

"Wait," Sterling said, half-turning, his glove pressing the weapon down, pointing it to the ground.

He faced Babe again. Their eyes locked but Sterling could see the mutt appeared confused. After a moment, Babe began to peer about. The dog staggered to the side, its front legs collapsing.

The rear limbs followed. The animal lay panting, blinking, until his eyes closed, head resting on front paws.

Sterling looked at the man at his side then down at the shotgun. "What are you doing here?"

"Kevin said sometimes you're funny, do stupid things," Noel Parenteau replied. "Like forget your gun."

"I don't own a gun."

"He said that, too."

Sterling glanced at Babe. The attack dog appeared content, eyes shut, gentle breaths, snowflakes clinging to his black fur like a blanket.

"We better move. I think someone's been shot," Sterling said. "I found blood."

Sleet bit into their faces as the two men leaned low into the storm as they ran towards the maintenance and repair garage. They darted between the stilts of raised storage tanks decorated in tall black stencil announcing either DIESEL or GASOLINE.

In front of the door, Sterling breathed deep. Was this going to be another Zeke and Zak hoax? The key inserted, a gentle turn produced a click.

Inside, they waited until their eyes adjusted. In only a few metres, blackness smothered the light of the bulb above their heads. The auto garage odour of petroleum lay heavy in the air.

Another dim light struggled in the distance of what looked to be a hallway. Down this corridor, according to the map, they'd find the hidden room.

His hand on the wall, Sterling stepped into the inky space. The muted light blinked ahead. One slow step after another and the bulb became less blurred, began to define itself.

Without warning, Sterling's Kodiak slipped out from under him. He teetered on the other boot until Noel's vise grip came to the rescue.

The elder Parenteau knelt, removed his glove and wiped the concrete floor with his fingers. He raised them to his nose.

"Blood," he said.

They made their way along until, at last, the cobwebbed light flickered above. Just as the map claimed, a double padlocked steel door blocked the visitors.

Sterling retrieved the keys from his parka pocket. He inserted the one marked "storeroom" into the first padlock, twisted. The heavy gauge resisted then snapped open. He hung the device on the freed latch and frowned: one key, two locks? More games? Foul up? To come only this far would be infuriating. Into the second lock, he slipped the same key. For a moment, it wouldn't turn, then clicked, parted.

The ponderous door swung open to a blaze of illumination. Both men shielded their eyes. Row upon row upon row of banquet table-sized wooden planters filled the room, about the size of the main floor of a small house. Above, banks of high-wattage lighting burned.

Sterling stepped up to the garden, listened. A mountain stream gurgled. A trough ran under the plants, their bare roots bathing in a flowing green liquid. A light, sweet aroma laced the air.

Noel walked down an aisle, poked a plant stalk with the barrel of his twelve guage. "In my day, we called this ganga." Like a farmer judging his yield, he surveyed the crop. "I don't know much about this stuff but I'd say harvest is over."

Only then did Sterling see what the elder Parenteau noticed. On some plants, only the odd leaf hung among the bare stems and branches of the crowns. Underfoot, dirt, empty pots and hand tools littered the floor. The cannabis had been reaped in a hurry.

Sterling followed his row to the rear of the room. A chain and padlock through the push handle of the two doors under the exit light prevented them from fulfilling their role, kept out the curious. The area looked to be used for storage at one time. Several one hundred gallon oil drums lined the wall. Rusted transmission gears, radiators, camshafts and the like spilled out the open barrels. The words *used oil* marked one lidded container.

Beside the drums, a door opened into a darkened room. Sterling felt along the inside wall until his fingers flipped up a switch illuminating a fluorescent ceiling lamp. It looked as if he'd come upon a laboratory. Several tables sported some sort of apparatus of propane burners and glass vessels connected by tubing along with stacks of plastic mixing bowls. Stoves and sinks lined one wall. On the floor sat a large barrel. He peeked inside. He guessed the white powder to be either finished crystal meth or its main ingredient, ephedrine.

He stepped up to a shelf of chemical bottles — iodine tincture, red phosphorus, methanol, acetone, muriatic acid. The final bottle read: "red lye drain cleaner." The *Sun* story said police found heavy traces of lye in the toxic crystal meth samples. Sterling shook his head. It wouldn't be hard to mess up a soup of this stuff.

Turning off the light behind him, Sterling walked to door signed "washroom" at the far corner of the rear wall. The knob wouldn't turn. One after another, none of the three keys fit. It didn't matter, the story could write itself now. Let the police investigate the bloody truck seat, the bullet hole in the trailer. Get out while the getting was good.

He retraced his steps along the row of oil drums past the spill on the floor. Crimson tributaries coursed through the thick inky liquid. He lifted the lid. The heavy steel banged hard on the floor.

Oil matted the twins's hair, their closed eyelids, sheened their skin in a dark hue. Sterling looked away then back again, bewildered. Crazy, random thoughts tripped over each other. Two grown men squatting in an oil drum. Why? How could they both fit? Were they sleeping? One head toppled over, floated on its cheek, the severed neck exposed. A slick blackened forearm, hacked at the elbow, bone jutting, bubbled to the surface. The awful realization flooded his brain. The other skull listed, flopped on its ear. Only one man could have done this.

"My Lord!" Noel uttered the words like a prayer.

The elder Parenteau began to sniff. Was he crying? Sterling turned, followed his friend's line of sight upward focusing just under the ceiling. Wisps of smoke curled around the air vent's metal grate. The trickle grew to a stream then a flood, dark and acrid — the black smoke petroleum combustion produces.

Sterling's eyes stung, the air scratching his throat. He covered his mouth. The vent banged, echoed a muted roar, the tin expanding with heat.

At the front of the room, steel slammed on steel. Sterling scrambled down the aisle, pulled on the handle, shook the door. It wouldn't budge. Someone had padlocked it again from the outside.

Black smoke whirled in clouds along the ceiling, the vents on both sides of the room spitting orange flame. Sterling's throat constricted, strangled by an invisible hand, its fingers gouging his lungs. He crouched, crabwalked to the nearest planter. Grabbing a pile of rags littering the floor, he opened the sprinkler faucet, soaked the cloth. He covered his mouth with one of the wet masks and made his way back to Parenteau.

Had the old man gone nuts, had the smoke fried his brain? Shoulder down, Noel rammed the washroom door again and again, kicked at the knob. Shoving Sterling aside, he raised his shotgun, fired. The battered handle dangled.

"Someone's inside," he coughed and pushed his way through, Sterling on his heels.

A grey haze blanketed the bathroom. In the corner, a figure sagged against the toilet, coughing, cheek on his shoulder. His eyes drifted half-lidded, closing.

Sterling knelt. "Staff Milburn, can you hear me?"

The policeman stirred, straightened his body, moaned. His head lolled over, eyes blinking. He drifted in and out of consciousness.

"Ed Braun," he mumbled.

"Is insane," Sterling whispered and swallowed.

The staff sergeant's hands clenched his thighs. His legs splayed on the floor at nauseating angles.

"We have to get out of here." Noel urged, blinking back stinging tears, wheezing through a wet rag over his mouth. Roaring orange tongues flared across the ceiling. Smoke clawed at their throats, raked their breathing. Sterling glanced at Milburn's crooked limbs. The fire left no choice. "Crawl," Noel said.

On their knees, each man gripped the mountie under an arm and pulled. At the first movement, he screamed. Then he passed out.

Out of the door, they edged along the row of oil drums along the rear wall of the grow room. A thick sheet of flame danced overhead, searing down, spitting and crackling. Patches of the corrugated steel walls glowed red and white, heat waves billowing the air. The coal-coloured smoke whirled, enveloping the room. Sterling felt his way along, wiping his eyes with the drying rag, his skin hot like a blister.

All of a sudden, the weight in his grip halted, refused to move. He looked back. Panting, choking, Noel huddled alongside Milburn. The exertion, the heavy ingestion of smoke in breaking down the door had taken its toll.

Panic grabbed at Sterling's brain. First you asphyxiate, then the flesh melts off the bones. He dropped the useless, withered, smoke-soaked mask. His lungs blazed with the fire that crept ever closer. He pushed, pulled but neither Parenteau or Milburn moved. The chained exit doors taunted, stood before them. Through the haze, the shotgun lay on the floor beside Parenteau. Reaching over the two prostrate men, Sterling grabbed the weapon, rose to his knees. Lack of oxygen strangled his brain. Thoughts slowed. His fingers fumbled over the safety. On or off? One shell gone, one left?

Clinching the stock to his shoulder, he aimed at the padlock, pulled the trigger. The explosion blasted his ears as his shoulder hit the floor, the kickback bowling him over. He looked up, straining to see. Pellet gouges circled the doors above the handles. Below them, the lock dangled intact.

Sterling moaned. The gun had punched the oxygen from his lungs. He wheezed short breaths. If he could just stay concious. He pushed his chest up from the floor.

"Noel. Another shell." The words scratched like hot coals.

Parenteau lay flat on the floor. His breaths laboured, irregular. His eyes opened, focused on Sterling, then shut.

All of a sudden, a firefight erupted — the staccato cracking of machine guns, light flashes, flares overhead. Hugging the linoleum, after a few moments, Sterling raised his head. There were no bullets. Then flash and crackling traced along wire and another high-watt lamp exploded.

Sterling fell back. The room grew darker, the lights extinguishing one by one. Some kind god was turning down the volume, the horrible roar dying away. Sterling closed his eyes. A short rest and then he would move.

A good idea that, the hot shower bathing his face, caressing his singed skin. He opened his eyes, licked the drops splashing down his lips. Overhead, a pipe spewed and hissed. The system feeding the hydroponic network had burst in the heat. For a moment, the fire hesitated, looked unsure. The flames, however, thrust up again, tossing aside the moisture into steam.

Again, the incendiary din bombarded Sterling, a new urgency infusing his muscles, his mind. Rousted, too, by the deluge, his glistening hair matted to his skull, Noel pushed himself upright, pointed at the exit doors.

"The padlock," he shouted. "The key."

It took a moment for the words to make sense. Sterling's hand slipped into his pocket, his fingers wrapping the thin billets of metal. Was it possible. The storeroom key fit both locks on the entry door. Was it a pass key?

Reaching up, Sterling's fingers jumped back from the hot bar handle. The key slipped in, no resistance. The lock parted at a twist, the chain rattling to the floor. Shoulder down, Sterling fell forward. The doors whipped apart, slammed against the outside wall. Sleet peppered his face.

The two men stared into the night heaving fresh air. The inferno, too, gulped oxygen, roared its approval with a tidal wave of combustion. Each man covered his face with one arm, the other under Milburn's shoulders as they dragged the limp body through the doorway, flames licking all around.

Outside, orange pincers flared up the corrugated metal building, glowed against the stainless steel of the diesel and gasoline storage tanks. The oven lit, the fuel waited just metres away.

Noel's large brown eyes darted about. He pointed to a snowdrift. "We'll use that."

Sterling wrestled a wooden loading pallet from its resting place, flipped it upside down at Milburn's side. The mountie moaned as they shifted his body onto the the slats. His twisted legs rested on the makeshift sleigh. From under his parka, Parenteau pulled out his scarf and tied an end to the two-by-four frame. Sterling watched, did the same.

They leaned into the wind and trudged with their load. Although his legs rode above the snow, the policeman groaned in concert with each bump of the rough hewn runners.

About fifty metres away, power still fed the main office building and garage. The front area shone like a sports stadium bathed in a soup of twirling sleet. Something flashed. One of the overhead repair bay doors scrolled upwards revealing a pair of headlights. Rolling out into the yard, a blue GMC sparkled, preened as if on parade. Even unlit, the roof rack of driving lights glittered chrome. The pickup eased through the open gates, turned onto the road in the direction of the lake. The truck's tail-lights blinked into the night.

By the time the sleigh rested outside the fence, sirens whined in the distance, growing louder. After laying his parka over the prone passenger, Sterling began to punch numbers into his cell phone.

Milburn's eyes opened. "You can't let him get away." The voice scratched, ravished by smoke. "He's not finished." For a moment, the cop's lips moved but emitted no sound. He coughed.

"Braun bragged about killing Fredericks, ranted about devil sons betraying him."

The mountie began to choke, cleared his throat.

Kneeling, Sterling said, "It's okay. Take it easy."

Milburn's hand grappled the reporter's sleeve, wrenched him closer. "Listen." The injured man's eyes glistened. "He said there was one person left who knew and then he was free to go back." The staff sergeant coughed once more. "Bonnie Matheson."

His hand fell away.

Sterling looked down the road travelled by the GMC. Zeke and Zak supplied her with the dope she trafficked. Her trashed car, the threatening note, she knew too much.

Sterling shot up, tossed the phone to Noel and began to run toward the Triumph. "Call the police!"

Behind the wheel, Sterling cursed the narrow tires, their shallow tread, the skating rink that called itself a road. He jerked the steering wheel hard turning off Highway 265. Again the rear end broke loose, its momentum wrenching the TR6 into a four wheel drift across the oncoming lane, ploughing into the far ditch. He rammed the accelerator. The sports car jacked through a shallow drift and careened back onto Lakeview Drive.

Sterling eased up on the gas. He would do no one any good stranded in a snowbank. Peering out the windshield, he strained to see through the reeling white eddies. His fingers locked around the wheel. Even at the slower pace, the ice-humped ruts tossed the little vehicle about like a bobsleigh.

How does one get someone else so wrong? Braun was the iron man. Was that it? Because he didn't bend, he'd snapped. The vision flashed — Zeke and Zak, their heads in the barrel, slick, bobbing on a sea of oil. Is that how Sterling would find Bonnie? The inline six growled, the reporter's boot urging the accelerator closer to the floor.

At last the Matheson home rose out of the storm's whirling haze. Sterling braked, killed the lights and eased the car to the side of the road. Braun had spent most of his life as a soldier, a man trained to kill. The only ally Sterling could muster would be surprise.

He jumped from the idling vehicle, ran to the neighbour's pine bungalow and flattened himself against the wall. Breaths short, heart pounding, his body shook. The impromptu shower that had saved his life in the fire now stiffened his clothes, his hair. He blinked ice drops from his eyelashes.

No blue GMC hunkered in front of the Matheson home. Perhaps Braun had changed his mind or his ranting was meant to mislead. More likely, though, the consummate professional preferred to stalk like a ghost.

Sterling vaulted over the picket fence sepa-rating the two yards and ducked into the fire-wood lean-to attached to the back shed. About 100 metres down, the path from the street cut between two residences to the beachfront. Sterling remembered tramping the trail in the dawn twilight a few days before. A three-quarter-ton would fit snug there tucked among the larch and pine.

He scanned the expanse of glass; no light shone from within. About the property, those strange white-blanketed gargoyles —Brendan's sculptures — stood vigil. All, that is, except Brendan's favourite — the fish. The steel jack lay in the snow, its belly ripped open where the spear had once quivered.

Hard packed paths cris-crossed along the beach and up the yard to the house. If Braun came this way, he'd leave no boot prints. If he hadn't arrived yet, the seconds ticked away for Bonnie's escape.

Sterling studied the black windows. He ran across the ground floor balcony to the rear door. It opened without a sound. Down this hall Bonnie and Sterling had chatted in front of the fireplace.

Sterling stole along the thick shag carpet. Faint light framed the door that hung ajar. He pushed it open.

She sat in a chair wearing jeans and a heavy sweater, her back to the fire, her hair shimmering in the glow. Eyes wide, unblinking, she looked straight ahead.

"Bonnie," Sterling whispered, stepping forward.

She turned, her eyes enlarging like those of a frightened fawn.

Something small and hard poked his back.

"You left the barbeque early." The familiar voice spoke low.

He raised the round steel to Sterling's ear and pushed him to the middle of the room. Bonnie rose, took the reporter's hand. Captain Ed Braun stood before them in khaki fatigues. His crew-cut flat as a runway, the middle-aged man's face shone. His cuts healing, the black eye now the pale green of his field uniform. The barrel of his C7A1 assault rifle pointed chest-high.

His face had the grin of a man no longer burdened, set free. "You'll look sweet together when they find you." Shaking his head, he said, "What is it with you kids that you never listen? I tell the twins not to sell around here, don't crap in your own yard, we're doing fine on the road." Still smiling, the back of his big hand wiping the corner of his eye. "But no, greedy and stupid, they don't listen. And when trouble comes, my own flesh and blood, evil as the day they killed their mother, try to take everything I've worked for, run like scared rabbits, leaving me behind to rot in prison." Laughing, tears flowed as the words raged. "As if those two could fool their old man." He studied Bonnie. "You didn't deserve to lick John's boots. He isn't even in his grave yet and you're taking up with a coward who gets his kicks watching real men in uniform draw blood." His eyes shifted to Sterling. "Even when I ran you off the road, practically spit John's murder in your face, you still didn't get it." Braun snickered, his eyes filled, his cheeks slick. "John McTaggart was a real hero. You'll never see another like him."

The assault rifle wavering before them, Sterling couldn't keep the exasperation from his voice. "Why did you kill him, then?"

The mirth that danced in the soldier's weeping eyes died. "Kill my colonel?" The barrel raised, pointed at the reporter's head. "Are you crazy?"

A blur through the air slammed into Braun's thick neck. The thud, like a maul punching hard wood, twisted his body. A sack of loose bones, he slumped to the floor.

The firelight dappled Brendan's pale face as he stood in the doorway, liquified his translucent hair. A metre-long rod of steel in his grip, he stared at the fallen man. Sterling knelt, two fingers searching for a pulse on Braun's wrist. "He's alive."

The words pushed Bonnie back into her chair, her hands veiling her face.

Her brother pursed his lips, exhaled, the sound almost a whistle. "Thank God that's over."

He stepped back to the couch, sat down and rested his chin on the steel rod. The end had a rubber hand grip, the other a sharp point. Sterling studied the weapon and the realization hit him. McTaggart's spud, his winter walking stick, had hidden in Brendan's sculpture as the spear. The young artist took inspirational forest walks at four in the morning.

Are you crazy? Braun had said. He would never kill his hero.

"Can I see that?" the reporter asked, pointing.

Brendan raised his head, wrapped his fingers around the shaft. "Why?"

"That's the question. Why did you kill him?"

The albino's soft pink eyes widened, incredulous. "The man was about to shoot you!"

"Why did you kill McTaggart?"

Brendan rose to his feet. "Braun was right. You are crazy."

Bonnie's hands fell from her cheeks. She shot up from her chair. "What are you saying?"

"Scrape away the solder and paint," Sterling said, "and I think we'll find Captain Braun's engraved dedication to his colonel."

Turning back to her brother, Sterling asked, "What do you think, Brendan?"

Bonnie stared, her eyes travelling up and down the spear. Her palm raised and covered her mouth. "John's walking stick," she whispered.

Brendan hoisted the chisel-ended spud, stepped toward Sterling. He reared, arm raised.

"No!" Her voice sharp, Bonnie stepped in front of her brother.

Brendan froze, a killer in statue. Then a slow wave of pain and confusion swept away the anger in his face. His hand fell, the walking stick slipping from his grip.

"Why?" His sister's voice broke. "Why Brendan?"

The weapon on the floor, Sterling stepped forward and Brendan retreated a couple of paces, his bloodshot eyes darting, feverish.

"Where would I be without this house, my studio?" he said. "The whole neighbourhood could have heard him shouting after the party. You don't marry me and you can kiss your precious little house, your brother's hideaway goodbye." Brendan took another step back. "If he

Scott Gregory Miller

couldn't have you, it didn't matter if the bank kicked me out into a snowbank. At least now, you have his will."

Bonnie's eyes filled. "I would have taken care of you."

"You were the one who got us into this."

He ran out of the room.

Sterling scrambled through the kitchen and out into the yard. He stopped, looked about. The wind ripped at his shirt, keened in his ears. Rippled sheets of white squalled across the frozen lake.

Chasing up behind him, Bonnie's fingers gripped his wrist. "Please," she cried. "Go after him!"

Out front, an engine howled. Only the Triumph's inline six screamed to its redline like that.

Sterling reached the street. The Triumph twirled out of control on Lakeview's slick surface. At last the sports car came to rest. Sterling released a long breath. The motor gunned once more, spinning the rear tires, jerking the TR6 rut to rut down the road.

His car headed for the highway without him. Above, the sky glowed orange crowned by roiling black clouds. The inferno at Braun and Sons Trucking made daylight of the night over Candle Lake. The chorus of sirens grew.

Undulating waves of blue and red light rolled over Sterling as the RCMP patrol car slid to a stop. The driver's side window lowered and Constable Cuthand's face appeared.

"What's going on? We received a 911 to this address."

Sterling looked toward the house. Bonnie stood on the front step, the blizzard tossing her hair, stoning her face with sleet.

"Larry Frederick's killer is inside. It's Ed Braun, he's hurt bad."

"We detoured an ambulance from the fire," Cuthand replied. "It should be here any second."

Sterling ran around to the passenger side, wrenched open the door and jumped inside before Cuthand could say another word.

Sterling shivered. "Bonnie's brother murdered John McTaggart. He's driving a mustard yellow 1976 Triumph TR6 sports car, headed west out of town on Highway 265."

The cop stared at his passenger, motionless.

"Go!" Sterling barked.

The mountie's lips pursed, eyes steady. After a moment, he nodded. The sedan lurched forward, the rear tires keening as they spun grooves in the snow.

Sterling's teeth chattered. He fanned his icey pink hands over the heat vent on the dash.

Turning onto 265, the patrol car slowed, maneuvered past parked vehicles lining the roadway. A growing throng of gawkers, a giant milling snake, moved toward the conflagration of Braun and Sons Trucking. The sky's wavering brilliance drew their eyes like a hypnotist.

Emergency lights flashing, siren blipping, Cuthand nosed the sedan through the crowd to where a roadblock halted progress. Behind the wooden barricade, a police van, its blues and reds dancing, straddled the highway. In front, his reflective yellow and orange vest a beacon in the swirling snow, a traffic cop waved through his fellow officer.

Sterling wiped the windshield with his sleeve. Brendan wouldn't have been able to get past this way. He must have followed a residential road further down to the highway, the only route out of town. Without the delay, he'd have gained minutes, time enough to slip the TR6 down some country back road where he'd never be found.

The way clear for half a kilometre to the far roadblock, the car accelerated. Across the snow-crusted ditch and parallel service road, acres of truck yard burned, a mountainous pyre. Sterling lowered his frost-glazed window. From a hundred metres away, earth core-like heat radiated through the storm to feather his face. Every building, every tractor, every trailer ablaze, flames spit their sacrifice to the heavens above. Across the highway, an arc of liquid from a single pumper truck washed over a lone building.

Constable Cuthand followed Sterling's eyes. "The village's only fire truck, it's fifty years old. With those big fuel storage tanks in the compound, all we can do is clear the area, wet things down."

They approached the second road block. The people of Candle Lake stood in awe. Wailing, the patrol car wormed its way through the mass of bystanders. Cheers erupted with every splatter of sparks across the sky.

When they had passed the last straggler, the patrol car accelerated down the empty road. Only darkness, sheets of whirling snow lay ahead, no Triumph, no Brendan. Behind, the horizon glowed.

The mountie flicked a switch on the dash. The siren died but the pulsing blue and red lights still splashed against the towering sentinel of trees guarding the highway. The muffled pounding of the engine sounded far away. The windshield wipers scraped one way, screeched the other. The inky night's white blankets devoured much of the headlights's glow.

Sterling's vision settled into the speckled darkness. Brendan fought to protect his home, his sister. Bonnie's lover, for a time generous and

371

kind, had succumbed to the poison in himself, became desperate, evil when he couldn't have her on his own terms. Her brother killed the man who threatened to rip him from his cocoon, obliterate his world. Tossed behind bars with no hope for much of the rest of his life, could the young man's future be counted in anything more than months, even days? Before the fireplace, Bonnie had spoken of suicide as an escape from the darkness. Would her death not soon follow her brother's?

Sterling studied the young policeman's stern face: "I was surprised it was you Bonnie wanted me to call from the Wheelhouse tonight. Then I remembered Kevin saying G. A. got you through a bad time."

Constable Cuthand nodded. "I wouldn't be here today otherwise."

"Do you think Bonnie can beat it?"

"It's tough. A gambler has to hit rock bottom before it becomes obvious quitting is the only route. She's been under an awful strain for a long time, her parents, her fiancé, now this tonight." He shook his head. "I only wish I'd insisted on going for coffee instead of letting her beg off at her house. At least she'd have avoided Ed Braun."

Sterling thought for a moment then said, "Then we may never have known Brendan killed the colonel."

The big sedan bumped along, ploughing through snowdrifts building on the pavement. A sudden dreariness swept over Sterling. With all focus on the fire, Brendan had a sporting chance. In her heart, Bonnie would cheer her brother as he ducked the arms of the law. Just be gentle with the TR6, hide her in a safe place, please.

"Look!" Constable Cuthand's eyes bore straight ahead. Spots of scarlet flickered in the distance. Sterling's stomach sunk.

The force of authority wailing once more, the big police mill growled pressing the reporter's back to the seat as the car descended the long hill. The ephemeral specks grew into solid red disks dashing any hopes he had of them not being from the Triumph. Even in black silhouette, like a lady, her sway, her profile didn't lie.

Sterling bolted upright. Beyond the hill, lurked the bad camber corner, its iron fist guard rail. The sports car skidded left, the tail-lights swinging, steadying, disappearing into the trees.

Light flooded around them, the sky flashing brilliant. The reporter wrenched around, peered through the rear window. A fireball rocketed to the moon, muted thunder slipping over the forest. For a breath, the car vibrated. The ignited storage tanks at Braun & Sons Trucking smattered the horizon with their fireworks. Falling back, a steady luminescence painted the sky above the forest.

A sharp boom ahead snapped the reporter's head forward again. A twisting ocher tongue licked the sky, it too striving for the moon, but spent, dropped again out of sight. The sedan eased around the corner. Sterling stared, his mind numb, riveted. Ahead, the Triumph blazed, the flames of her pyre reaching for the stars.

Afternoon March 11

Red, blue, yellow and green lights blinked and the regular cadence of beeps signalled that the patient's vital functions pulsed steady. Tubes stuffed his nostrils, his mouth, flowed red or translucent from his arms. Only the inhuman burps and beeps of computerized wizardry broke the grey silence of the hospital room.

Ed Braun's chest rose and fell with the forced induction of oxygen. With his spine snapped, no muscles moved. His blackened eye already a lighter blue, his cuts would heal, only a scar or two would mark his skin for the rest of his life. Inside his brain, however, he lay helpless, trapped amongst the demons that raged there.

The words of the doctor, his judgement, trod through Sterling's mind as he sat by the bed: "It would be a miracle if the patient ever moves a muscle again."

In the basement morgue of the hospital lay the charred remains of Braun's attacker, Brendan Matheson. Bonnie had bluffed, put up a brave front when she said she didn't fear for her life. The threat and her vandalized car had sent her scurrying to Milburn with the whole story. They could make a deal if she co-operated and testified. When the major crimes task force out of P.A. took over the Meath Park detachment, the staff sergeant decided to slip away, sniff around the Braun Trucking compound. That's where Babe caught Milburn's scent and Ed took a steel pipe to his legs.

Sterling's vision rested on Braun's hairless skull, shaven for surgery. When did such evil infest his mind? Was it in Rwanda where he pedaled dope to killers who macheteed their way to genocide? Or was it twenty years before in this very hospital where newborn twins cried at the death of their mother?

Captain Braun had professed the utmost respect, even love for his colonel. Yet, why hadn't McTaggart recognized the monster in his officer? For that matter, why hadn't a keen international correspondent seen the sickness. Was it because, in one form or another, it had infested all of them?

Sterling rose from the chair. One fact remained: three of them had walked through the blood of Rwanda's madness. Only one still had a chance at a normal life. Could he keep the devil from the door?

Sterling turned away, unable to look any longer at the body stretched, silent, on the bed.

Under the closed lids, the eyes never stopped bouncing, darting, searching for escape.

Up the stairs to the fifth floor, Sterling found Staff Sergeant Milburn's room. He stepped inside to find Megan holding her father's hand as he lay sleeping, his legs suspended above him. Sun poured through the window bathing the pair. She put her fingers to her lips for silence.

At that moment Milburn opened his eyes and said, "You're about the last person I thought I'd ever have to thank for anything."

"How are you doing?" Sterling asked.

"They tell me it will be quite a job to get me walking again." His hands rubbed the white plaster casts. "But I'll do it."

"I just saw Ed Braun. He'll probably never move again."

Megan let her fingers slip from her father's and sat in a chair beside him.

Milburn turned his head toward the sunshine. "His boys tried to save me. They wanted it known they didn't kill anyone." He paused as if soaking in the warmth. "They told me when Fredericks lost his job, he threatened to turn them in if they didn't cut him in deeper. Their old man wanted the newsman taken care of but they refused." Milburn blinked several times, his eyes seeming to grow heavier but he continued. "The twins were going to stash me somewhere around

377

here until they were long gone. Then they'd make a phone call so I could be found. They were just loading me into the cab of the semi when Braun caught us."

Megan stood and said, "I think we should let Dad rest now."

"Sure," Sterling walked to the door and opened it. "I don't understand one thing. Why didn't Braun kill you, too?"

"He said I was a man of uniform." Milburn reached for his daughter's hand. "Like him."

Afternoon March 17

"Can I have a balloon?" The little tyke stuck out his stubby hand, fingers muddied in chocolate.

Sterling slipped the nipple over the helium tank hose, pressed. A wheeze of gas plumped the latex fat in seconds. Sterling knotted the string and sealed the opening.

The boy shook his head. "I want a red one."

"No."

Shrugging, the child said, "How about green?"

"No."

The kid's hand glided across his upper lip clearing away a curl of snot, leaving a brown stain on his nose.

"Can you breathe in that stuff and talk funny like Donald Duck?"

"No."

"Let me then."

"No."

The child's smile faded, his lower lip protruded. At that moment, the string slipped from his mucky paw and his new toy, a gorgeous yellow colour that any kid would love, floated

Scott Gregory Miller

to the ceiling. The sensitive little guy burst into tears, scrambled over to his mother and leapt into her arms. Stroking her baby's hair, clutching him to her bosom, she glared at Sterling.

He turned away and surveyed the community hall. Doesn't she know all that sugar creates monsters of them?

Hordes of children, the occasional adult in tow, screeched and screamed, battled and rough-housed, dashed and crashed about the polished wooden floor. Fun Day wouldn't be over for hours yet.

A solemn procession moved through the giant rumpus room. In its midst, a swatch of blonde caught Sterling's attention. Four men in black leather, flicking their hair from their eyes, escorted Bonnie. She nodded at Big Jim McLeod and the boys in his band as they parted a path for her. The motley group's tough veneer dissolved with the tender looks each one gave its newest member.

Bonnie approached. "You look funny."

"I'm paying back a debt." Sterling said. "I got your cheque in the mail. Thanks."

"Sorry I couldn't double it like I promised." Her gaze met his for a brief moment then fell to the floor. "I came to say goodbye." She gestured at the musicians, her band. "We're going on the road for a couple of months."

Words seemed tiny, useless. "I heard. Good luck."

"I'm sorry I didn't return your calls." Bonnie's white teeth grazed her bottom lip, bit down. "I needed to be alone."

Sterling nodded.

"I just wanted to tell you I don't blame you for Brendan's death." She folded her hands together, stared at them. "It might sound like a horrible thing to say but I'm glad he didn't have to go to prison. It would have been the worst kind of torture for him."

Her parents, her fiancé, her brother all taken from her yet she still reached for any light in the darkness.

"It's not horrible if that's how you feel."

Her blue eyes regarded Sterling. A sparkle, not large but it was there, ignited.

"I've been good so far," she said. "No VLT's, nothing."

"I'm glad,"

Bonnie's looked through him to somewhere else. "One day at a time," she whispered. She glanced over her shoulder, shrugged. "I have to go." She looked up at him for a long moment holding his eyes in hers. "That night with you, I hadn't felt so safe and warm in a long time." Their gaze remained steady, unflinching. "In the morning, I just panicked. You'll never know how sorry I am."

Sterling nodded.

"Is it okay if I kiss a clown?" she asked.

He grinned. Bonnie stretched up on the silver toes of her fancy-stitched cowboy boots and, for a brief moment, their lips touched.

She stepped back and studied him. Her head bowed as a sad smile crossed her face. "Perhaps . . . " Her voice trailed off.

Bonnie turned and walked back to the four blues players who closed around her like a cocoon, her new family. Instead of gambling, music would swallow her. Would that world take her through to the other side? He hoped so. The procession moved to its own slow cadence through the raucous life playing around it. What had she wanted to say? Sterling eyes didn't leave her until the crowd digested the band.

"Can I have a red one?"

He looked down at a little girl in pigtails, freckles. "No."

Moments later, even though tugging the string of a beautiful new blue balloon floating above her, the spoiled child stomped away.

"How's it going?"

Sterling preened in his big white floppy shoes, his rainbow-coloured pantaloons and ruffled blouse and said, "Great! The kids love me."

"I knew you were the man for the job," Kevin said.

"Every Sunday for three months and we're even, right?"

Parenteau laughed. "Even! Interest is what's on the table here. We'll talk principal later." He patted the clown on the back. "I see you're driving the Bumbler again. Fortunately, I was able to find a spot for the Jag way on the other side of the lot with everyone else."

Sterling eyed his so-called boyhood buddy.

Kevin returned the look. "I hear Dan Farrow is stepping down, claims all the lies you wrote about him turned the people against him."

"So sue me."

"I doubt it. He'll be too busy counting his money. People saw him cheering his burning building after the Braun fire jumped the highway."

Sterling rolled his eyes, disgusted.

"Word is his dealership was insured to the teeth." Kevin put his hand on his friend's shoulder. "Isn't life grand?"

Shaking his head, Sterling said, "At least your casino deal is dead."

"It always was."

"Is that what you wouldn't tell me?"

"Farrow caught wind of an early draft of our land claim. It was just a wish list, not the one we filed. But the mayor flew with the notion that Candle Lake was about to be confiscated by the Indian band. Of course, only his casino deal could stop the takeover." Kevin looked to be enjoying the telling. "All the ruckus and panic he raised brought the government to the negotiating table, something it avoided for years. Since we'd finally caught some ears in Ottawa and Regina, we didn't feel it was our place to set the mayor right with the facts."

"So the both of you used the ignorant media to further your own causes?"

"We like to learn from our white brothers"

The lawyer beckoned to someone in the crowd and said, "Our neighbour is very interested in meeting you."

A tall, elegant woman in a suit tailored for business, auburn hair upswept, approached with her companion, a little man in a rumpled coat busy on a cell phone.

Kevin bowed at the waist, swept his arm. "This is your man, Mrs. Lord, Myles Sterling."

Turning to his friend, the lawyer said, "Meet the publisher of the Prince Albert *Sun*."

"At last," Mrs. Lord smiled. "This is my editor, Joseph."

Muttering into his phone, worrying the few strands on his shiny pate, at last, Joe rang off. He studied Sterling for the first time, his pink rubber ball nose, his flaming orange hair.

In a voice deep with authority, Joe said, "Mrs. Irene Dankewics is tired of being a secretary, has just thrown her hat in the ring for Mayor of Candle Lake. I need twelve column inches by deadline."

"Would you like a nice red balloon?" Sterling replied. "I've saved one special."

Like his protagonist, **SCOTT GREGORY MILLER** pounded the pavement as a reporter for fifteen years and is now a free-lance writer/journalist. He has previously published in *Storyteller* (Summer 97), *Grain* (Winter 01) and onewheeldrive.net (March 2004), and participated in the *Friday After Five* (Thistledown, 2000) and *Great Earth Excavation Company* (2002) anthologies. He lives in Estevan, Saskatchewan.